Office Slave

Other books by J.W. McKenna:
"The Hunted" with Jaid Black
"Darkest Hour"
"Slave Planet"
"Lord of Avalon"
"The Cameo"
"Naughty Girl"
"Wanted: Kept Woman"
"My Pet"
"Controlled: Programmed for Sex"
"Boarding School Slave"
"Sold into Slavery: Novel of the Bangkok Brothels"
"Out of Control" I and II

ISBN: 1-4196-1214-X

To order additional copies, please contact us.
BookSurge, LLC
www.booksurge.com
1-866-308-6235
orders@booksurge.com

Office Slave
Books I and II

J.W. McKenna

2005

Office Slave

Chapter 1

"Come in, Ellen," Jack Sawyer said, working to keep his voice even. "Did you have a nice vacation?" He stood in front of his pool-table-sized walnut desk, a manila folder tucked under one arm.

Ellen Sanchez, Sawyer Metalworking's attractive, dark-haired financial officer entered her boss's spacious office smiling. "Oh, yes, Jack. The beaches are wonderful in the Bahamas. It was very relaxing." She paused, noticing Jack did not return her smile, and asked tentatively, "Did everything go all right here while I was gone?"

"Sort of," he said vaguely. "There's something we need to discuss. Here, have a seat." He indicated the chair across from him. She eased down onto it, folding her skirt primly in front of her.

Jack glanced at the figure of his employee and admired it anew. Ellen was a beautiful Latino, a rich combination of Incan and Mexican ancestry. Her smooth high cheekbones gave her face a sharper, more exotic look, offset by a cascade of dark hair. She kept herself in good shape, he noticed, which was surprising from someone who made a living sitting at a desk, poring over figures.

"How's Bill?" Jack asked suddenly. "He find a job yet?"

She glanced up, suspicion in her eyes. "Um... No, not yet. He's in a specialized field, you know..." Her voice trailed off. Her eyes darted away, as if she wanted to escape.

Jack sat down across from her, putting the folder deliberately on his lap. "How long has he been out of work, this time?" he pressed, emphasizing the last two words. He knew Bill had been fired from his last two jobs.

Ellen stared at him for a minute, as if she couldn't believe his impertinence. When it was clear he really wanted to know, she licked her puffy red lips and said, "Oh, let's see... About a year now, I guess."

"Must be hard to make ends meet."

Her eyes fluttered and she grew pale. "Oh, not really, we're pretty thrifty, so—"

Jack interrupted her, his voice taking on a harder edge. "It's surprising that someone whose husband hasn't been able to hold a steady job is able to drive a Mercedes and take vacations in the Bahamas."

The remaining blood drained from her face. "It's a very old Mercedes," she said softly, as if that excused her. She stared at the folder in his lap. The silence stretched on for several seconds before Jack explained his rude behavior. "While you were gone, I had the books audited."

Ellen's mouth dropped open. "But, but—there was no need—"

"No need! Sawyer Metalworking's profits have been eroding for years, yet we have plenty of business! I asked you to explain that and you gave me nonsense about higher taxes and greater costs of materials." He picked up the folder and tapped it on his leg. "But not once did you tell me that you've been stealing from me!"

"No!" Her denial was automatic.

Jack opened the folder and handed her some sheets of paper. "Don't bother denying it. Here are the dummy companies you set up, copies of some of the checks you wrote to them for 'services rendered,' and, finally, a copy of a check to an 'Alice Edwards' that you cashed at First Federal Bank. That's your handwriting, is it not?"

Her cheeks flushed with color. "No! No, you're wrong! I don't know who this 'Alice Edwards' is, but it isn't me!"

Without a word, Jack slid another item from the folder—a five-by-seven photograph of Ellen, walking out the door from First Federal Bank, dressed casually in shorts and a tee-shirt. It was unmistakably her.

"The teller ID'd you from a photo. Please have the decency not to continue your lies."

Ellen reeled and nearly fell off her chair. She grabbed the edge and steadied herself. Jack observed her carefully built wall of denial crumble. She burst into tears. "God, Jack, I'm so sorry! I didn't mean to do it—I was just so desperate! We were about to lose the house. I only intended to borrow it!"

Her mood suddenly darkened. "That goddamned Bill! I told him to work harder at getting along with people!" Her mood shifted again, back to contrition. "I'm so sorry. I'll pay you back, I promise!"

With that, Jack took out the remaining item from the folder. A single sheet of paper. "This has been going on for more than three years now. Right under my nose. By a woman I trusted. My own CFO." Each word hammered at her. "You'll see by this document, you've embezzled a total of two hundred, forty seven thousand dollars from me."

She held the paper in shaking hands. "T-that much?"

"That's equivalent to five workers on the factory floor. As you know, we only have about two dozen workers there, covering two shifts. Would you like to go down with me and pick out five of them that I'll have to lay off, thanks to you?"

"No! You can't!" She buried her face into her hands. "Please don't."

Jack waited for a few minutes while she cried. He felt cold. Angry. And to think he used to fantasize about her! Now he only wanted revenge for her betrayal. When her crying diminished, he leaned in again. "I'm going to call the police now, Ellen. Embezzling this amount of money is probably good for five years in prison. I only wish it could be more."

She looked up, eyes red-rimmed, a shocked expression on her face. "But—but, you can't! I'll be ruined! Besides, if I'm in jail, I won't be able to pay you back! I said I'd pay you back and I meant it!"

Jack scoffed. "How? You're certainly not my CFO after today. And I doubt you'll be able to get any kind of accounting job once word gets out about your tendency to steal from those who hire you."

The word made her wince. Clearly, she hadn't thought of herself as a criminal until this moment. Jack knew her story: She was only "borrowing" the money until Bill got another job, or she got a raise, then she'd pay it back, quietly and over time. Sure she would've. He knew that most embezzlers convinced themselves that they would pay it back. Nine times out of ten, they never get around to it—unless they were caught.

"Please don't say anything. I can get another job and pay you back out of that!"

"Do you really think I'd let you loose on another company knowing what I know? And how would you pay me back, by stealing from them?"

"No! No! I wouldn't! I'd work overtime. I'd take a second job. I'll never do anything like this again. Please."

With elaborate slowness, Jack reached over and secured a small calculator from his desktop. He looked over it to Ellen's tear-stained face. "And just how much, approximately, do you think you'd be able to pay me each week?"

"Well, if that bastard husband of mine gets a job..."

She stopped, as if she realized that wasn't Jack's problem. "I think I could manage, um, two-three hundred a week." Her eyes were bright as she contemplated a way out of this mess.

Jack punched in the numbers. "Let's see, two hundred, forty seven thousand, divided by three hundred..." He looked up. You could pay me back in sixteen years. That's assuming I don't charge any interest, which I'd be a fool not to. So, with interest, let's say an even twenty years, shall we?"

Ellen looked blank, her reddish brown eyes opened wide.

"So how old are you now?"

"Th-thirty-two."

"So you expect me to keep quiet and hope that you continue to pay me until you're fifty-two? The statute of limitations runs out in five years—you could just stop paying me then and I'd have no more leverage. I'd be stuck for most of the loss. What kind of a fool do you take me for?" He reached over his desk and turned the phone around to face him. He picked up the receiver.

"Please! What are you doing?"

"Why, I'm calling the police, as I told you I would. I see no way out of this."

Suddenly, she came off of the chair and kneeled in front of Jack, putting a hand on his leg. "Jack, I know you find me attractive. I could make it worth your while to wait."

Jack paused, holding the phone halfway to his ear. He turned and leveled his gaze at her. "You're kidding me."

"No, I'm not. Anything but ... the police."

"You really think your pussy is worth a more than two hundred grand to me?" She jerked back as if electrocuted. "I mean, don't get me wrong, you are an attractive woman.

But if I need to get my dick wet, I can find a dozen elegant call girls for, say, a thousand a night—that's a far cry from two hundred-plus grand."

"I-I didn't mean just for one night. I'll be yours, to do what you want, until you feel I've paid you back."

"Well, that's a very tempting offer, I must admit." Ellen's eyes grew hopeful. "But let's run the math again, shall we? Since you aren't a professional, let's say I pay you five hundred a session and we fuck twice a week." He used the crudest words on purpose, just to watch her face flinch. "That's two hundred forty seven weeks to pay off your debt, or about five years. Plus interest, we'd have to make it about seven years. That's a long time to be my whore. What would your husband say?"

She made a face. "He wouldn't care, not if it meant I'd be taking care of our money problems, as usual."

Jack laughed. "You don't really expect me to believe that'd he'd just sit by and let me fuck you anytime I wanted for the next seven years, do you?"

"Well, if he doesn't like it, he can leave. It's about time he carried his own weight."

"Okay." Jack let the matter of her husband drop for now. He could tell there were a lot of cracks in the Sanchez marriage. "But what about me? I'm forty, and still dating women, one of whom might end up being my wife someday. What if I found someone in the next seven years? How would I explain you to her? 'Oh, don't mind Ellen, I'm just fucking her as part of a business deal.' I don't think that would go over too well."

"Please, Jack. We can work something out. Just tell me what you want."

Jack's ear was assailed with the beeping tone of a phone that had been off the hook too long. He realized he was still holding it mid-air. He quickly hung it up. "What do I want? I want my money back. One way or the other. Either I get it in cash, or I get my pound of flesh by seeing you sitting in prison."

Her face fell. "So you aren't interested in me, um, you know, sexually?"

Jack locked his eyes on hers. "I didn't say that. I admit to being attracted to you. But I don't let that interfere with business, you understand?"

She nodded. "All right. So you want to do this from a business perspective. Let's talk business. What will it take to keep me out of jail and my CFO reputation intact?"

"You're not serious."

"Yes I am! I'm very serious. I mean, I'm serious in finding out your price. I'm not sure I'll be able to agree to it, but I'm willing to listen."

"Okay. I could ask you to sell your car and give me the money," he said, keeping his gaze steady on hers. "Your house too, for that matter. What do you think they're worth now?"

Ellen just stared back, unable to speak. She took a deep breath. "That won't help much."

"Oh? Why not?"

"The car is eight years old, you'd probably get six thousand for it. The house is heavily mortgaged. If we sold it now, with the market conditions currently, I'd probably only clear ten thousand, which I'd have to split with Bill." Tears came to her eyes. "Then I'd have to find another place to live anyway, so some of that money would be spent on rent and moving expenses."

Jack waited, watching her. He wanted her to come up with another solution. When she didn't say anything, he prompted her. "Well, I guess that's it, then."

"No." Her voice was small. "I-I could be your girl, do anything you wanted me to do."

"What does that mean, exactly?"

She blushed pink. "You know, anything you wanted. You could, um, make love to me anytime, like right here, in your office."

"So you're offering me your services as a sexual slave?"

She just nodded, worrying her lower lip with her teeth.

"What's that? I didn't hear you."

"Yes, I'd be your sex slave. Anything but be arrested for what I've done."

Jack sat back in his chair, his hands crossed over his stomach. He knew this was every man's dream, to have a woman willing to give herself to him in every way imaginable. When he'd first learned about her duplicity, his immediate thought had been, turn her in. Let the police handle it. But later, when he'd had time to think about it, he had to admit, he'd entertained fantasies about her as a subservient woman. Of course, he'd dismissed them as just that, fantasies. Now she was asking him to express his deep hidden desires. Dare he speak them out loud?

"Take off your clothes." The words erupted from him as if he were possessed. He bit the inside of his cheek, expecting her to scream or stalk out. Instead, she simply stared at him.

"That's your price?"

Jack made a dismissive sound. "No, that's good faith bargaining on your part. You brought it up. I'm the wounded party here, you understand. I want to see what you're offering. When you're naked, we can begin negotiations in earnest. If not..." He nodded toward the phone.

Her eyes bored into his for a long moment, then she stood and shucked off her suitcoat and began unbuttoning her ivory silk blouse. Jack watched, mesmerized, as her lacy bra came into view. Ellen separated the last button and pulled the sides apart, giving him a full view of her heaving chest, mottled pink with embarrassment. She paused, trying to catch her breath. Ellen shrugged her shoulders and let the blouse slip down her tan arms. She folded it and carefully laid it over the back of her chair. With her back to him, she unclasped her bra, shrugged out of it, and placed it over the blouse.

She turned back to Jack and allowed him to stare at her erect breasts. He noticed how her skin coloring gave them a bronze tone and the areolas were light chocolate brown. Her breasts hung perfectly, defying gravity. Jack realized his mouth had come open, so he closed it with a nearly audible snap.

Ellen unzipped her skirt. She stepped out of it gracefully, as if she'd put on a show many times before. He stared at her panty hose-encased legs, the white triangle of her panties above. He found himself getting a little short of breath as well and his cock swelled and threatened to burst from his pants. He shifted in his seat and waited.

Ellen hooked both thumbs into the waistband of her pantyhose and tugged them down over her hips. Her panties were caught up along with them, revealing the dark furry mound between her legs. She sat on the edge of the chair and removed the pantyhose, one leg at a time. She averted her eyes, clearly embarrassed, but determined to get it over with. He wondered how the Faustian bargain he'd entered into here might end. Would it ruin his career as well as hers? He knew he should just call the cops, but seeing her obeying his commands, he thought he might play it out a little longer. Just to see how far it would go.

Ellen finished rolling the hose down her long, copper-colored legs. She picked up the discarded garments and piled them onto the back of the chair, on top of her other clothes. Then she turned and sat, facing Jack, her legs casually crossed at her knees.

"Like this?" She asked, her voice quavering. She took a deep breath.

"Yesss." He found the word came out elongated, despite his efforts to be cool. He mentally shook himself, trying to get back on track. After all, he was in charge. She would do anything he demanded, rather than face ruin.

"No," he contradicted himself. "Put your feet flat on the ground, let your legs come apart."

Ellen did as he asked, letting him get a good view of her bushy vee, the enticing folds of skin below.

"That'll have to go," he said, pointing.

She looked down. "That? You mean...?"

"Yes. I want you to keep it shaved from now on. Or maybe get one of those Brazilian waxes."

She shook her head slightly, as if in disbelief, but didn't argue. "Okay."

"You'd no longer be my CFO, of course. Instead, you'd be at my beck and call for whatever I wanted. I'd move you into the smaller office next door." Ellen glanced over at the door where Jack's former secretary had worked in the office beyond. She'd left two months ago to get married and Jack hadn't yet filled the position. "I'd want you to wear sexier clothes too. Shorter skirts, smaller tops, or at least blouses with a few buttons unbuttoned. And no underwear. Ever."

Ellen's face grew red. It was as if she could handle being naked in front of Jack in the privacy of his office, but the thought of her parading around the plant dressed like a slut got to her.

"E-Everyone will know," she sputtered.

"Know what? That you're a slut or an embezzler? It's either one or the other at this point." Jack shook his head. "Come to think of it, go ahead and get dressed. Let's forget the whole thing. I'd just as soon call the police." He reached for the phone.

Ellen stood up quickly and placed a delicate hand on his forearm. The sight of all that naked flesh so close to him made him pause. "Please." She was begging him. Ellen, the cool, beautiful and unapproachable woman, was begging him. He looked into her eyes, gauging her sincerity there.

"I'll do anything you say, Jack. Anything. I just can't be exposed for embezzling. Please. It will ruin me." She came closer until her legs touched his. Her breasts were just inches from his face. He couldn't help himself; he reached up and touched one lovely mound, feeling the electricity in his fingers.

"Okay," he breathed. "Have a seat. Let's continue our negotiations."

She returned to her seat and sat down. For a moment, she crossed her legs again, then caught herself and brought her foot back to the floor. She deliberately spread her legs apart and waited, arms crossed under her breasts.

"Okay. As I said, I want my money back. Having you as my personal sex slave isn't worth the money." A frown slipped across Ellen's face. "But having you earn back the two hundred, forty seven thousand, plus interest, has a certain amount of appeal."

Her eyes widened. Jack could tell she now had an inkling what he was getting at. Her blush began anew. "You can't mean..."

"Mean what? That there are certain things you won't do? You'll steal but you won't fuck, is that it?"

"But I thought—"

"What? That I want you for myself? Sure, I want you. I'm a man. You're a beautiful woman. And I would fuck you whenever I wanted to. But that doesn't get me my money back, does it? No, for that, we'd need to hire you out."

"But—but you can't! I'll be arrested!"

Jack pointed a finger at her. "Not if you're careful. Besides, which would you rather be arrested for, prostitution or embezzlement?"

Ellen chewed on her bottom lip. "But I'll be ruined, either way! I can't earn your money back if I'm in jail! And I could be killed on the streets!"

"Oh, don't worry, I won't put you on the streets. No, I see you as a classy call girl, working on behalf of the company. Or, on occasion, I might want to farm you out to a brothel."

"But what about, you know, diseases and such! I could die from something."

"Hey, no one says you have to go bareback. You can make them wear condoms."

She had another argument ready. "But Bill would freak out! He'd divorce me and tell everyone what a slut I've become."

Jack just shrugged with one shoulder, as if it made no difference to him. "Like I said, you have a choice." He tipped his head toward the phone.

He could see she was wavering. "And what about ... us? What would you demand of me, when I'm not out fucking every manufacturing rep in the Midwest?"

"Total obedience."

She seemed dissatisfied with that answer. "W-what would that entail?"

"Just as it sounds. You do anything I tell you to do, without argument. If you disobey me, you get punished, or I'll just forget the whole arrangement and call the cops."

"Punished?"

"Yeah, like spankings. Nothing you couldn't handle."

"And these, um, duties—I hope you don't expect me to run drugs for you or something!"

"I'm not talking about anything like that. Just sexual things."

Ellen pondered that information. Jack could bet she was running sex acts through her mind, trying to decide which ones were beyond her abilities to stomach. "You mean, like, uh, making love to another woman? Or a gang-bang?" Her voice quavered.

"Maybe. You'd do whatever necessary to keep the customers or employees happy."

"But I could have you arrested too!" The angry words slipped out. She seemed to gather her nerve and rush ahead. "I mean, setting yourself up as a pimp is illegal too! How would that play at the Chamber of Commerce?"

"You're right, of course. If you got caught or turned in, I'd probably be arrested too. Then the entire sordid story would come out. While you're on trial for embezzlement, I'd be on trial for pandering or the like. But I think I'd get off and I don't think you would."

"After they hear that you forced me into this, they'd—"

"I haven't forced you to do anything, Ellen. This was entirely your idea. I've said several times, I'm fully prepared to call the police. You're the one who's prolonged this conversation by encouraging me to think of alternatives. And frankly, there aren't many when you've admitted you've stolen such a large amount of money."

She shrugged, trying to maintain her dignity while naked. "It'd be your word against mine. I'd tell them you forced me. I may go to jail for a couple of years, but you could get more time for running a sex shop!"

"I wouldn't call it a sex shop. It's only you, trying to do what you can to pay me back. Besides, I'm not a fool. I took the liberty of filming this meeting." He pointed to a vent, high up on the wall. Ellen, her eyes wide, looked over and spotted the small lens of a camera pointing through the slats at her.

She stood and turned away, grabbing her clothes to shield her nakedness. "You can't. That's illegal." She struggled to put on her clothes. Jack didn't try to stop her. He merely stood, picked up the phone and began to dial.

"W-what are you doing? Stop that!"

Jack ignored her, the phone pressed to one ear. "You understand that this tape will become evidence. It could even be made public, unless you hire a sharp attorney." He turned his attention to the phone, where a recorded voice was telling him the correct time. "Hello, police?"

Ellen lunged for the phone cradle, cutting off the connection. Her clothes dropped to the ground." Let's not do that ... um ... yet," she begged. "Let's talk a little longer, okay?"

"Last chance," he said. "I don't want to play games any more. Either you agree to use your 'personal assets' to pay me back, or this conversation is over."

She stood, trying to maintain what dignity she had left. Silence filled the room, stretching time. Jack watched as she wrestled with her decision.

"All right," she said at last. "I'll do your dirty work. I'll be your, uh, slave. It will cost me my self-esteem and probably my marriage, but I'll agree to, um, work for you until I've paid my debt."

"Plus interest," Jack put in, "which we'll set at seven percent a year, a true bargain, considering. Agreed?" He pointed at the camera.

She squared her shoulders and looked up at it. "Agreed."

"Good." He got up and walked around to his desk. "I'm shutting down the camera now. I don't think we'll need it any longer." He pointed a remote unit at a bookcase and Ellen could hear the VCR click off.

She watched as Jack retrieved the tape and immediately locked it into his safe, mounted behind a painting along one wall. He turned back to Ellen.

"From now on, your name will be El. I don't think a slut like you deserves a complete name. We'll announce tomorrow that you're changing jobs, going from CFO to secretary. You do what I tell you to do, without question, no matter how embarrassing. You'll call me 'Mr. Sawyer,' 'sir' or 'master' at all times."

El blanched, but said nothing.

"I'm going to have a small camera and a light installed under your desk, with a feed into my office here. When you are sitting down, you are to spread your legs so I can see your naked pussy, which must be shaved daily or waxed smooth. Whenever I call you, no matter what you're doing or who else is in the room with you, I want you to put the fingers of your free hand on your pussy and rub it as long as we are speaking. However, you are not allowed to come by yourself. So if I catch you having an orgasm out there, you'll be punished."

Her mouth dropped open and the color began to drain from El's face.

"When I call you into my office, once that door is closed behind you, I want you to immediately remove all your clothes, come over to my desk and kneel, then ask, 'How may I serve you, master?' You understand?"

She nodded like an automaton. She appeared to be in shock.

"I may have someone in my office at the time. It doesn't matter to you. You strip naked. You might be asked to take care of them. If so, I'll reduce your debt at the rate of one hundred dollars for a blow-job and two-fifty for a fuck, ass or pussy. Any time I fuck you, it doesn't count toward your debt, that's just part of the overhead you pay for your new position. Sometimes, you might be asked to go somewhere to meet guests and do whatever they tell you to do. I'll keep track of your debt payments, and you can check them anytime." Jack smiled thinly. "Unlike you, I have no desire to cheat you."

"W-what—"

"Oh, that's another thing," he interrupted. "You are not to speak unless you are given permission or spoken to first."

She thought about that for a moment. "May I speak, sir?"

He waited a long beat, then: "Yes, my slut."

She blinked at the casual insult, and asked: "What about Bill?"

"That's your problem. You can tell him or not, up to you. But if you do and he gets the idea that he needs to come here and protect you from me, you'd better convince him otherwise. If anything happens to me, even a threat, I'll cancel the deal and a full accounting of your activities will be reported to the authorities, including that tape I just made."

She thought about that for a moment. Jack could see the wheels turning in her head. "So, you want me available at all times? Like days and nights?"

"Yes, although it will be mostly days. Think of it this way, the more you earn, the sooner you'll be done with this. I think if you really applied yourself, you could earn three grand a week. That'd mean you could pay me off in eighteen months."

Jack could see the information weigh heavy on her. Eighteen months probably sounded like forever. He figured she'd be a completely different person at the end of it.

"Okay, let's get started. I want you to suck me off." Jack splayed his legs apart. El hesitated, then sank to her knees and began fumbling with his pants. He could see her hands were trembling.

"Do you suck your husband's cock?"

She didn't look up. "Y-yes, sometimes."

"Well, you'd better get used to it. You're going to become an expert."

El managed to free his flaccid cock and bent down to take it into her mouth. Her licking soon caused it to swell, allowing her to draw more of it into her throat. She began to move her face quickly up and down his shaft, as if to hurry him along.

"No," he cautioned. "Take your time, like a high-class hooker would."

She slowed her pace immediately, but didn't stop slurping and licking. After a few minutes, Jack could feel his climax approaching. He grabbed her face and moved it up and down on his cock at his own rhythm. She struggled for a moment, then let him have his way. He felt his cock twitch, then explode into her mouth.

She gasped and tried to pull away, but Jack held her tight until his cock was spent. Then he allowed his soft cock to slip from her juicy mouth. Ropes of his seed ran down her chin.

"That was a fine first effort, except that you MUST swallow cum at all times. Do you understand?"

She nodded, unable to speak. She closed her mouth

and Jack could see the muscles in her throat working. He pointed to the drool on her chin and she wiped it up with her fingers. He made her suck them clean.

"All right." He pushed her away from his lap. "I want you to get dressed. I never want to see you in a business suit again after today, unless I order it. I'm giving you the rest of the day off so you can go shopping for the types of outfits appropriate for a slut. You know what to buy: short skirts, skimpy tops, high heels."

Jack watched, unmoved, as tears began to flow down her cheeks. "M-master, may I speak?" Her voice caught.

"Yes, slave."

"H-how will I live? If all my money goes to pay off the debt, how can I make my house payments, pay utilities, buy groceries?"

Jack had been ready for that question. "First of all, tell Bill he needs to get a job, any job. His free ride is over. And he'd better not lose his next job. For now, I'll let you keep the house. I want you to bring your receipts for your mortgage payment, and other routine bills. I will pay half of your living expenses, and add the totals to your debt. Billy boy can pay the other half or he can move out. There'll be no money for extras, such as vacations or fancy cars. You'll have to sell your Mercedes and bring me the money to help offset the cost of keeping you."

"But, master, how will I get to work?"

"Either I'll pick you up, or I'll send a car."

He asked her approximately what her monthly household expenses were, and she gave him a figure. Jack ran the totals on his calculator. "Looks like that's going to add at least another year to your debt."

El's head sagged in defeat. One of her tears fell unnoticed onto her breast.

"Any more questions?" He could tell she had several, but she merely shook her head. "All right. You may get dressed and go. Be ready for your new position at 8:30 tomorrow."

She nodded and stood up, seemingly no longer concerned about her nakedness. Her shoulders slumped. Jack could see some of his semen, mixed with her saliva, spotting her heaving breasts. Before she could step back, he reached out and grabbed one of them. She froze, a questioning look on her face. "Looks like you forgot some," he pointed out.

She looked down, and used her fingers to scoop up the fluid and lick it. He released her and she began putting on her clothes. Jack felt a bit of sadness, watching this magnificent beauty cover up her nudity. He much preferred her naked and vulnerable. When she was dressed, she asked for permission to go. Jack smiled and nodded.

Chapter 2

Jack parked outside El's house at 8:35 the next morning and honked. Her Mercedes still sat in the driveway with a "For Sale" sign stuck in the back window. He wondered if she had told Bill the news, or if she was going to try to hide it from him.

The door opened immediately, and El came out, peering anxiously around her neighborhood, as if afraid someone might see her. She looked like a different woman. She was dressed in a red skirt that came to mid-thigh, a white tank top and black pumps with two-inch heels. Jack thought the shoes could be a bit higher, but overall, she looked good, in a trashy sort of way. As she approached, he could tell she wasn't wearing a bra, just as he had ordered. He could easily see the nipples poking tents into the cloth. He suspected she wasn't wearing panties, either. He'd find out soon enough.

She raced down the steps and got in the passenger seat quickly. Jack waited, staring at the door to see if Bill would come out, angry and shouting. Nothing happened.

He turned to El, noting that her makeup was the same as yesterday, not nearly slutty enough. "Did you tell Bill?"

"Um, sort of. I told him I stole some money to cover for his being out of work and I'm going to have to pay it back. I didn't tell him exactly how. He still thinks I'm the CFO."

"Dressed like this?"

She could see the flush creep up her neck to her ears. "He didn't ask a lot of questions. I think he's in shock about the whole thing. I know he feels partially responsible."

Jack nodded, staring at the house. That made sense. But he'd have to monitor the situation. It wouldn't do to have an irate husband stirring things up. He turned back to El. "Okay. You look pretty good. But there are a couple of things." He ticked them off his fingers. "One, you're not wearing enough makeup. You look like the businesswoman you used to be, not the slut you are. You're going to need more lipstick, eyeliner, the works. Two, whenever you come into the car, I want you to spread your legs apart and show me your cunt. Sit bare-assed on the seat."

She made a small noise in her throat, and lifted her ass up off the seat. She pulled the back of her skirt out of the way, then sat down again. Jack peered closer, noting that she had attempted to shave her mound, but had left quite a bit of stubble. "You call that shaved?"

She flushed even redder, if that was possible. "S-sorry, sir, I did it myself and it's hard to reach everywhere."

"You didn't tell your husband that you were shaving it?"

"No, sir. Not yet."

That caused Jack to think of something else. "How often do you and Bill fuck, on average?"

El looked at the floor. "Um, about once a week. It used to be a lot more, but because he's been out of work lately, I'm not often in the mood for him, you understand."

"Yes, I do. Does he use a condom?"

She glanced up at him, as if considering whether she should challenge him for his prying questions, but his look told her he was serious. Before she could answer, he grabbed her upper arm. "Don't every try to lie to me or conceal facts. You have no privacy or secrets from me now, do you understand?"

"Yes, Ja—I mean, Mr. Sawyer."

"Okay, answer the question."

"No, sir. I'm on the pill."

"Okay, from now on, you are to inform me whenever you fuck Bill—or anyone else. I want to hear details."

She took a deep breath. "Yes, sir."

"I will decide later if I want you wearing yourself out on your husband, when you could be letting that pussy earn my money back."

"Yes, sir."

"Now, as to these other things. I want you to go back into your house and bring a bag containing your makeup kit, shaving cream and a razor."

She blanched and Jack thought she was going to refuse, but she didn't. She seemed to gather herself, then unlatched the door and got out. He watched her adjust her tiny skirt, then trudge up the steps and disappear inside. She came out onto the porch a few minutes later, followed by Bill. He seemed upset, or at least filled with questions.

El brushed him off and hurried back to the car, a small paper bag clutched in one hand. Bill stared at Jack, then shook his head and retreated inside. Jack wondered if he intimidated Bill. After all, Jack held their future in his hands. And Bill was not a big man, so he didn't seem to be much of a threat. Jack knew Bill would be wrestling with his demons over this and wouldn't be sure what to make of it. Eventually, Jack believed El would have to tell him, and there could be trouble if Bill decided to go after him or call the cops.

El had reseated herself, remembering to pull up her skirt. Jack put the car into reverse and backed slowly out of the driveway. He turned and started forward, glancing down occasionally to check out El's bare pussy. He reached over and let his fingers touch her slit. She jerked slightly, then settled down and let him stroke her.

He didn't say anything to her during the drive and she seemed to know better than to talk first. Whenever he glanced at her face, she was staring straight ahead. She tried hard to ignore his fingers.

He pulled into the plant and parked in his reserved spot, right near the door. He got out, paying no attention to El. She struggled to get out, holding the bag in one hand, and trying to move her skirt down quickly with the other. Jack could see a flash of her bronze bottom before she could cover it.

She followed him inside, walking quickly with her head down. She avoided the stares of the few others she saw on the way to his office. El started to follow Jack inside, but he stopped her immediately. "Your office is ready for you, just down the hall. I want you to enter through your door. I'll call you when I need you."

She nodded vacantly and left. Jack could only imagine the sight that greeted her. While she had been gone yesterday, he'd had her desk turned so it faced the glass door into the hallway. Her modesty would be protected by the kick panel in front, but he knew she'd feel more on display this way. He'd had a tiny camera installed underneath her desk, and another one high up behind her.

He went to his desk and unlocked the top right-hand drawer, where the small flat-panel screen had been installed. He flicked a switch. The screen came on, showing the view from the overhead camera. He watched as El walked around the room slowly, as if she couldn't believe this was to be her prison for the next couple of years. It was much smaller than her CFO's office, consisting of little more than a desk, a chair, a computer and a phone. Everything in the office could be seen through the glass door from the hallway outside.

He observed her as she put down her bag on the desk, empty except for the phone and a computer monitor. Nervously, El pulled the chair out and peered underneath it, noticing the small spotlight there, chair high. She looked more closely and spotted the camera, then shook her head. El sat down and scooted herself up close. Jack flipped over to the other camera and observed her legs open in front of him, giving him a good view of her naked loins. The light illuminated her perfectly. Still, that stubble bothered him. At least she had remembered her orders. He wondered if she would remember them all.

He flipped back to the other camera and waited until someone walked by and spotted her in the former secretary's chair. It was Gloria Murphy, Jack could see, from human resources. She came in, clearly stunned. They chatted. Jack turned a knob next to the screen and the words came through a small speaker.

"—you doing here?" Gloria seemed flummoxed.

El fidgeted. "Um, I'm Jack's new secretary."

"What about your job?"

"I don't know what's going to happen with that."

"You mean, you-you've been demoted?"

"I'd prefer to call it a mutual decision."

"But why? And why wasn't I informed?"

"I'm not at liberty to say. You'll have to ask Jack."

Jack smiled, watching the scene. Her first mistake, calling him Jack. El's embarrassment pleased him. He picked up the phone. He watched as it rang on El's desk. She jumped, then reached for it with her left hand. Gloria watched her, waiting for her to finish so she could pepper her with additional questions.

Jack observed that while El's right hand strayed to her

lap, her fingers didn't touch her pussy. He had expected as much. Her second mistake.

"Yes, sir?"

"Yes, El. I wanted you to take some dictation. We're going to have to come up with something to say about your change of job assignment."

"Yes, sir." She started to hang up.

"Oh, and El..."

She froze in place, then brought the receiver back to her ear. "What did I tell you to do whenever you were on the phone with me?"

"Um, yes, sir. I'll do that right away, sir."

Jack switched the camera and watched as El's right hand crept closer to her groin, finally reaching in and just brushing her slit. He switched back in time to catch Gloria staring at her as if she'd lost her mind.

"Well, I have to go," El was telling her. "I've got to see Ja –, er, Mr. Sawyer."

Gloria stood there, speechless, as El rose, adjusting her small skirt with as much dignity as she could muster. Then she came to the door connecting the two offices and entered.

Jack flicked off the screen and pushed the drawer back into place.

El seemed grateful to be able to close the door behind her, shutting Gloria out. Jack imagined that Gloria would waste no time in spreading the news about Ellen's bizarre new behavior.

"Yes, sir?" she said, standing by the door.

"You seem to have forgotten the rules of your employment."

El started, taking a step back. Then she immediately began stripping off her clothes. In seconds, she was naked.

She came over by Jack's chair and sank to her knees. "How may I help you, master?"

"Knees wider apart. There, that's better." Jack let her stew for a moment. "Let's take care of this memo to employees, shall we?" He handed her a pad and pen.

She took it, still on her knees, her face blank. He dictated a short note about El's job change without giving any details. He told her to use her "new" name in the release, El Sanchez. She wrote down the information with a shaky hand. Jack could've dashed out the note himself in far less time, but it pleased him to have her be the author of her own demotion notice.

When he was done, he told her to write it up and sent to him for approval. She started to get up, and he stopped her. "I can't very well let you get away with your bad behavior, now can I?"

"B-bad behavior?" To El, no doubt her failures to obey were minor transgressions, easily forgiven. Jack had to let her know where she stood.

"Yes. You called me Jack in front of Gloria. You failed to rub your pussy, even when I reminded you. And you didn't strip immediately upon entering my office."

"S-sorry, sir. It won't happen again."

"And then there's the matter of your sloppy shaving job. I guess I'll have to correct that mistake myself, won't I?" He paused. "Unless you want Gloria to do it."

She rocked back onto her heels. "Oh, no, sir! Please. I'd rather you did it."

"You know, of course, that what you'd 'rather' have happen is no longer important."

"Um, yes, sir."

Jack thought for a moment. "I'll give you a choice of punishments. You can either work in your office naked for the next two hours, or you can submit to a spanking with my belt."

El looked horrified. "No, Sir! Master! You can't! Please, I beg you,"

"Which is it to be, El?"

Her eyes roamed around, as if looking for an escape. For the first time, Jack believed she was finally realizing what she had gotten herself into. "I'll-I'll take the spanking, sir. Anything but w-work naked in front of anyone walking by! I'd just die!"

He nodded. "Place yourself over the desk." He stood and removed his belt.

She obeyed warily, spreading herself flat and gripping the far end of the desk as if her life depended on it, her eyes never leaving the belt in his hand. When she was in position, her lovely rounded ass up and ready for him, she suddenly blurted, "Master? May I speak?"

He sighed as if greatly bothered by her interruption. "Yes, what is it?"

"W-won't people hear us? That could prove, um, hard to explain."

Jack pretended to think about it. "Yes, you're right. I'm not so concerned about the slapping of my belt on your ass, but your screams could cause problems. Go get me your top."

She sprang up, as if grateful for the reprieve. It was a short one, however. When she returned with the scrap of cloth, he indicated she should reposition herself. When she had done so, he made her open her mouth and pressed part of the wadded up shirt inside.

"Try not to make too much noise," he said. She nodded, her eyes wide with shock. He wondered how she was going to explain this to her husband.

He stood back and let her have a crack with the belt. She screamed into the gag, clearly startled by how hard he struck her. Jack admired the nice red welt it raised on her honey-toned ass. Already sweat was beading up on her forehead and her eyes pleaded with him to stop.

He struck her again, and again, moving the belt around each time to cover all the unmarked areas. He let out some of his anger at her betrayal. He stopped at five, deciding to go easy on her. Jack wasn't surprised to see the spanking had caused her slit to expand. Her juices glistened in the light. Despite her protestations, this seemed to turn her on.

"Okay," he told her, putting the belt back into the loops on his pants, "that will do for now. If you are disobedient again, I'll have to give you ten strokes."

She shook her head wildly, as if she'd never consider such a thing. Jack leaned down and pulled the top from her mouth. The breath exploded from her. "Oh, master! May I speak?"

"Yes, slut."

"That really hurt! Please, I'll be good. I promise!"

"You'd better be."

She rubbed her ass gingerly and whimpered.

"Now that that's out of the way, I think it's time we took care of your other problems."

"Other problems?"

"Yes. Go bring me the bag you brought from home."

Her eyes flew open as she realized she'd left it on her desk. She grabbed her top and went to the door, stooping to pick up her skirt. Jack's voice stopped her in her tracks. "I didn't say to get dressed first."

She froze, the clothes bunched in her hands. "You-you want me to walk out there n-n-naked?" She couldn't believe it.

"Yes."

She turned and as if on stilts, walked stiff-legged to the door. Jack took the opportunity to open the desk drawer and turn on the main camera. The hallway outside her office was deserted.

El peered through. Jack could see her face appear on the left side of the screen. She checked the corridor through the glass door. When it seemed safe, she bolted through, snatched up the bag and ran back to the safety of Jack's office. He smiled and carefully shut the drawer.

"Here it is, master." She put the bag on his desk and stood back, waiting. Her obedience seemed much improved.

"Go into my washroom and put on more makeup. I want you to look like a hooker. After you're done, bring me a hot, wet towel and a dry one," he ordered, opening the bag and handing her the makeup kit. She wiggled her way to the bathroom. Jack grinned at the stripes on her ass. She disappeared inside. It was quiet for several minutes. Then he heard water running. A short time later, she returned. Her face had more rouge and her eyelids were blue. Red lipstick had been slathered on her mouth. He nodded his approval. "That's a good start. It would help if you got some false eyelashes."

He took the dry towel from her, folded it and laid it right at the edge of his desk. "Here. Back up against this, then lean back until your shoulders hit the blotter."

Warily, she obeyed. When she was in place, Jack could see she didn't know what to do with her legs. Letting them hang down assuaged her modesty, but the desk rubbed against her welts. Raising her legs and hooking her heels on the edge of the desk eased her pain, but exposed her private parts directly to his leering gaze.

He watched while she wrestled with the dilemma.

Finally, she decided the pain won out over modesty, so she let her heels rest on the desk, splaying her legs wide. Jack nodded in agreement at her decision and rolled his chair in close. He was sure she could feel his breath on her pussy. It remained wet and slightly open. Her breath was shallow.

"You didn't do too bad on the top, but you missed a lot down here," he commented, as if he were talking to a barber about a haircut. She blushed red.

Jack placed the hot towel on her loins to soften up the hairs. He left it there for several minutes, whistling softly to himself. Once, he reached up and tweaked one of her nipples, causing her to start. He noticed both her nipples swelled.

He removed the towel and squirted a good portion of shaving cream into his hand. He carefully spread it above and around her slit, noticing how his touch further excited her. Her clitoris swelled until he could see it poking out from under its hood. He wondered how it would look with a gold ring through the skin above it. He glanced up at her nipples, imagining them with similar gold rings. Nice.

He took the razor and began to shave her, starting at the bottom and working against the grain. He carefully folded her labia to the side to get into the creases. El said nothing, but she began to breathe more heavily. Jack knew she was really becoming aroused now. He could see it in the amount of fluid that was dripping from her slit and collecting on the towel below.

He shaved carefully. Once the phone rang, and he stopped, pulling away just in time to prevent nicking her. She acted as if she was going to get up, but he held her in place with one hand while he answered the phone.

Jack could see it was an internal call. "Yes? Oh, yes, Gloria. Yes, her job has been changed. I just decided I needed her in this position." He winked at El, his head framed between her obscenely splayed legs. She looked away in embarrassment. "Oh, salary? Well, don't worry about that for now. Yes, I'll let you know. Yes, we're working on a memo now."

He hung up. "Looks like the natives are getting restless. They want an explanation. I wonder if the memo will satisfy them?"

El just shook her head.

Jack returned to his work. He was enjoying himself immensely. He shaved her until he was sure he had gotten every stray hair, then wiped her down with the damp towel. "There," he said, sitting back and admiring his handiwork. "That's how I want to see you from now on."

"Um, master, may I speak?"

"Yes, slut."

"It's hard for me to reach everywhere. But if you enjoy it, I-I would be happy to make myself available to you every day."

That didn't surprise Jack. He could see she was turned on by the attention. But he didn't want to be working for her, even in this small way. "That could become tiresome, slut. Tell ya what. You got a beauty salon you go to?"

El paled and shook her head.

"Really?" Jack seemed nonplused. "I thought every girl had a salon."

"Well, Ja—I mean, Mr. Sawyer, I have a woman who cuts my hair, but she ... she would never ... I mean..."

"Hmm, that's too bad. So you need to find a full-service beauty parlor. I wonder if Gloria could help." He picked up the phone.

El shot bolt upright. "No sir! That's not necessary. Um ... maybe I can have Bill do it."

Jack smiled. Somehow, that appealed to him, to have Bill be complicit in his wife's sexual degradation. "Sure, whatever. Just make sure your pussy is shaved clean every day. If I decide I want to do it again, I'll let you know."

He pushed her back down. She didn't resist. Jack ran his fingers around the now-smooth surface. More fluids dripped from her slit. She squirmed, though she tried to hide it. "I'm going to be checking it every day, so don't disappoint me." He let his fingertips brush along the edge, gathering some of the clear fluid. He brought it to his mouth and sampled it. It had a sweet, pungent taste.

He could see her eyes on his face. Her lust was impossible to disguise now. Her hips twitched, her skin seemed to glow. He knew she wanted him and would do anything to have his cock thrusting into her in the next few minutes.

Perfect, he thought. He checked his watch. Ten o'clock. Just right. The phone rang again. An outside line, this time. El looked pained as he answered it.

"Jack Sawyer. Oh, yes, Bob. So glad you called!" The call had been prearranged for ten, but El didn't know that. Jack had been trying to land this client for a while now, but had been unable to pry him loose from Michigan Manufacturing. He had invited Bob Orley to stop by today, promising him a "deal he couldn't refuse." Jack had told him to call him at ten, when he was on his way to the plant.

"I don't know why I'm coming by, Jack," Bob said in his ear. "I told you I'm happy with Michigan."

"Yeah, but I'll bet they don't have the right package of incentives that I've developed," Jack replied. He noticed that El seemed to become alarmed at the direction this conversation was going. She tried to get up, but he put a hand on her hip, keeping her in position.

They talked for a few more minutes, then Jack said, "Okay, I'll see you soon," and hung up.

"Master, may I speak," El immediately said.

Jack thought about that. "No, slut."

El's eyes widened. He could tell she didn't know what to do now. Always before, when she asked to speak, Jack allowed it. Now, when she had some serious questions about "Bob," he shut her down. She tried to get up again, but he again stopped her with a hand.

"Don't get up," he ordered, and the tone of his voice conveyed to her that she might be in store for another whipping if she disobeyed. She lay back, panting. Jack ran his finger up her slit to the clitoris, causing her to jump. He reached into the center drawer and brought out a condom, still in its wrapper, and tossed it onto her stomach. Her face told him everything.

"Wait here. Don't move." He got up and went into El's office, closing the door behind him. He wondered if she would obey him or if he'd come back in a few minutes and find her hiding in the bathroom.

The glass door opened and Bob strolled in. Bob Orley was a big, handsome, good ol' boy, one who liked the camaraderie of his business pals. Jack believed that's why he'd stuck so long with Michigan Manufacturing—the owner was an old high school friend of his.

But a lot had happened in the years since, and Jack had heard through the grapevine that Bob's loyalty was beginning to fray. Perhaps he'd not gotten the terms he'd asked for, or perhaps Michigan had begun to take his business for granted. Either way, Jack thought Bob might be open to another offer.

Jack also knew Bob had been married to the same woman for twenty-five years, a real cow. Bob's extra-marital escapades were legendary and who could blame him? But Jack doubted Bob had ever experienced the delights of a slim young woman like El. She was about to pay back some of her debt, big time. If Bob agreed to switch to Sawyer Metalworking, it would bring in tens of thousands of extra dollars per year.

Of course, he wouldn't tell El that. She'd have to repay her debt one fuck at a time. She could keep Bob happy anytime he wanted to stop by, at two-fifty a throw.

Bob shook his hand and they chatted for a while. When the moment was right, Jack laid out his proposal, offering a slightly lower price and quicker turnaround time.

"Above all, Bob, I want you to know that Sawyer Metalworking really wants your business. We'd work hard to please you every day. I can guarantee you'd never be sorry you switched."

Jack could see the reluctance on Bob's face. Before he could respond, Jack added: "Oh, and to help seal the deal, I've got a little gift for you in my office. That's yours, whether you go with us or not."

Bob looked questioningly at the door. "You want me to go in?"

Jack nodded. "I'll just wait out here for a bit."

He watched as Bob opened the door and looked in. His mouth dropped open. That told Jack that El was being the obedient sex slave she should be. Bob shot Jack a big grin, then disappeared inside, closing the door softly behind him.

He sat on the edge of El's new desk and listened to the dim noises through the door. At first all he could hear was the alto of El's voice as she climbed toward an orgasm. He imagined Bob had just plopped down between her legs and dove in, lapping her to a quick climax. Now he could hear Bob's bass vocals, intercut with El's cries as she neared her second orgasm. He knew they were fucking in earnest now.

Jack's cock hardened and he wanted to fuck her himself, just as soon as Bob was finished. There came a muffled cacophony of sounds: flesh slapping flesh, cries, small objects falling to the floor. A crescendo of voices erupted, then silence.

In about ten minutes, Bob reappeared in the doorway. "That was right neighborly of ya," he said, a foolish grin on his face. "I'll have to think hard about this. Would you mind if I came back, say, day after tomorrow, to explore your offer further?"

"Sure. How about the same time then?"

His smile broadened. "I have to tell ya, Jack, I never got this kind of treatment from Michigan."

"Well, that's why our customers are one-hundred percent satisfied."

After Bob left, Jack returned to his office. Surprisingly, El was still on her back on the desk, her legs splayed out, her head tipped away from him. When she heard him, she turned toward him. Jack had expected tears, but was surprised to find her still panting from her orgasm. The skin on her chest and neck was mottled with pink.

"How did it go?"

Her mouth opened and closed as if she had trouble finding her voice. "It was ... incredible."

"Really?" He was surprised, but pleased that El had enjoyed it too. It would certainly make it easier for her to embrace her new duties.

"Yes, sir." She propped herself up on one elbow. "I've never had an orgasm like that before. Not with Bill, not with anyone."

"That's great, because he's coming back again the day after tomorrow."

El sat up. "Really?" Her expression told him she was looking forward to it."

"Yes, you did very well for your first effort. That's two-fifty off your debt. I'll make the entry now." He called up the Excel program and added the total. It made an insignificant dent, of course, but it was a start.

"Did he use a condom?"

"Yes, sir. I handed it to him first thing and he didn't object. It made me feel safe, you know. Maybe that's why I came so hard."

Jack nodded. El might prove to be excellent at her new job. "So tell me what happened."

El didn't even flush. "Well, first he went down on me. Being shaved so close, it was really sensitive! I liked it a lot. I came so hard I thought I'd pass out." She looked down as if she was too embarrassed to hold Jack's gaze. "He's really good at that." She looked up and Jack just nodded, so she continued. "Then he, um, fucked me. He has a very nice-sized cock. He hit all the right spots."

"That's good, El. You did well."

"Sir, may I get up now?"

"No." He unzipped his pants. She sighed and lay back flat, spreading her legs for him. "One more rule to remember, slut. While you may ask clients to use condoms, I don't wish to use one. Therefore, you should stay on the pill."

"Yes, sir."

"Good." He stepped up and aimed his rock-hard cock at her slippery entrance. He couldn't explain why fucking her after Bob enticed him so. Perhaps it was the "naughty factor." Or perhaps that her actions might result in Sawyer winning a big contract. Either way, it excited him. He pressed his cock into her, watching as the folds parted and the juices flowed around him. He continued to press until his balls slapped gently against her ass, then he pulled back and began thrusting, grabbing her hips for leverage.

El began to get into the action, rocking her hips in time with his movements. Jack could feel himself rising to a powerful climax. He didn't hold back, he didn't care for her pleasure, only his own. When he was ready, he thrust hard against her and squirted his seed deep into her.

In seconds, El came as well, grabbing his forearms so tightly he though she might cut off the circulation to his hands. They clung together while the orgasm ended. Finally, Jack pulled away. He could see the mixture of fluids pour out of her gaping slit onto the towel.

"Okay, you can get up now," he gasped.

She rolled over onto one elbow and pushed herself the rest of the way up. "May I go to the bathroom, master?"

"Clean me first."

She dropped to her knees and took his cock gently into her rosebud mouth. It felt good to have her lips around it, even though he was quite sensitive. When she was finished, she sat back.

He nodded. "Okay, go ahead."

"Thank you, sir," she said before she disappeared into the bathroom. Jack buttoned himself up and sank back into his chair. He checked his watch. Eleven-thirty. A lot had happened and it wasn't even noon yet.

Chapter 3

El stared at the face of a harlot in the mirror above the sink. It made her feel like she was somebody else. The Ellen she knew from before seemed to recede in her mind. She used a damp towel to clean up her pussy. It felt good now, being shaved so close. Of course, it also felt good to have been fucked so completely. Bill had never made her come like this. No one had. Was it because Jack had spanked her first? Teased her? Was it because she really enjoyed being taken by a stranger, at the orders of her boss?

She couldn't explain what had happened to her. She told herself she had agreed to this crazy, illegal scheme only to avoid prison for embezzlement. But deep down, she knew there was another reason, one she couldn't articulate at first. It was her id—it needed the raw, powerful sex, the submissiveness that Jack demanded. This part of her had been long suppressed. Now it had come flooding to the surface, not to be denied.

She cleaned herself up as best she could and came back out to face whatever Jack had in store for her. But now she wasn't afraid, not like she had been yesterday, when he had confronted her with the evidence. For some inexplicable reason, she felt free for the first time in her life. Maybe it was because she no longer had to be making any decisions.

Bill had let her do that. She'd been taking care of him for years. The thought of her lazy husband tarnished her mood. She knew he was eventually going to find out just exactly what she'd been doing to avoid arrest and she doubted he'd be able to handle it.

"El."

She shook off her thoughts and came to Jack's side. "Yes, master?" She knelt down, knees wide apart.

"You were very good this morning. Beyond my expectations. But now I'm behind in my work, I'm afraid." El shot him a worried expression. "No, no," he said quickly. "It's not your fault. It just means I'm going to have to work through lunch hour. I'd like you to order me something from the deli. Turkey sandwich will be fine and some iced tea. Order yourself something too."

She nodded. She knew the deli. They delivered, which meant she didn't have to go outside and endure looks from strangers. Despite her enjoyment of slutty sex with Bob and Jack, she still felt embarrassed for others to see what a slut she'd become. It didn't make a lot of sense, but there it was.

"May I put on my clothes?"

He nodded. She got dressed quickly and returned to her office. Her pussy still leaked some fluids and she worried that it would stain the back of her dress. She took some tissues and folded them, tucking them between the crack of her ass and the miniskirt.

As she scooted up close to the desk, she remembered to spread her legs, so he could see her. Before she could pick up the phone, the intercom buzzed. She picked it up, her other hand automatically moving to her clit, where she rubbed it vigorously, even though she was somewhat sore.

"Yes, sir?"

"I just wanted to see if you remembered," her master said over the phone. "And what's that under your ass?"

El paled. "Oh, um, that's some tissue. I didn't want to stain my dress."

"No," she heard him say. "Remove it. If your dress gets

stained, if everybody can see, that just proves what a slut you are. They don't have to know that you're doing it to repay what you stole, but I don't want you to hide what you've become."

She found herself nodding and reluctantly removed the now-damp tissue. She knew her skirt would soon be soaked through. Whenever she walked down the corridor, people behind her would point and laugh silently. The image of it both excited and embarrassed her, and her fingers rubbing her clit only made it worse.

"Yes, sir. I'm about to order your lunch now, sir."

"Go ahead." He hung up.

She pulled her hand away from her aching slit and called the deli. She ordered two turkey sandwiches and two iced teas. She wondered if she was going to have to pay for it and how she might do it—she didn't have any money. She reached for the phone, ready to call Jack, but then held off. He wouldn't want to be bothered by something petty like this.

The delivery boy came in twenty minutes later. He couldn't have been older than twenty. He still had a spray of acne across his face. He had long hair, tucked up under a reversed ball cap, jeans, and a blue shirt with the name of the deli on it.

He smiled when he saw El's skimpy top and the nipples poking through. "Order here for Sawyer," he said, holding up the bag. "Comes to seventeen-fifty-seven."

"I don't have any cash on me. Can you put it on the company tab?"

He shook his head. "We don't do that anymore. Too many people tried to stiff us."

"Well, I could get it from Jack, but he's busy right now. Can you wait until later today?"

"Sorry, ma'am." His eyes never left her breasts.

She took the hint. "Isn't there something else we could work out?" She scooted back from the desk, letting him see her short skirt. His eyes grew wide. "What'ya have in mind?"

"A blow-job?"

The deli boy looked around. "Here?"

"You can sit at my desk. I'll go underneath. No one will notice, unless you cry out or something."

His face brightened. "Sure." She got up, turned around and backed down under the desk. It caused her legs to splay apart, hiking up her dress. When he sat down, El could tell he could clearly see her bare pussy, distended and reddened from recent fuckings, still dripping fluids. She allowed him stare for a few seconds, then signaled him to move up. He scooted up close until his groin was right in front of her. She unzipped him and let his swelling cock spring free. But the desk was too low; she kept banging her head when she tried to envelope the mushroom head.

"Lower your chair," she said to his penis. He fumbled for the lever and soon he dropped down to a more manageable height. Now she could reach him properly. She took him into her mouth, sucking and licking. He tasted like she might've imagined a young man would, all sweet and sassy, full of energy and need. She teased him for less than a minute before he spasmed, shooting his seed into her mouth. She swallowed it easily, although some spilled onto her chin.

He scooted back a bit, a big grin on his face. He zipped up. "Wow! That was really great! Anytime you want to order anything, just ask for Frankie!"

"Okay, Frankie. I'll do that." She used her finger to scoop up the remaining sperm and suck it clean. She started to get up, but Frankie blocked her way.

"Uhh," he said, staring down at her.

"What?"

"For a tip, could you let me see your ... uh, you know ... again?"

She gave him a knowing smile. "Okay. Since you've been so nice." She couldn't believe she'd stooped so low so quickly. It was as if that person she'd been yesterday was a distant memory. Now she was on her knees, showing a boy her pussy that had just been royally fucked by two men.

She squatted on the carpet, spread her legs wide and pulled up the front of her dress, letting Frankie get a good look. He just stared, his mouth partially ajar. Then she pushed her skirt down and he wheeled back, letting her out. He stood and nodded to her.

"Thanks for your order."

"You're welcome."

After he left, she thumbed the switch on the intercom.

"Yes?" His voice sent chills down her back.

"I've got your food, sir. Would you like it now?"

"Yes."

She clicked off, then froze. She suddenly realized, she had forgotten to rub her pussy while she spoke to him. Damnit! Would he notice? She couldn't stand another spanking—her ass was already too sore.

Squaring her shoulders, she marched in, hoping for the best. She remembered, just after she shut the door, to put the bag down on a nearby chair and remove all her clothes, the few that she had on.

She approached Jack, holding out the bag, pretending that nothing was wrong. She dropped to her knees. He eyed her carefully. "How did you pay for this?"

"Well, sir, I didn't have any money, so..." She hesitated, not sure if he'd be mad or not. The words came out in a rush. "I blew him for it."

Jack laughed. "I know, I watched. I just wanted to hear you say it. Remember, don't keep any secrets from me."

"Will that count toward my debt?"

He cocked his head to the side. "Why, yes, I think it should. I didn't ask you to do it, but I admire your initiative." He turned to his computer. "That makes three-fifty you've earned so far and the day's only half over!"

He unwrapped the sandwich and took a bite. El, not sure if she would be allowed to eat, remained at his side on her knees, waiting for instructions.

"Despite your initiative, I am disappointed in you," he said, his mouth partially full. El froze. He knew!

She tried to pretend ignorance. "Wh-what do you mean, sir?"

"You know perfectly well what I mean."

She caved in. "You mean because I didn't touch my pussy when I called about the food?"

"That's right. And you called me Jack to the delivery boy." He shook his head in mock sadness. "I was hoping you'd learned your lesson."

She started to beg, and immediately realized it would be useless. She could only wait and hope he wouldn't spank her any more today. Her bottom was already well marked!

His eyes softened and he appeared to read her mind. "No, I don't want to spank you again. I'll tell you what, instead of a beating, which you richly deserve, how about this instead: You stay at your desk for the remainder of the day without your skirt on. You can leave it here. And I want to see your one hand on your pussy all the time. Okay?"

El felt her heart hammer in her chest. To be naked all afternoon, covered by nothing but her skimpy top? Anyone who came in would notice immediately, even if she scooted up right close to the desk. And how was she supposed to get any work done with one hand on her pussy all day?

She started to protest and realized the alternative was another spanking. She couldn't bear that. "Yes, sir," she said in a tiny voice.

"Good. Carry on." He returned to his food. El took the bag containing her sandwich and the other iced tea and walked over to the door. She stopped long enough to pull her top on over her head, then opened the door and peeked out. Her office was empty, but occasionally people would stroll by on their way to lunch. She waited until the coast was clear, then bolted for her chair. She had it scooted all the way up and was trying to decide how to eat with one hand when the intercom buzzed.

"Yes," she said, making sure her fingers rubbed her clit.

"You forgot to close the door."

She turned, chagrined, to see he was right. She looked up at the glass door, and saw two people walk by talking to each other. They paid her no mind.

"All right, sir. I'll close it."

"See that you do—oh, and slut?"

"Yes, sir?"

"Keep one hand on your pussy while you do."

She made an inarticulate sound and hung up. She stared at the hallway outside, trying to decide how best to time this. After watching the door and seeing no one, she jumped up, her right hand cupping her mound, and ran to the office door. She closed it with a nervous slam and jumped back into her chair.

The intercom rang again. Her heart sank.

"Y-yes, sir?"

"There's no need to slam the door. Do it again, only this time, close it softly."

"Ye-yes, sir." She gritted her teeth. Her lunch forgotten on her desktop. Her stomach churned. She watched the glass door until another person walked by, then got up quickly, one hand covering her privates. She opened the door to Jack's office and quietly closed it again, then turned and headed back for the chair.

She glanced up to see Scotty, the ruggedly handsome day shift foreman, standing there, open-mouthed. El wanted to die from embarrassment. She slouched down and rapidly duck-walked to her chair, trying to hide as much of her lower half as she could. She wanted to wave him away, but he came in before she could move.

"Ellen, is that you?"

"Um, yes, Scotty." Her face was beet red.

"What are you doing here? I heard you changed jobs, but why? And what's with..." He waved at her face and outfit.

"Oh, I just decided I needed a change." It was a lame excuse and Scotty wouldn't be fooled by it for a minute.

"You, um, you don't seem to be wearing any, er, pants."

She cradled her head in one hand, and stared at the blotter. The other remained in her lap, as ordered, lightly stroking her pussy, though it was driving her crazy. She just knew Jack was watching her through the camera. "No, Scotty, I'm not."

"But, why?"

Before she could answer, the office door opened and Jack walked through. "Scotty!" he said with false cheer. "Just the man I've been wanting to see. Come in!"

Scotty walked by the desk, his face a mask of confusion. As he passed by, she knew he could see the naked roundness of her hip, the way her hand disappeared under the desk.

Jack turned to El. "Carry on," he said. They both disappeared into the office. She pushed her right hand farther into her wet pussy and let her tears of shame flow.

Chapter 4

Jack brought Scotty into his office and guided him to a chair. He sat down across from him.

"What the hell is going on around here? I've never seen Sanchez acting so weird. And why isn't she in her office? What's with that outfit?" The questions spilled out of him.

"It's a long story, one that I can't tell you because of a confidentiality agreement. But I can tell you that Ellen, whom I'm now calling 'El', has agreed to help us incentivize the plant."

Scotty's expression made it clear that Jack's explanation meant nothing to him. "Incentivize? What are you talking about?"

Jack gave careful thought to what he was about to say. He knew Scotty had been divorced for ten years and didn't have a girlfriend at the moment. Not surprising because he was rather set in his ways. He liked to smoke cigars, so his clothes reeked all the time. He shaved only about every third day. He seemed to enjoy his new-found bachelor life. But Jack suspected he might be interested in some free pussy. His team might like it as well.

"As you know, we've been pitting the day shift against the night shift for years, trying to get you guys to outdo each other, with limited success. I guess it's hard to get up the energy to outdo Tom's team when all that's at stake are sets of steak knives or frozen turkeys. So I've come up with a plan to really make for an interesting contest."

Scotty seemed puzzled. "Yeah?"

"Yes, and that's where El comes in. She's agreed to be the prize for which team has the best productivity at the end of the quarter. That's just six weeks away."

Scotty shook his head. "Prize? What do you mean, prize?"

Jack leaned forward. "Perhaps you'd like to see for yourself." He reached over the desk and hit the intercom. "El?"

The strained voice came back. "Yes, sir?"

"Could you come in for a minute?"

There was a momentary silence. Then: "You mean, right now?" The voice almost sounded panicked. Scotty just stared at Jack.

"Yes, right now."

"Y-yes, sir." The intercom clicked off.

Scotty turned toward the door, watching with rapt attention. In a few seconds, the door cracked open and El came in, one hand attached to her privates. She stopped just inside the door, unsure what to do.

Jack said nothing, he just stared at her. Finally, she whimpered deep in her throat, closed the door behind her, and pulled her top off over her head. Now naked, she approached the two men, shoulders slumped. She knelt in front of Jack and asked: "How may I serve you, master?" Her face was scarlet. Her right hand never left her pussy.

Scotty's eyes bulged out. "Ellen? What's going on? Will somebody tell me what's going on?"

"Like I said, these are positive changes that have been arrived at by mutual consent. El here has agreed to help out the company in any way she can and this is one of the ways."

He turned to Jack. "But she's ... she's naked!"

"Yes, that's part of the incentive program. Wouldn't

your team like to share in her delights? All you have to do is beat Tom's team."

"But she's married!"

"Yes that's true. That's not going to be a problem, is it, El?"

El shook her head, her face down, her hair partially covering her features. Jack stood up. "Now, I'm going to leave you two alone for a while, Scotty. She wants to show you just what is at stake. And she'll do the same for Tom, so both of you will have a clear understanding of the contest."

He walked to the door and left, closing it softly behind him.

El's embarrassment burned like a brand on her skin. At the same time, her body betrayed her by producing more fluid along her slit. She could feel her labia engorge, her heat rise. She waited until the door closed, then she lifted her head and looked at Scotty.

"I-I know this is a shock, Scotty."

He stared at her body, his eyes roaming up and down until she felt she'd already been violated, and yet, she felt her desire grow.

"Come on, Ellen. You can tell me. What the hell is going on? This isn't like you! What's Jack done to you?"

"N-nothing. I mean, I really can't explain. It's a secret. But he's right in that I've got a new job now and it's to help this company really grow." *What have I gotten myself into?*

She put her hand on Scotty's arm. "You know, you can, um, do what you want with me. That's why I'm here now."

Scotty looked around suspiciously. "Is there a camera here? Am I being set up?"

"No, nothing like that." For a moment, El hoped the camera in the vent had been turned off. "It's just as I've said. I'm yours if you want. All I ask is that you wear a condom."

"You really want me to ... you know..."

She looked up at him. "Only if you want to."

He reached down and tentatively touched her breast. "I don't know what's going on here. I think you both have lost your minds. But if this is on the level, I'm not going to pass it up." He leaned down to kiss her on the cheek. El could smell cigar smoke and bad breath, but she didn't say anything.

"There're condoms in the center desk drawer," she said. "You want me on the desk or the couch?"

"Jack's desk? Nah, that'd be too creepy. Let's use the couch." El went over and lay down on her back, allowing her legs to splay apart. Scotty found the condoms and held one up to show her as he walked over. He unbuckled his pants, his eyes never leaving her bare cunt.

"You can kiss it, if you want," she said, watching him.

He ducked his head sheepishly. "Ahh, no, I'd better not. I wouldn't know what I was doing."

"You never did that with your wife, back when you were married?"

"Naah. She thought sex was, you know, dirty."

No wonder they got divorced, El thought to herself. "Well, it's not. If you want to try it, I'd help you." She decided not to tell him their boss had recently come inside her.

"Really?" He looked like a schoolboy, told he could kiss a girl at the dance.

"Sure. There's nothing to it. Just lick it, right in the folds of skin."

He paused, his face a foot away from her smooth pussy. "I'd never imagine that our CFO would be encouraging me to do all this," he said, half to himself.

"Ex-CFO. I know it's a hard adjustment. After all, it's my first day in my new job, too. It'll take some getting used to."

Scotty stretched his tongue out and flicked at her slit. El shivered. Being naked, exposed, and used by men she hardly had spoken to in the hallways really affected her in ways she'd never imagined. He licked her again and she felt her cunt respond, opening up to him.

She closed her eyes and let the sensations take her. Scotty kept licking, sometimes with the flat of his tongue and sometimes just with the tip. Her clit, she could tell, had poked out and was begging for some attention.

"Lick the top," she breathed. "Come from underneath or it'll be too tender."

She felt Scotty follow her instructions and it was delightful. She began to breathe shallowly. She could sense an orgasm approaching. El wondered if Scotty would be patient enough to let her have one.

He didn't seem to be in a hurry. He kept licking and teasing her until she knew it was close. She'd never felt so sexually alive before. He licked her again, flicking her clit and she came in a sudden rush, grabbing his head and holding it close.

"Oh God! Oh God! Oh God!" She didn't care who heard.

When she finally eased down from her climax, she realized she was still holding Scotty's face close against her sopping wet pussy. She released him and he let out a breath.

"Whew! I thought I was about to be suffocated!" he

joked. She looked down to see his face smeared with her juices. Then she looked further down and spotted his hard cock thrusting out from between his shirttails.

"Looks like you've got a problem that I can solve," she cooed. She opened her arms to him. He crawled up on her, his cock just inches away from her wetness. "Condom," she reminded him. He nodded and slipped it on.

Now she could relax. She felt his thin cock slide into her. He tried to kiss her, but she just turned her head aside. He seemed to get the message. He pounded away energetically for a few minutes, then came in a rush. El could feel his cock twitch inside her. She didn't have a second orgasm, but that was all right, as long as Scotty was happy.

She whispered in his ear after his breathing slowed: "Now do you understand what's at stake if your team beats Tom's?" She could feel him nod. He climbed off her. He tossed the condom, pulled his pants up and gave her a mock salute, then left by the door to her office. Jack came in a moment later.

He saw her sprawled out on the couch, naked and sweaty, still flush from her orgasm. "I take it things went well," he said dryly.

"Yes, sir. Scotty seemed 'incentivized,' I'd say."

"Good. Tom's shift starts at four, so I'll have him stop by then. You might as well get cleaned up and report back to your desk."

For the second time that day, she found herself cleaning up in Jack's bathroom. When she emerged, Jack was sitting at his desk, working on some papers. He ignored her until she began putting on her clothes by the door. She had just pulled up her skirt when Jack caught her eye.

"Remember what I told you?"

She blushed. "Sorry, sir." She let the skirt drop then

went through the door—closing it softly behind her!—and found her seat. Her embarrassment wasn't as acute now; she hardly glanced at the glass door to see if anyone was passing. Perhaps she was getting used to it.

El scooted the chair close and wiggled her ass on the cool leather seat. She spread her legs and imagined Jack was looking at her "desk cam" at right now. Her hand drifted to her pussy and she stroked herself softly. She wondered if Bill would ask her how her day had gone and what she'd tell him.

"Oh, it was great, hon, I got fucked by a client, my boss and two shop foremen! And I blew the delivery boy! How was your day?"

Gloria stopped by about a half-hour later. She had more questions about El's new job. She was such a nosy bitch! El tried to keep as much of the desk between them as possible, but it was hopeless. When Gloria caught sight of El's nakedness from the waist down, and her hand disappearing under the desk, she gasped.

"You're naked, you slut! How dare you! Does Jack know about this?"

El's heart began to pound. "Yes, he does."

"But, why?"

"I just decided I wanted to be Ja—Mr. Sawyer's secretary, that's all. And what I wear is between me and him."

Gloria wouldn't give up. "You can't dress like that here!"

"He ... said it was all right."

Gloria turned and marched into Jack's office. El wondered if she was supposed to be the gatekeeper and check with her boss before admitting anyone. But Jack hadn't told her to, so she let Gloria barge in. She tried to hear their voices, but it was hard to make out through the closed door. She could only hear Gloria's insistent voice and Jack's calm responses.

In a few minutes, it grew quiet. Her intercom buzzed. Sighing, El wondered if she would be forced to make Gloria come as well. She'd never eaten out a woman before. Would Gloria be the first? She stood and went to the door, one hand on her pussy, as required. She opened it and stepped through. She was surprised to find Gloria had already left by the main door. She stripped off her top and came to Jack's desk, then kneeled.

"Was Gloria angry, sir?"

He glanced over to her. "Is that the way you're supposed to announce your arrival?"

"No, I'm sorry, sir. How may I be of service, Master?"

Jack looked up from his work. "To answer your question, yes, Gloria is upset. She doesn't seem to be interested in my explanations. She could prove troublesome.

"But that's not why I called you in. Scotty called, said none of the men believe him about the new incentive program, so I'd like you to get dressed and go down there and let them know it's legitimate." He looked pointedly at her. "You don't have to fuck anybody, just let them know you'll be available when the time comes."

El felt relieved to be able to put on her skirt again. She dressed quickly, afraid Jack might change his mind. Then she was out the door and into the corridor. She went downstairs to the plant floor and sought out Scotty. Her presence—and the way she was dressed—drew attention almost immediately. She heard wolf whistles as she walked around.

"Anyone seen Scotty?"

The comments and questions flew back at her. "What's going on, Ellen?"

"Why're ya dressed like that?"

"Is it true what Scotty says?"

She stopped at the last question and faced the man. He was a sallow-faced, heavyset middle-aged man, name of Richards. For some reason, El suddenly pictured him on top of her, grunting his way to a climax. "Yes, it's true," she told him matter-of-factly. "If this shift beats Tom's shift, you guys get to spend some time with me."

"Spend some time? What's that mean?"

She leaned in close to his ear, her embarrassment rising anew. "You guys can all ... have sex with me."

Richards took a step back in shock. "You're joking!"

Two others rushed up. "What's this? What's happening?"

Richards explained. The others didn't believe him. They turned to El. "Come on! This has got to be a joke! We aren't allowed to do that!"

El assured them it was true. She kept an eye out for Scotty, knowing he'd back her up.

"Come on, if it's true, show us what we'd get!" one of the men said.

She turned to them. Her face felt hot. She knew she was blushing again. El looked around and saw she was too exposed here, so she pointed to the tool shop and headed that way. The three men followed her, and soon were joined by several others, like a pack of rabid dogs.

Scotty was in the tool shop, talking to another man. He looked up over the top of the Dutch door and smiled when he spotted El. "Well, lookie who's stopped by. I told you guys."

"They don't believe me, either, Scotty. Mr. Sawyer said I should convince them it's for real."

He opened the half-door for her. "Well, you'd better

come in here, or you'll get mobbed." The other man just stared at her, as if he wasn't sure if she should be allowed to invade his tiny shop. Scotty closed the half door behind her, keeping her safe from the other men.

El turned around the faced the men crowded around the door. Slyly, she raised her top until her breasts came into view, then quickly dropped it. The men hooted and whistled.

"Come on, show us the rest!"

El shook her head in resignation and reached down to the hem of her skirt. Then she raised it up to expose her naked pussy and pushed it down again. She felt light-headed.

"I didn't see! I didn't see!" someone shouted from the back.

"Last time," she warned, and flashed them again. The group went wild.

"Now the ass! Show us!"

El turned around and let them see her well-marked ass. The crowd grew quiet when stripes from Jack's belt came into view.

"Goll-lee! Wudja look at that!"

"She's been whipped. Musta done som'tin bad!"

El smoothed down her skirt, her face flush with embarrassment. She just wanted to return to the safety of her office. Scotty helped her get out through the crowd. Behind her, she could hear, "No way Tom's boys are going to beat us!" She smiled to herself, knowing Jack would be pleased.

When she returned, she buzzed Jack to let him know. Then, without being asked, she removed her skirt and dropped it onto the desk. She sat, bringing her right hand back to her pussy. She was rather sore now. She had to fuck Tom in an hour, and she hoped he would be the last today.

She didn't know how she was going to survive two years of this. Her emotions were all mixed up. On one hand, she had the most powerful orgasm she'd ever had when being fucked by Bob, but on the other hand, the embarrassment she had to endure was taking its toll on her. In a very short time, all pretense that El had been a woman of substance and value would be gone, and everyone would treat her like the whore she'd become.

Chapter 5

El got out of the limo and walked tiredly to her front door. Raphael, the driver, waved as he pulled away. Following Jack's orders, she had given him a blowjob to thank him for the ride and now her mouth tasted bitter. She wanted to shower and have a drink.

Bill opened the door before she could reach the doorknob and stepped aside, a concerned look on his face. "Ellen? Are you all right?"

"I'm fine," she said. The last thing she wanted right now was to try to explain her behavior to her husband.

But Bill wouldn't let it go. "I've been worried about you—that you've been reassigned, the way you dressed today. What's going on?"

"Did you get a job?" El tried to short-circuit the conversation.

"No. It's only been one day, Ellen."

Her temper flared. "I can't support you any more, Bill. You have to make enough to pay half the expenses! Take anything! Don't let your pride ruin everything."

"I don't understand why you're still working there! If they caught you stealing, why haven't you been fired? Or arrested? Tell me what your situation is, dammit!"

El sighed. She knew she'd have to tell him eventually. Right now she was just too tired. "Let me take a shower, then fix me a drink and I'll try to fill you in."

As she headed toward the bathroom, an image flicked through her head: Bill, after being told the whole sad story, crouching between her bare thighs, carefully shaving her pussy for Jack. She shook her head, ridding her mind of the thought.

She took a long, hot shower. When she washed her sensitive pussy and ass, she was reminded of her long day. She might've made the wrong choice. Being disgraced and jailed could well be preferable to this.

After drying off, she wrapped herself in a thick terrycloth robe and came out to the living room. Bill was waiting there with a scotch on the rocks, her favorite drink.

She took a sip and sat on the couch. Bill hovered expectantly nearby.

"First of all," she began, trying to set some ground rules, "you should know that this was all my decision. No one forced me to do anything." She took another sip and began her story from the beginning. She had told him yesterday (was it just yesterday?) that Jack had caught her stealing and she'd been reassigned, but she hadn't provided any details.

Now she told him she was being used to entertain clients and workers, without going into a lot of detail about her humiliating treatment at the plant. Bill sat there, his mouth ajar, his eyes wide. He seemed too shocked to be angry at first, but then his mood darkened.

"That bastard! He can't get away with this! That's extortion!"

She put a hand on his arm. "You can't, Bill. You can't do anything rash. Promise me."

"You don't have to do this, El," he said, using his nickname for Ellen that had now been corrupted by Jack. "We can move away, start fresh somewhere else."

"No. You haven't been listening. I have to pay him back or he'll call the cops. If I run, they'll track me down and I'll be arrested and my life ruined. No one would hire a CPA who's been convicted of embezzling! This is the only way out, don't you see?"

Bill shook his head. "No, I don't see. There must be another way."

Her anger flared anew. "You could get a fucking job!"

Bill turned away, hurt "I'm going to, I promise. Tomorrow."

She softened a little then. "Good. Otherwise, we won't make it."

Bill's head swiveled around. "Is he paying you?"

El hung her head. She told him of the arrangement she had with Jack and that she hoped to be able to pay him back within a couple of years.

"A couple of years? That's impossible! I'm not going to stand by while my wife becomes the sex slave to a maniacal businessman."

"Yes you will. You'll do nothing to disturb our arrangement. You can help me or you can divorce me. Those are your choices."

Bill sat back, stunned. El could read his face: He felt guilty for being out of work for so long. He probably had suspected El was bringing home too much money, but he'd never asked her about it.

"Well, what's it going to be? Are you in or are you out?"

Bill locked his eyes on hers. "When I married you, I promised to stick by you in sickness and in health, good days and bad," he began. Ellen's heart lept with joy. He was going to help her. "But those same vows said something about being true to each other, forsaking all others, right? If you think I'm going to be able to sit by while you get fucked by strangers, you're mistaken. I don't care if you did steal money to help us."

El opened her mouth in shock. The joy she briefly felt vanished along with her remaining dignity. Then she became angry. She had gotten into this situation because of him and now he was getting 'holier than thou' on her?

"You bastard. You lazy bastard! You think I like this? You think I get off on this? I'm doing this for us, don't you see? I found a way out of an impossible situation and all you can do is sit there and act pious?"

Bill shook his head. "You're not doing this for us. You're doing this to save your career. My career will get started again. I haven't stolen anything—or fucked anyone. Above all, you didn't talk to me about this before you started spreading your legs!"

He stood up. "You can fuck Jack and anyone he chooses, but if you think I'm going to play cuckold, you're out of your mind." He stalked out of the room.

El sat there, unable to think clearly. She was still angry with him for getting her into this mess, but she had to admit, he was right: she had made the decision unilaterally. She told him the way it was going to be. For some reason, she thought he would understand, that he would feel remorse for his lack of effort. That he would abandon her had never seemed like a real possibility.

She got up and went to the bedroom. Bill had a suitcase on the bed and was packing. "Where are you going?"

"For now, back to my parents." He looked up. "I know, I'm too old to be running home to mamma, but I don't have the funds to start myself up somewhere else right now. Once I get a job, I'll find a place."

"Just like that, you're throwing six years of marriage out the window?"

"No, not 'just like that.' It took a stunning act of betrayal to do it."

El's mouth worked, but no sounds came out. Her anger, her humiliation, her fear all combined and contradicted each other in her mind. Then another voice, a tiny, wicked voice called out: *Now you can do what you've always wanted to do.* She shook the stray thought out of her head. She didn't want to do this, how crazy that idea was! But it was like an itch she couldn't scratch.

Bill finished packing. El stood there, trying to think of something to say. Did she want him to go? She could cancel the deal, go to prison. Would Bill wait for her?

No, she decided. He wouldn't. Their marriage had been rocky before, now it had finally shattered. She couldn't save it by herself. She was truly on her own.

At the door, Bill turned to her. "Goodbye, Ellen. I'll miss you, I really will. I'll come by later for the rest of my things. Good luck with your new job." He said the last with a sarcasm that burned Ellen's soul.

She stood there, mute and shaking, as Bill loaded up his car and drove away without a backward glance. She shut the door and leaned against it. Now she really was screwed, she thought, not even smiling at the irony of that phrase. Jack had only agreed to pay for half the expenses—there's no way she could cover the rest. She'd have to sell the house for sure.

Maybe that wasn't such a bad thing. That meant that Jack wouldn't have to pay nearly as much for a cheap apartment as a house. She could wrap up her ordeal in far less time. She'd have to do the math.

"Jack will know what to do," she whispered to herself. "I'll ask Jack." She caught herself. "I'll ask Mr. Sawyer." That she would defer to her boss didn't seem strange to her. In just twenty-four hours her life had fallen under his control, and she seemed ready to give him all her problems.

She couldn't eat, her stomach was too upset. She had another scotch and went to bed. Her only thought before she fell asleep was: *I hope I can shave my pussy properly by myself.*

The next morning, El was groggy when the alarm went off at seven. She got up late and took another shower. She sat on the closed toilet seat afterwards and shaved herself as carefully as she could. Using a hand mirror, she thought she reached nearly every bit of stubble, but it was awkward and took far too long.

It was 8:15 by the time she raced into her bedroom to pick out an outfit. Her "new" wardrobe consisted of a few short skirts and tops; she'd have to buy more soon. She threw on a denim miniskirt and a light blue top. Since she didn't have to worry about underwear, she could be dressed in minutes. Remembering Jack's comment about her shoes, El chose a pair of tan sandals with three-inch heels. She had bought them before she'd gotten married and rarely wore them. Now she felt tall and shapely, if a bit unstable.

With a sudden bolt of fear, she realized she had forgotten to put on her makeup. She looked at her watch: 8:25. There was no time to put on a foundation. Quickly, she smeared on some eyeliner and rouge and coated her lips. She wished she'd remembered to buy false eyelashes. Maybe Jack would allow her to purchase them during the workday.

She heard the car horn just as she finished brushing her teeth, so she dropped everything and ran out the door. It was Jack, not Raphael, she was happy to see. She got in and, without being asked, pulled up her skirt and sat on the seat. She spread her legs for him. His hand reached over and rested against her pussy. It made her feel hot and lightheaded.

"You seemed to be running behind today," Jack said, his fingers teasing her.

"Um, yes. I had a little trouble getting up."

"How did Bill take it last night?" He made no move to drive away.

Well, might as well tell him, she thought. "Not well. He left me, went home to his parents'."

Jack glanced at her. "How does that make you feel?"

"Like a failure. Like I've been abandoned. 'Course, I can't exactly blame him. As he pointed out, I made this decision on my own, without any input from him. So I got what I deserved."

"I guess that changes things—concerning the house, I mean."

"Yeah. I'll have to put it on the market now. Of course, I'll give you anything I make from it—unless you want me to use that money to get a cheap apartment."

What was unspoken, of course, was: Are you going to help me pay for my living expenses?

Jack was silent for a time. He simply stroked her pussy. She found herself getting lost in his attentions. Finally, he said, "Yes, you should put your house on the market right away. I know a realtor who might be willing to help you out."

El knew what that meant—more sex in exchange for services. Her stomach fluttered and she wasn't sure if it was from the thought of her ever-expanding list of "clients" or Jack's fingers rubbing her clit.

He suddenly stopped and El opened her eyes to look at him. "Rather than get an apartment, I've decided to move you into my house—temporarily. I have plenty of room. That way, you won't have to pay rent and all the money you earn can go right into paying me back. We can sell your furniture or put it into storage."

El mulled that over for a minute. She visualized herself, waking up on clean sheets, next to Jack, having him roll over and fuck her hard before she got up. She liked that idea. "Yes, sir."

El waited for Jack to start the car. Then he said: "So Bill's gone? The house is empty?"

She looked at him. Did he want to fuck her here? "Yeah, it's empty."

"Good. I need to find you another outfit."

"You don't like this?"

"No, it's fine. I want you to wear that. But we have a client meeting this afternoon and I want you to have something more conservative to change into."

That told El that this client may not be interested in a sex slave.

They got out. El had to adjust her skirt. Her pussy tingled. She led Jack up the stairs, wondering what her neighbors must think. First they see her husband leave, now a stranger goes inside with her.

Jack picked out a nice business dress—if she was Ally McBeal. The skirt was too short, but not obscenely so. Not like the one she had on. The top consisted of a light blue rayon blouse and a suit jacket that matched the skirt. No underwear, however. He didn't let her wear the outfit, he just brought it along on a hanger.

Back in the car, Jack's fingers went back to work. They rode in silence for a bit. El's pussy was beginning to grow wet and she could hear the occasional squishy sound as Jack's probed her. Surprisingly, she wasn't too sore this morning. His ministrations were beginning to turn her on again. She closed her eyes and leaned back against the car seat.

"I feel some stubble here," Jack's voice interrupted her daydream.

"Oh! I'm sorry, sir. I spent a lot of time on it. That's why I was almost late."

"Well, we can fix that."

She wanted to ask what he meant and she visualized him shaving her on his desktop every day. The thought excited her. But before she could speak, they bumped over the entrance leading to the plant. El sat up and automatically started to adjust her skirt before realizing that was the actions of the Old Ellen, not the new, slutty El. Jack parked, but before he got out, he raised his fingers to her mouth. Without thinking about it, El licked her own juices off them. Jack got out, again without a word. She got out and tugged her skirt down over her ass cheeks. She reached into the back seat and retrieved the outfit.

She heard a wolf whistle and turned to see Tom, the night foreman, just getting off work. He leered at her and winked. She briefly smiled back, remembering Tom's visit yesterday afternoon. He'd come swaggering in, his big stomach leading the way. He had to be fifty. Like Scotty, he was divorced and had let himself go. From what she'd heard, Tom liked to say he had two hobbies: drinking beer and eating.

Fortunately for her, Tom didn't want to fuck her. He only wanted a blow job. Because Jack was busy in his office, she had to blow him while he sat in her chair, just like she'd done for the delivery boy. Only this time, she wasn't wearing her skirt. Tom stared at her pussy for a long time before he let her get started. Once her mouth was on him, he'd come in just a few minutes—apparently, it had been a long time since he'd gotten laid.

"Thanks, slut," he'd told her and she almost got angry. It was as if only Jack could call her a slut. The ludicrousness of her situation had stopped her, however. After all, she *was* a slut. It might as well be on her job description.

She tried to push the image of fat Tom out of her mind. As she went down the corridor to her office carrying the dress, she passed a couple of factory workers on the way. When one of them, a big black man she knew as Jim, slapped her on the ass, she turned and glared at him, then stalked off. In her office, she hung up the suit and had barely gotten to her seat when the intercom buzzed. She reached for the phone and her pussy at the same time, without thinking. Her training was taking over.

"Yes, sir?"

"Come in, El."

She got up and went through the door, stopping suddenly, mouth agape. There stood the man who had just slapped her ass in the hallway. Both of their eyes were on her and they didn't seem pleased.

El closed the door and removed her clothes, her hands shaking. She approached Jack and kneeled.

"How may I help you, master?"

"El, I asked Jim here to give you a slap on the ass this morning as a test to see how well you're fitting into your new job. Would you tell me, please, your reaction to Jim's actions?"

El knew she was in trouble. Her ass still ached from yesterday's spanking. "Um, sir, I, um, glared at him."

"Why did you do that?"

"I was caught off-guard, sir. I wasn't thinking."

"That's right. What's your role here?"

El thought she might faint. She glanced up at Jim, who seemed bemused by her predicament. "I'm ... a sex slave." She heard Jim chuckle.

"Right. What should you have done when Jim spanked you, do you think?"

El thought hard. "Um, smiled at him?"

"Yes, that would've been preferable. Or wiggle your hips or blow him a kiss—anything that indicated to him that you appreciate his attentions. Do you understand?"

"Yes, sir."

"This tells me you need some additional training, doesn't it?"

"Yes, sir."

Jack nodded. "Jim has been kind enough to offer to administer the punishment."

El paled. Jim stood six-two with biceps like footballs. If he spanked her, he'd probably kill her. She made a low sound in her throat.

"I realize your bottom must still be sore from yesterday, right?"

"Oh, yes, sir!"

"So I'll give you a choice. You can either let Jim spank your tits with a ruler..." He pulled one from his desk drawer and held it up. El felt her breasts ache at the very thought. "...or you can let Jim fuck you..."

"Oh, I'll let him fuck—"

"Wait, you didn't let me finish. You'd have to fuck him in your office, not mine. And he'd tie you spread over your desk, ass toward the glass door. When he's finished, he's going to leave you like that until I come out and untie you."

El paled and nearly fainted again. To be on display like that! Yesterday, she'd been mortified to be seen without her skirt on in her office, now she could be publicly humiliated in front of whoever passes by. And she knew that once word got around, everybody would be stopping by for a look at her naked body. Some might even fuck her again.

"Oh, sir...please." She wasn't ready for that!

"What's your decision?"

"Sp-spank my tits, sir." Jim sighed and looked disappointed.

"Very well. Turn and face Jim." She moved her knees

around a quarter turn. She felt Jack grab her arms and tie them with a section of cotton rope he pulled from his desk. "Just so you won't try to cover yourself," he told her.

Jim took the ruler in one large hand and approached her. El closed her eyes and steeled herself. "Open your eyes, El. While he's administering your punishment, I want you to think about how you treat your fellow employees."

She did, just in time to see him strike her left breast. Whack! The first blow took the breath from her lungs. She shuddered and wiggled, trying to lessen the pain. Whack! Now on the right breast. El didn't know if she could stand it. Maybe letting him fuck her and being on display would have been a better choice.

Whack! Whack! Whack! Whack! Top and bottom of her breasts. She was crying now, tears flowing freely down her cheeks. She nearly sobbed with relief when Jack told Jim that was enough.

He untied her. She sagged down, caressing her tender breasts, her eyes blurred by tears.

"I'm going to go get a cup of coffee. You may thank Jim for helping with your training while I'm gone." He left.

"Th-th-thank you, Jim," she said automatically, without looking up.

Jim's deep voice startled her. "You need to be more polite, slut. Look at me."

She raised her eyes and through the fog of tears, she saw his long black cock, sticking out of his pants, right at the level of her mouth. Now she understood what Jack had meant by "thanking him." She opened her mouth and took Jim's thick cock inside.

He was too large for her to deep throat him, but that didn't seem to stop him from trying to force himself on her. She used one hand to stroke him in an effort to bring him off more quickly. That seemed to pacify him. She rubbed the shaft and suckled the head for several minutes while Jim built up a head of steam. El's pussy began to throb of its own accord and she felt her wetness grow. It surprised her because she suddenly realized she wanted the big man's huge cock deep into her pussy. Would Jack allow it?

Within a few more minutes, Jim came in great quantities. El choked on his sperm, much of it running down her chin and splashing on her breasts.

When he pulled back she immediately began wiping up his precious seed with her fingers and sucking the fluid from them. He tasted good. She looked longingly at Jim's softening dick. She wanted to get up and lay down on the desk for him, but she knew he'd already been satisfied.

"You're a real sweetheart," Jim rumbled as he zipped up. He turned and left. El felt her heart lurch when the door closed behind him. Jack must've been waiting outside, for he came in at once, a cup of coffee in one hand.

"Now, what have you learned from this?" Jack spoke to her as if she were a recalcitrant child.

El turned to attention to Jack, hoping he'd fuck her now. "To be nice to workers, no matter where I meet them." She put her hand on his leg.

Jack ignored the effort. "That's right. I'll take off another hundred off your debt. You may go."

She scurried back to the door and put on her clothes. She winced as she pulled her top down over her sore breasts. She knew by tomorrow, she'd have bruises on them to match the ones on her ass. She decided to do whatever it took to avoid further punishments.

Chapter 6

El sat at her desk with very little to do, but she wasn't complaining. After all, her job required she be available to anyone who wanted her, as long as Jack said it was okay. She mulled over the amount of money she'd made in the past two days. Let's see, it was two-fifty each for Bob and Scotty, and one hundred each for the delivery boy and Tom. Oh! And Raphael. That's eight hundred. And another hundred today, so far.

The numbers encouraged her. If she averaged eight hundred a day it would total four thousand a week. She took out a calculator and ran the numbers. Two hundred, forty-seven thousand at nine percent interest, comes to about two hundred, seventy thousand. Divided by four thousand a week and that's....

She smiled when she saw the numbers come up. Fifty-seven weeks! That's just a little more than a year. And if she gave Jack the proceeds from the house and car, even less time.

Now she knew what she had to do. Rather than "endure" the fuckings and the suckings, she must encourage those opportunities. Of course, she never wanted to have sex without getting credit for it. Every cock she sucked brought her one day closer to being released from her servitude. And fucking was even better. She could make them wear condoms, rather than suck down a man's raw seed into her belly. And at two-fifty a pop, she could be making five thousand a week, if she worked at it.

She replayed the scene in her mind this morning. When

Jim slapped her on the ass, she should've turned and asked him if he wanted a blowjob or, better yet, to fuck her—as long as Jack agreed, of course. And when Jack offered her the choice of being fucked and put on display, she should've accepted the fucking. Not only would she have earned two-fifty, but no doubt others would've come in and fucked her. She could've made a couple of thousand before noon!

It occurred to her she was rationalizing her actions, embracing her new life as a slut. And yet that voice deep inside her encouraged her: *Don't forget how strongly you came when Bob fucked you.*

Her face grew hot. How could she be thinking about that? She'd been used, it wasn't right. Yet, it had been a powerful orgasm. The best by far.

The intercom buzzed. This time, her hand reached for her pussy before she picked up the receiver. "Yes, sir?"

"I'm expecting a client at ten. I'd like you to bring us some coffee, but don't strip unless I tell you to."

"Yes, sir." She looked at her watch. It was barely nine-thirty. Coffee sounded pretty good to her, so she decided to get herself some. She rose and went into the corridor. When she entered the lunch room, there were three other employees there, two men and a woman. All conversation immediately ceased. They stared at her.

El knew they'd been talking about her, about how far she'd fallen. Rumors must be rampant, since neither she nor Jack would talk about why she had become the company slut. That was the choice she'd been given—company slut or public thief. If she ever wanted another job as a CPA or a CFO, she had to endure this.

"Hi," she said brightly and poured herself a cup of coffee.

"Is it true?"

El turned. The question had come from Darlene, a heavy-set woman who worked the day shift.

"Is what true?"

"That you've resigned from your position as CFO so you can...um, er..."

El flushed. "Yes?" She wasn't going to let Darlene off the hook.

"That you, um, provide favors for workers?"

"Yes, but only with Jack's permission."

"Why?" The woman was baffled.

El shrugged. "I like it."

"You like to display yourself too," said one of the other men, an immature young man she knew only as Steve. "I was there yesterday when you came down."

"Sometimes," she said simply. It wasn't true. She only did that at Jack's order. Being on display, naked or half-naked in public, had proven to be much harder than simply fucking someone, she'd found.

"Prove it. Show me your tits."

El almost refused the boy's impertinence. Then she remembered Jack's edict and the result of her rudeness toward Jim. She put down her cup and pulled up her top, giving him a brief display of her bruised tits.

"God! What happened to them?"

This from the third man, Ed, whose eyes seemed to bulge from his head.

"I was ... punished."

"Why?" Darlene asked.

"I was rude to one of the workers."

"Really, how?" Steve again.

"I ... He slapped me on my ass and I glared at him." El knew her face was red. She tried to cover it up by taking a sip of coffee. She regretted coming in here. All she wanted to do was retreat to her office. She started for the door.

Ed grabbed her arm. "So if I wanted to slap your ass..."

"Or grab your tits," the boy put in.

"...you'd have to let us?"

"I...I think so. Mr. Sawyer just said not to be rude."

"But if I wanted to bend you over the table and fuck you, Jack would object to that?" Ed moved closer.

"Ahh, yes. Jack's in charge of all that." She realized she'd forgotten to call him by his proper name.

"So if Jack says you have to do it, you have to do it, right?"

"Right."

"But short of that," the boy said, moving close to her other side, "we can fondle you, make you show us your body?"

"Um," El's confusion registered on her face. "I think so. I'm not sure. I'd have to ask Ja –, Mr. Sawyer."

"But you just said you have to be nice to us," Steve said. He reached out and stroked one of her breasts through the thin material.

"It would be nice," Ed said, emphasizing the word, "if you would show us your pussy." He turned to look at Darlene, as if seeking approval.

"Yeah, sure, I'd like to see it too." El suspected the rumors about Darlene being a lesbian were probably true.

El felt defeated. "Okay, but only for a second. Mr. Sawyer's expecting me back to meet a client."

That elicited a lot of derisive comments about what she was going to do with the client. But they stepped back slightly to give El some room. She put her coffee down on a nearby table and hooked her hands under the hem of her skirt.

"No grabbing, okay? I don't want to be late."

She pulled up the cloth and let them see her bare pussy

and bruised bottom. Steve and Ed whistled. Darlene looked wistful.

When she pushed down her skirt, Darlene said, "It's not fair."

"What's not fair?" Ed asked.

"You guys get all the breaks. What about us girls?"

El felt dizzy.

"Yeah, what about the girls," Steve asked. "I mean, if Jack told you to go down on Darlene here, would you do it?"

She stared at the floor. "I guess so."

Darlene brightened. "Really? You swing both ways?"

"I've never done it before…" The way she said it made it clear that she'd be willing to try it.

"So in this contest with the night shift, you'd let the guys fuck you, but for me, you'd do what I wanted?"

"Yes, I guess so. I mean, if Mr. Sawyer said so."

"All right, Darlene!" Steve cheered.

Darlene nodded, her face beaming. "Well, that's all right then." She turned to the other guys. "So what say we beat those sluggards on night shift and get us a piece of ass?"

They laughed and El walked out, returning to her office. It was nearly ten. She sat and waited nervously. At ten exactly, she got up and returned to the lunchroom. Thankfully, it was deserted. She fetched a pot of coffee and two clean mugs with the Sawyer Metalworking logo on them.

She returned and knocked on the interoffice door, then entered. Jack was sitting in one of the easy chairs across from a well-dressed man in his sixties.

"Oh, good, coffee's here."

El resisted the fleeting urge to strip off her clothes, remembering Jack's orders. That was strange. Yesterday, it seemed so odd to be naked in his office and today, the opposite is true. She poured two cups and placed them on the low table between them and stood back. When she looked up, she found the visitor staring at her. She blushed and looked at the rug.

"This is my assistant, El," Jack was saying. "She helps me in many ways. She's part of our new 'customer satisfaction' effort."

El's color deepened.

The man didn't seem to understand. "Well, she's a pretty one, that's for sure. You married, honey?"

El looked up, startled that he would speak directly to her. "Well, separated." It embarrassed her to tell this stranger about her crumbling marriage, but she suspected Jack would be angry if she didn't tell the truth.

"Well, that's too bad for your husband, but great for all the other young men out there," the stranger said, smiling.

"Oh, she likes older men, too, don't you, El?" Jack patted her ass lightly and rubbed it possessively.

"Yes, sir."

The man started to catch on—he just couldn't believe it. Jack jumped in to explain. "As you know, we've got the same capabilities as our competitors. Our prices are about the same, our work is excellent and so is our customer service. Others make the same claims, I know. But we have something they don't have." He pulled El to his side and ran his hand slowly down her body, from her breasts to her pussy. El tried not to move.

"We treat our customers right. We want you to be completely satisfied. Are you interested in finding out what Sawyer Metalworking can do for you?"

The man's mouth opened. His eyes grew wide. "Are you telling me what I think you're telling me?"

"Only if you're interested. I wouldn't want to insult you."

"No, no," the man waved a hand. "I'm not insulted. I'm sixty-one years old. My wife gave up on sex ten years ago. I just find it hard to believe that you'd offer this lovely girl to me as an inducement to get my business."

Jack turned to El. "Show him your charms."

El's mind went blank as she stripped off her top and let her skirt puddle around her feet.

"She's all bruised!"

"Yes," Jack said with a show of regret. "She's still in training. She needs punishments on occasion. But she still fires on all cylinders." Jack gave her a little push from behind.

El approached the man and sat down on his lap, then reached down to unbuckle her sandals. The visitor began rubbing his hands all up and down her body.

"So you're telling me that if I sign with you, you'll let me fuck this beautiful girl anytime I want to?"

"Well, not anytime. She has other duties she must attend to. But we can put you on her regular schedule."

The man rubbed El's sore tits, but he addressed his question to Jack. She was merely an ornament. "How badly do you want this contract?"

"Badly enough that if you agree to give us a portion of your business, I'll let you enjoy her talents right now."

The well-dressed man thought for a minute. "Tell you what, Jack. We've got a ball-bearing deal with Ashton that's coming up for renewal, and I'm not happy with their terms. If you can beat them, I'll give the contract to you."

Jack thought it over. "I'm familiar with Aston's overhead.

They've got a lot of debt they're carrying. I'd want to look over the figures, of course, but I'd say we can beat them easily. You've got a deal, Walter."

El sat there, thinking how easy it was to do business when one side had a willing, naked female to use as bait. Her cunt had just tipped the scale for Jack. Idly, she wondered what the contract would be worth. Would he reduce her debt by that amount? It was something she hadn't thought of before.

Jack stood up and shook Walter's hand. "I'm going to step out for a while to give you two some privacy. There are condoms in the desk drawer, if you need them. Have El call me when you're done. I'll be on my cellphone."

He left, humming to himself.

Walter turned to El. "Okay, let's get started. I want a blowjob as a warm-up to get me hard, followed by a good fucking."

El thought: That's three-fifty off my debt!

Chapter 7

Jack continued to hum as he strolled through the plant, checking on supplies and greeting workers. Many pulled him to the side to ask privately if it was true—that Ellen had gone from CFO to slut, available to them as a perk. Yes, it was true, he told them, but only if we can get productivity up and accidents down.

"She's not going to just drop her drawers for anyone in the hallway," he cautioned. "You've got to earn it."

His cellphone rang after about forty-five minutes, and he noted it came from his office, so he returned immediately. Walter was just leaving, promising him he'd send over the details of the contract for Jack to study. Jack told him he'd have an answer in less than a week.

Jack couldn't help but notice the big grin on Walter's face as he left.

El was facedown on the couch, somewhat breathless, her legs splayed apart. He went to her side, noticing the sheen of sweat on her body, the redness of her pussy, the bluish marks from her punishments. It bothered him that El bruised so easily. He'd have to come up other punishments. He didn't want clients being put off by her bruises.

"Give me all the details, so I can put it in your debt record."

El sat up gingerly, but made no attempt to close her legs or cover herself. She told him that as soon as Jack left, Walter had her suck on his cock until he grew hard. "It took a long time, master," she said. "He was kinda old."

Jack knew she was finagling for a blow-job credit. That

was fine with him. He never would have had a shot at the contract if not for her.

"Once he was hard, he had me climb up on the couch. I asked him to use a condom, but he refused, telling me that this contract is worth enough so that he shouldn't have to wear a raincoat." She sniffled, as if it bothered her greatly. "I didn't know what to do, master, so finally I let him. I thought you might be mad if I didn't. He, um, fucked me hard, from behind. It kinda hurt, since my ass is still a little sore."

"You did fine. Is his sperm still leaking out of you?"

She bit her lip. "Yes, sir."

"Show me."

She reached down between her legs and brought up a glob of sticky fluids from her pussy. Jack could see the whitish mix of sperm within. "Okay, that's worth two-fifty, but I'm not so sure about the blow-job, since he didn't come."

"But master!"

"Tell you what. You scoop that from your cunt and swallow it, and I'll consider counting that as well."

She paled, but did as he said. For several minutes, she brought her hand from her pussy to her mouth until Jack was satisfied.

"Okay, come and look at how you're doing."

She got up eagerly and kneeled next to his chair while he called up the spreadsheet. So far, El had reduced her debt by twelve-hundred-fifty dollars.

"Um, master, may I speak?"

"Yes, slut."

"These new contracts, contracts that I helped bring to you, like Walter's and Bob's. Will I get any credit for that extra revenue?"

Jack had expected this. Sure, it would seem fair to reduce her debt—he never would've gotten that business without her. But that would mean a much shorter time that she was here, working for him, pleasing him, increasing productivity and bringing in even more clients. He hated to lose her too quickly. There was also her betrayal to take into account.

"No, El, you won't. You agreed to pay off your debt at two-fifty a fuck and one-hundred a suck. I think any extra business you bring in will be your penance for being a thief for the last three years."

"But that's not fair!"

"Fair? You want what's fair after three years stealing from me, betraying this company?" He felt a flash of anger and decided he didn't want to get into an argument over what was fair. Jack went to the safe and removed a videotape. "I'll show you what's fair." He put it in the VCR.

El shook her head. "I don't need to see it. I remember it."

Jack smiled thinly. "This is a different tape. I edited it myself."

The images came up: El, on her back with Bob pounding away at her, her mouth open wide in ecstasy. Then another shot of her and Scotty as he fucked her, her legs up high in the air like an energetic whore. Another cut: Then an over-the-shoulder shot of El giving head to an anonymous penis under her desk.

El stood up, shocked. "You taped everything?"

"Of course. Consider it protection. You stick by your agreement. When you've paid off your debt, I'll destroy all the tapes and write a nice recommendation for you. If you make any more noise about what you're 'owed,' I'll have you arrested. While your trial is going on, I'll send an edited version of this tape—with the images of the men blurred, of course—to the news stations. I doubt they'll be able to use it, but word about your little adventures will get out and you'll become a laughing stock. You'll never work for anyone ever again—except maybe as a hooker."

She lowered her head and cried.

"I don't want to hear any more about this, all right?"

El nodded, tears streaking down her face.

"Now that that's out of the way, this little talk has made me horny. Lie on the desk, face-down."

She looked up through her tears. "But, Walter just fucked me..."

"That's all right with me. I don't mind."

She got up and splayed herself over the desk, ass in the air. Jack reached down to stroke her pussy, feeling the wetness there from her previous fucking. For some reason, it turned him on. He thrust himself into her immediately and reached around to rub her clit while his cock sawed in and out.

She seemed to like that. She pushed back against him and pressed her head down on the blotter. She began moaning and moving her hips in rhythm with his thrusts. Jack couldn't hold back, he came with a rush. He kept rubbing her clit and in a few seconds, she came too. He could see a deep flush spread over her neck and cheeks.

When he was finished, he pulled away, watching the drool of fluids leak from her wide-open pussy. God, she was a hot lover! He wanted to push her further, if he could.

He allowed her to rise and go clean up in the bathroom. When she came out, he stopped her. "Let's talk about your stubble."

She blinked. "Yes, master?"

"Don't bother shaving tomorrow. I want you to have

a Brazilian wax at a salon I'm going to send you to. They need some hair to work with, they tell me."

Jack could see the color drain from her face. "But, sir— won't that hurt?" Her knees came together involuntarily.

"It's possible, but I think they try to keep the pain to a minimum. But if you'd prefer, we could have one of the workers shave you every morning. I'll bet that would be a great incentive, huh?" Jack pictured her on her back on her desk, her pussy facing the door, while a different worker shaved her every day under the gaze of others in the corridor.

El clearly didn't like that idea. "No, that's okay. I'll go to the salon."

"Great." Soon, he planned to add other changes to her body, but that would have to be arranged later. Ever since the idea had come to him yesterday, he'd wanted to add body jewelry to his company slut. It would make her more exotic and desirable.

If he handled it right, it would also kill two birds with one stone. Jack remained dissatisfied with the bruises he and Jim had left on her body. It worried clients and it made him seem like an overly cruel master. But he was sure she'd need additional punishments. After her beatings, he'd bet she'd choose almost anything but that, including piercings. She didn't have to know that he no longer wanted to bruise her.

"You may go," he said, dismissing her. He returned to his desk, not bothering to look up as El quickly dressed and left. But he turned on his camera and watched as she settled in, her legs spread wide for him under the desk.

Chapter 8

El's stomach was growling. She checked the clock: one-ten. She hadn't heard anything from Jack for more than two hours and wondered if she should just go to lunch on her own like she used to do or wait for his instructions. Remembering her many painful lessons, she decided to do nothing until he told her to.

Suddenly, the intercom buzzed. Breathing a sigh of relief, El's hand dropped to her lap and began rubbing her damp pussy even as she picked up the receiver.

"Yes, sir?"

"El, I've been remiss. I should've sent you to lunch. Are you hungry?"

"Yes, sir. Would you like something, sir?"

"No, I'm fine. I'm meeting a client for a late lunch. Go ahead and take forty-five minutes." The voice paused. "But first, come in for a minute."

El's heart began to pound. *Now what?* She dutifully entered the office and stripped, then knelt; it was becoming routine.

"You've had kind of a light day today, haven't you? Just one fuck and two blowjobs. So I've got a way for you to earn some extra money."

El didn't know how to respond. She wanted to turn him down and just be left alone for lunch, but she knew better than to refuse.

"Thank you, sir. What can I do?"

"You probably have forgotten, but Hank's retiring Friday. I told him to stop by my office at two today for a special thanks from me. Will you take care of him?"

El's mind recoiled. A bigger pig than Hank she'd never met. He was a profane, loud misogynist who thought the world had been ruined when women got the vote. To be Hank's plaything worried her.

"Hank, sir? He's kinda rough, isn't he? He might hurt me if you're not here to protect me."

"Hank? Nonsense. Sure, he's a little rough around the edges, but he knows better than to hurt our slut."

With a sinking feeling, El knew she was trapped. "Well, all right, sir. I'll do my best."

Dismissed, she dressed and escaped. She had no car, so she had to walk to a nearby restaurant. She had barely made it to the sidewalk when a car pulled up. Inside, she recognized two men from the day shift, on their way back from lunch.

"Hey, Ellen!" The driver, a squat black man, grinned at her. His name came to her suddenly: Duane.

"No, she's called El now, aren't you, gal?" the other worker put in, a skinny white man named Ralph. He'd apparently read the interoffice memo.

"Er, yes. Mr. Sawyer calls me El now." She waved and started to walk away, hoping they'd let her go. But Duane backed up the car to catch up with her.

"I also understand that you have to be nice to us workers," he said, leering.

El tried to set him straight. "Jack's in charge of all that," she told him. "You have to clear it with him."

"That's true," Ralph added, "but the way I hear it, you gotta show us your goodies whenever we want."

"Well, not out in *public*," El responded, feeling the heat rise in her chest. "I mean, I don't want to get arrested."

Duane reached around behind him and opened the back door. "Get in. Or we'll tell Jack how you weren't very nice."

She wanted to refuse but feared additional punishment. She climbed in and closed the door. "Don't you guys have to be back at work?"

"Yeah," Ralph said. "But first, we want to see a little show. Let me see your tits and pussy."

She pulled up her top, letting them have a good look. They whistled and high-fived each other.

"Now the rest," Duane said. She left her top propped up over her breasts and lifted her ass up off the seat. She raised the hem of her dress, pushing her bare pussy out for them to see. Ralph reached out to touch her, but El didn't want to offer her services for free. She yanked her skirt and top back down and opened the door.

"Hey, that's not very friendly," Ralph said.

"Like I said," she told him. "You have to talk to Jack about that. I'm not supposed to just let everyone have at me all the time."

They didn't try to stop her as she got out. As the car drove back into the lot, El could hear them hooting and hollering. For some reason, it made her horny.

She walked to the deli. She still had no money of her own, so if she was going to eat, she'd have to find Frankie. It wasn't so bad, she told herself. He's a sweet kid. Jack might even give her credit for blowing him again.

Frankie was behind the counter when she entered the nearly deserted deli. His face lit up. "Hey, the Sawyer secretary! Glad to see ya!" Another young man just stared at her. El surmised that Frankie had spilled the beans.

"What can I get for ya?"

She ordered a tuna salad sandwich and an iced tea. "Can I get that to go?"

"Well, sure. In fact, I woulda delivered it!"

"No, I wanted to get out and stretch my legs." For some reason, both boys thought the line was hilarious.

"Um, do you have any money?" Frankie whispered as the other man prepared her food.

"No, I don't," she whispered back, feeling the color rise in her cheeks. "I was wondering if we could have the same arrangement?" She couldn't believe she was offering to trade a blow-job for a sandwich.

"Well, what about Sam?" He pointed over to the other young worker, a thin young man wearing glasses, who stopped making her sandwich long enough to tip an ear in their direction.

El shook her head. "Only one of you. That's more than fair."

"Well, ya gotta give him something or he'll tell the boss that I'm giving away food. I'll get fired."

El thought for a moment. "Would you mind if he watches?"

Frankie gave a shrug and went over to talk with Sam. Sam said something back and Frankie came over to El. "He says if you're naked, okay."

She nodded, sighing to herself.

Frankie had to help another customer, but when the deli was empty, he lifted a section of hinged countertop and motioned her inside. They all went through the door into the kitchen area in back.

"Okay, strip," Frankie said.

El yanked off her skirt and blouse, thinking how many times she'd stripped naked in the last two days. She couldn't even count.

Sam stared at her when she was naked. "You're all bruised."

"Oh, that. I bumped into a door," she lied.

Frankie opened his pants, while Sam watched from a few feet away. He seemed fascinated by El, but didn't want to get too close. He must be really shy, she thought.

She took Frankie into her mouth and began licking and sucking. Like most young men, he was rarin' to go, even though she'd performed this same act just yesterday. She stroked her wet mouth up and down his shaft, both her hands holding tight to his ass. Within a couple of minutes, he came into her mouth. She swallowed the sweet cream, not letting a drop loose.

When she was done, she stood and turned toward Sam. She felt kind of sorry for him. He made her sandwich, after all.

"How about you?" she asked. "You want one?"

Sam looked at Frankie, then at her, and shook his head. She could tell he was embarrassed to show his cock to his workmate. Just then, the bell over the door inside rang and Frankie grinned. "Don't worry, I'll get it." He winked at El.

El walked up to Sam. He stood about her height. She knew that he'd probably been dismissed by many of the girls of his age group because he wasn't as big and strong like other boys his age. A classic nerd type.

"It's all right, Sam. I won't hurt you," she cooed. She felt Sam deserved a little attention in his life. Here he was, probably all of eighteen years old, and she doubted he'd ever had a serious relationship with a girl before. Now he was confronted with a naked woman, who seemed eager to seduce him. She could understand his confusion and reluctance.

Sam looked at her nervously, and occasionally peered over her shoulder toward where Frankie had gone to help a customer. "Maybe Frankie needs some help," he stammered.

"You don't think Frankie can make a sandwich by himself?"

He nodded and looked away, as if afraid to stare at her

naked body. She decided to take it slow. "You don't have to do anything. But if you'd like to touch me, it's okay."

She took his hand in hers and placed it on her breast. "How does that feel?"

"It's ... nice," he said, letting his fingers gently stroke her. Emboldened, he brought up his other hand and touched her other breast. He watched, fascinated, as her nipples stretched out.

"See, you're turning me on," she said. In that moment, she knew if he asked her to fuck him, she'd do it. She wouldn't even mention it to Jack to get credit.

But Sam was far too shy. He touched her, but he couldn't talk at the same time. It was as if his voice had seized up. She tried to draw him out.

"Do you like them?"

"Er ... yeah, I mean, sure..." he stammered.

She captured one hand and brought it down to her hot, wet core. His eyes opened wide when he felt her wetness, the slippery fluids that coated her sex. "See? This means I'm ready for you," she whispered. "Whenever you touch a girl here and she's wet like this, it means she wants you."

"You, uh, want me?"

She leaned in close, so close one of her breasts brushed his chest. "Yes."

"You mean, you'd like to, um ... you know."

She spoke directly into his shell-shaped ear. "Never be embarrassed to say what you want, especially when you've got the clues in hand." For emphasis, she drew his fingers again across her dripping slit.

"You uh ... want to ... make love to me?" He said it as if he didn't believe it.

She breathed into his ear. "Yesss. Where can we go?"

He pointed to a door. "There's a storage room. It has big sacks of flour and such."

"Let's go."

Sam escorted El into the room and closed the door. To make sure they'd have some privacy, he dragged a heavy sack of potatoes up against the door. El looked around and spotted some flat sacks of grain along one wall that would do in a pinch for a bed. She lay back on them and spread her legs.

For reasons she couldn't quite explain, this felt so right. It was something she never wanted Jack to find out about. This was for Sam, a boy she'd just barely met but understood completely. This was his therapy, his training. He needed this in order to feel like a man.

He came over to her and looked awkward. "I don't want to hurt you," he said, pointing to her bruises.

"Don't worry, they've faded. I'm okay." She didn't know if he believed her lie, but it didn't matter. She had given him permission.

He unbuttoned his pants and pushed them down a bit. She could see his small cock sticking up, hard and ready. "Oh, what a wonderful cock," she said, trying to make him feel more confident.

"You really think so?"

"Oh, yes. It's just the right size."

He carefully spread himself over her. She could feel the head of his cock tickling her labia. He leaned in to kiss her and she accepted it gratefully. His breath was sweet, not sour like so many of the men she'd fucked lately. Their tongues intertwined. She felt his cock rubbing up against her. She spread her legs farther apart to make it easy for him.

At first, he didn't seem to be able to find the right passage, so El reached down and helped him along. His cock slipped in. She could hardly feel it, except when it rose up and stroked her g-spot. She shifted her position so he would stroke it often as he moved.

Sam didn't last long. He was so excited by his first fuck that he quickly spasmed inside her. She could feel their fluids leak out around his softening cock. She feigned a climax so he wouldn't feel inadequate.

"Oh, Sam, that was wonderful!" she gushed. "You're a good lover."

He seemed thrilled. "Can we do it again?" Already his cock was started to regenerate. El couldn't believe it. Ah, youth!

"Um, no, I've got to get back. As it is, I won't have time to eat the nice lunch you made. But I'm sure I'll come back for a visit again."

That seemed to satisfy him. He got up and tucked his wet penis into his pants. She waited while he moved the sack of potatoes, then walked out to see Frankie standing there, a frown on his face.

"Hey, when do I get my turn?"

She walked up to him and placed a soft hand against his cheek. "Soon, Frankie. It's just that Sam really turned me on and I couldn't help myself. Your turn will come."

Frankie was speechless. No doubt his estimation of his nerdy co-worker rose considerably. She dressed, picked up the sack of food, winked at them, and left. She had checked the time and knew she had less than ten minutes to get back before Hank was supposed to show. Though she hated the thought of him, she didn't want to be late. That would only cause more punishments.

She hurried back as fast as she could, but her sandals were not made for walking quickly. In her office, she dropped her uneaten lunch off at her desk and checked the time. Five after two. Dammit! She went into Jack's office and spotted Hank standing there, looking around the empty room. He was a big, barrel-chested man, with a thinning shock of white hair and bandy legs.

"Oh, there you are. You're late. I was beginning to think you stood me up," he said in a loud, angry voice. "Okay, let's get busy. I know what you are and you know what I want. Strip off those fuckin' clothes and let's get busy."

El couldn't help but contrast the gentle loving of Sam from this profane jerk. Still, she had a job to do. Sighing to herself, she stripped off her clothes for the umpteenth time that day. "Where do you want me?"

"On the couch, bitch. Up on your hands and knees."

"Would you wear a condom, please? They're in the top drawer."

Hank sneered. "From the way I hear it, you'll fuck anything that moves, so what do you care about condoms?"

"Jack asked that everyone wear condoms," she insisted. "If he hears you refused, he'll be upset."

Hank laughed as he unbuckled his pants. "Honey, I'm retiring in three days. Tell Jack he can kiss my grits." His hard cock sprung free.

Before she could protest further, Hank had grabbed her around the waist. She felt his hard cock bump up against her ass. She realized she could hardly protest—she'd just fucked a deli worker without a condom. Still, she didn't like to lose control like this.

She tried to resist him, but he was far too strong. His cock found its target and thrust inside her in one stroke. Once he was inside, she gave up struggling and let him have his way. It helped that she was already slippery with Sam's seed, mixed with her own lubrication. Hank, the blockhead, never noticed he was having sloppy seconds. He pounded away at her for the longest time. Her clit ached to be touched, but her needs didn't matter.

When he came, he bellowed like a bull. El felt his seed fill her womb. Her pussy felt as used as a bowling shoe on league night. He held her tight to milk every drop from his cock, then pulled out. His sperm spilled out of her. Before she could move, he walked up to her face and grabbed it with a meaty paw. "Suck me clean," he ordered, pushing his semi-hard cock into her mouth. She dutifully cleaned him, hoping it would cause him to leave sooner.

When he was satisfied, he buckled up his pants and headed for the door. "Thanks for a wonderful retirement present, slut," he waved and disappeared.

El sank down on the couch, one hand cupped over her pussy to contain all the fluids. She decided to ask Jack for more money if people were going to refuse to wear condoms. Dammit, she has some rights, doesn't she? She didn't know the etiquette of being a sex slave for an entire company.

Wearily, she went to the bathroom to clean up and got dressed. By now, she was tired of her clothes, tired of the way her body smelled, tired of fucking and sucking and being punished. All she wanted to do was go home. She checked the clock in Jack's office. Barely two-thirty. God, these days were long!

Chapter 9

Jack came back from his luncheon meeting at quarter to three and immediately called El over. She came in, stripped off her clothes with a resigned sigh and assumed her position.

"Did Hank come by?"

"Yes, sir. He fucked me, doggy-style. You can add it to my book."

"Good. You fuck anybody else?"

El decided to keep Sam to herself. "No, but I had to give the deli guy another blowjob to pay for lunch—does that count toward my total?"

"No. I admired your initiative the first time, but I didn't authorize a repeat."

El had expected as much.

"Anything else happen while I was gone?"

"Well, there was one thing. It would help me if you would clarify my duties. On the way to lunch, I was accosted by two day-shift workers, who asked that I get into their car and show them my tits and pussy."

Jack sat up. "Did you?"

"Yes, sir. but they wanted more. One of them wanted to touch me, and I was afraid of where that would lead. It would help if you told me what you expect when you say I should be 'nice' to workers. I'm happy to give them what they need, but if I let them have me, then my value as a reward for increased productivity will vanish."

Jack nodded. It was a good point. "I think you did the right thing," he said. "When someone asks to see your body, you should show it. And under controlled circumstances, a little touching may be okay. But when it comes to fucking or sucking, you need to run that by me."

"So in the car like that, you'd prefer they didn't touch me?"

He nodded. "Yeah. If there's going to be touching, I want to have control of that. Otherwise, we know what that'll lead to."

El was satisfied. Now she'd be sure to get credit for every sex act. In that way, she could pay off her debt more quickly and leave Sawyer Metalworking forever.

"Yes, sir."

"Okay, you may go. But be ready at four to go with me to visit that client."

꿏

After she left, Jack turned on the camera. He never tired of seeing El's pussy spread open for him. He thought it might be a good idea to add a third camera, mounted over the glass door, so he could see her from all three angles. That way, if she ever was ordered to sit at her desk without wearing a top, he could see what passing employees would see. He so enjoyed humiliating her.

He heard a noise and looked back at the screen in time to see Gloria barge into El's office. That bitch is going to be trouble, he decided. She had threatened him earlier with all kinds of workplace violations, the main being sexual harassment. Jack didn't need the events of the past two days broadcast on the local news. He'd have to find a way of placating—or blackmailing—Gloria.

He could tell from their conversation that Gloria was demanding to see Jack once again. In a few seconds, his intercom buzzed. Absently, he flicked over to the other camera in time to see her hand drop down between her legs. Damn! He wanted to catch her in a violation, so he could add to her punishments. But she was being far too cooperative.

"Yes?"

"Sir? Gloria wants to see you."

"Send her in."

Gloria barged in. For a fleeting moment, Jack pictured her stripping off her clothes and coming over to kneel at his side. But, of course, if she did, he wouldn't want to see her naked. She was a sturdy woman. Not fat, just filled out by middle-age. She'd been at the plant nearly as long as Jack had owned it. She did a tremendous job in human resources, so he didn't want to rile her. Yet she clearly seemed riled.

"What the heck is going on around here, Jack? I mean, you've got Ellen acting like a slut, the workers are all distracted by her, and you have no CFO now. I'm afraid you're losing control of this plant."

Jack studied her carefully, picking his words. "I know my methods seem unorthodox and I know you don't understand what El is up to now. But I have to tell you, Gloria, since she started her new job, we have a very strong chance to pick up two million dollars in new business."

That took Gloria by surprise. But she recovered quickly. "What's she doing, fucking the clients?"

"Let's just say she's 'stimulating new business.' If just a few of these clients come on board, we're going to have to expand the plant. And that means new workers."

"Well, that's all well and good, but this is going to blow up in your face. You can't force women to be your company bimbo! What are you thinking? And why is she going along with it?"

"That's confidential. I can tell you that this has been

done by mutual consent. No one's forcing El to do anything she doesn't want to do."

"Oh, I can't believe that. She was a well-respected CFO. No woman wants to become a man's slave!"

"You'd be surprised. She seems to be enjoying her new role." Jack paused, thinking carefully about his next statement. "As you know, we have the position of CFO open currently. Know of anyone who's qualified?"

Jack knew full well she did. She'd been hinting, long before Ellen had arrived, to hire her brother-in-law, Andy, who also was a CPA. Jack had found him worthy, but Ellen had slightly better qualifications. Plus, she'd been a lot better looking that Andy.

Gloria was no fool. "Are you suggesting that if I keep my mouth shut about Ellen, you'll hire Andy?"

Jack shrugged. "Andy was a strong candidate before. I would, of course, only hire him on merit, regardless of what you decided to do. However, if you raised a stink over this temporary situation, I think I'd be so distracted by the lawsuits, that I'd be unable to afford a CFO. We might even have to shut down the plant."

That reached her. She stared at him. Then she asked: "Temporary?"

"Yes. I'd say El's only going to be with us for a year or so. Then the plant can return to normal."

Before she could respond, Jack asked her: "Why are you coming to El's aid anyway? Didn't you tell me, when I hired her, that you thought she wouldn't be as competent as Andy?"

Warily, Gloria nodded. "I thought she had some flaws. I didn't know they were so big."

He nodded in agreement. "I'm going to post the position of CFO tomorrow. I hope, whatever you decide to do, you'll keep the best interests of the company in mind."

With that, he dismissed her. She went out the main door, avoiding El's office. It was as if she couldn't bear to see the tart again.

At quarter to four, Jack called El into his office and asked her to bring the other outfit. Once inside, she laid the suit on a chair and stripped yet again. She put on the conservative outfit. Jack could see that she felt more like her old self with the suit on. Jack picked up a folder on his desk and led her out.

They got into his car outside. Without being told, El pulled up her skirt and spread her legs for him. He absently stroked her naked flesh while he drove. She was quite wet to his touch.

"We're going to meet a man named Roger Andrews. He owns a plant that makes metal cabinets for various electronic devices. We have about twenty percent of his business and I think we can do better than that. However, Roger is ... well, let's say he's a contradiction. He spouts Bible verses and he's active in his church, but I know for a fact that he also hides a big secret. When he was a young, he joined the seminary for a time, thinking he wanted to become a minister. But he got caught fooling around with a young student, a teenage girl, and got tossed out. He's walked the straight and narrow ever since, been married for years, but I'll bet he'd love to sneak in some lovin' as long as he doesn't get caught. But we have to be careful.

"That's where you come in. As far as Roger is concerned, you are unmarried. I want you to find him so attractive you can't stand it. He's not an ugly man, although he's probably about twenty years older than you." Jack paused. "Now, one thing. I don't want you to pretend you're a deeply religious person because I think that could backfire. I'd rather he thought of you as a fallen angel, a troubled girl who needs to be redeemed."

Ellen blushed but said nothing.

"So flirt with him, but don't be too obvious. I'm going to make an excuse to leave the room, to give him time to talk to you privately. Give him your phone number, if he asks for it. Maybe touch his arm 'accidentally.' You know the drill."

El nodded. "You really think he might want to pursue me, even though he's married?"

"We'll find out. He may call you on some pretense, either at home or at the office. You are to be flattered and interested."

"And a little bit naughty?"

"You've got it. Ideally, he'll get into this thinking you need some counseling and he'll find out that you'd really like to fuck his brains out. Then we'll see what develops.

"Here," Jack said, handing her a small cell phone. "This is pre-programmed to my pager number—just press this button here. Keep this in your pocket. The volume's turned all the way down, so Roger won't hear anything. When you get what you need from Roger, you call me and I'll come back in. Okay?"

El nodded.

They arrived within thirty minutes. They were met by Roger's assistant, a matronly secretary named Gladys. She escorted them to his office, a rather colorless cube with windows looking out over the factory.

Roger rose to greet them from behind his plain, functional oak desk. He was a trim fifty, with salt-and-pepper hair combed straight back. He wore slacks and a polo shirt. Jack shook his hand and introduced him to "Ellen, my executive assistant."

Roger smiled and shook her hand.

❧

He really is quite handsome, El thought as he held her hand. She could picture him as a kindly minister, with a flock of adoring parishioners. She felt a little spark shoot through her. *This may be an easier assignment than I thought!*

Roger indicated they should all sit, then turned his attention to Jack. They were speaking in numbers: model numbers, profits, percentages—El tuned out. Instead, she concentrated on Roger, the way he moved, the words he used.

Once, while Jack was shuffling through some papers he'd brought, Roger glanced over at her, catching her staring at him. He smiled briefly and turned back to Jack. El worried that maybe he wasn't interested in her.

But a few minutes later, he glanced over again, this time letting his eyes lock onto hers, just for a second. El smiled back. It became a tennis match, serve and volley.

Jack wrapped up his presentation, offering to give them a better overall deal if Roger would let them produce a new line of products for them.

"What's your offer?" Roger inquired.

"Well, I can tell you in just a minute. My production manager promised me some last-minute figures before I left. If you'll excuse me for a moment, I'll call him and then we can talk business. Do you mind if my assistant stays here?"

"No, not at all." Roger flashed her another grin. El knew this was her chance.

Jack pulled out his cell phone as he left, pretending to call the factory. El watch the door close behind him, then turned all of her attention back to Roger.

"So," he said, breaking the ice, "how long have you been Jack's assistant?"

"Just a few days. He's bringing me around to some of

his clients so they can get to know me. I'm really glad he brought me today." She gave him her best, shy-but-sexy smile.

"Really? Well, I'm flattered. Tell me a little about your background."

El began telling her about her college education, but wove in a sad tale about coming from a broken home and how hard it had been, living on her own. When Roger inquired about her religious beliefs, she told him how she had lost her faith in the church when her mother died at the hands of a drunk driver.

"But God didn't cause that man to drink and drive," Roger responded.

"I know, but it was just so unfair. I felt betrayed. My father ran away when I was two and I've never seen him again, and my mom, my anchor, the one who took me to church every Sunday, died three months before I graduated from high school. I felt abandoned, not only by my parents, but by God as well."

"Oh, my child, this wounds my heart to hear your story! Have you had counseling to help you cope with your tragedies?"

"No, sir, I haven't." El blinked her eyes, trying to make tears form. "I probably should have. I went kind of wild after that, doing drugs and having affairs..."

"Well, I'd be happy to recommend someone—"

El blanched. "No," she said quickly. "I'm really rather shy about it. In fact, I don't know why I've been telling you all this. There's just something about you that makes me feel very comfortable."

"That's very nice to hear. You know, I almost became a minister at one time, way back when I was about your age."

"Really? I'll bet you'd have made a good one. You have a way of understanding people. I'll bet that's why you're so successful."

Roger was clearly flattered. They chatted a few more minutes, then Roger checked his watch. El knew too much time had passed—if she didn't entice him now, the moment would be lost.

"I've really enjoyed talking to you. If you had been my minister, I probably never would have left the church."

Roger cocked his head. He hesitated for a moment and said: "I'd be happy to talk to you again sometime, if you think it would help."

She feigned embarrassment, as if she were unworthy of his attention. "Oh, I'm sure you're far too busy to spend time dealing with my problems!"

"No, no. I'd like to help, if I could."

El pressed the button on the cellphone through the pocket of her suit jacket and told him: "Well, why don't I give you my phone numbers and you could call me?"

He readily agreed. She wrote her home and work numbers down on a piece of paper he provided, just as Jack came back from his "phone call."

"Good news," he said, eyeing El, then turning his attention to Roger. "My production manager says we can beat your other deal by eight percent."

Roger nodded and said that was certainly worth exploring. He promised to get back to Jack in a few days, after he discussed the offer with his executive staff.

On the way out to the car, Jack whispered to El: "Well, did he bite?"

"I think so. He has my phone numbers."

"Good, girl!" They got in. "Now show me your pussy."

Chapter 10

The next morning, Raphael, the Latino limo driver, picked her up. El was disappointed for some reason. Though Jack could be demanding at times, deep down she enjoyed being in his presence. She felt protected, somehow.

Then again, she told herself, riding with Raphael was good for a blowjob, so that's a hundred she wouldn't otherwise have earned. He drove her to the plant before accepting her services. He made her remove her top so he could fondle her breasts while she went down on him.

"Oh my pretty *puta*," he said, shortly before he came into her throat.

El dressed and got out, then went into the building. On the way, two co-workers asked to see her breasts, so she had to stop and flash them. Another followed her into her office and asked her to lift up her skirt. She obeyed, but when he put his hands on her ass, she told him to go talk to Mr. Sawyer, knowing that would cool his ardor.

The intercom buzzed. She reached over and answered it, letting her left hand rest against her mound. El absently began to rub herself, standing by her desk in full view of the corridor. Her action was automatic. The worker stared and backed out of the room, shaking his head.

"Yes, sir?"

"Come in, slut."

His tone of voice worried her. El came in right away and stripped. She wondered if she'd be better off just wearing a silk robe to work.

"How may I be of service to you, master?"

He pinned her with his stern expression. "You've violated more of my rules, slut."

Her mind raced. "What? What rules, sir? I've been very obedient."

Jack began to tick them off his fingers. "One, when you were in the car with Ralph and Duane yesterday, you continually referred to me as 'Jack,' not 'Mr. Sawyer', or 'master', or 'sir'. Two, you fucked a deli boy and didn't report it to me. Three, you were late for your appointment with Hank."

El could only stare. How did he know all those things so quickly?

"I-I'm sorry, sir. I didn't think you wanted to hear about the boy and I don't remember calling you Jack." She couldn't come up with an excuse for Hank—she had been late, after all.

Jack stood up and removed his belt. "I guess I'm just going to have to punish you until you learn."

El's eyes flew open. She had just started to recover from her last beating. The bruises were just now fading. "Please, no! Anything but that!"

He paused. "Anything?"

She nodded, suddenly feeling trapped. She hoped he wouldn't tie her to her desk naked, in full display of the corridor. He'd threatened that before.

"You didn't shave today, right?"

El was taken by surprise. "Uh, no, sir. You told me not to."

Jack made her get up and he inspected her stubble. He handed her a piece of paper. "Good. I'll have Raphael drive you to this salon. Ask for Angie. They'll do the wax job, and I'm going to call them and add something else."

El's hand flew to her mouth. "What? What are you going to do to me?"

"Don't worry, it's not permanent. Just go and obey them. If not, you may assume the position." He pointed to the desk.

She stood. "No, sir. I'll go." She visibly shook as she dressed and left.

Jack smiled. "My little plan is working perfectly," he muttered aloud. Of course, he made no call. It had all been arranged ahead of time.

El's skin felt cold and clammy with nerves as she rode to the address Jack had given her. She sat in the back of the limo, completely naked except for her shoes. Raphael didn't want another blow-job, so he made her strip and sit in the center seat, legs apart, so he could see her in the rear-view mirror. The tinted windows kept her safe from prying eyes.

They arrived at a strip mall and El got dressed. Raphael said he'd wait for her. She went into the salon and asked for Angie.

A thin, bleached-blonde woman in her mid-forties wearing too much makeup came forward. "Oh, you must be El," she said at once. "We're all ready for ya."

El noticed that Angie dressed a lot like she did—trashy and slutty. She had on a blue mini-skirt and a sleeveless white top, stained here and there with various potions and dyes. She took El into a private room. The act spoke volumes about what she might be in for.

"Take off your clothes."

El obeyed automatically. She was beginning to hate the bother of clothes. She found she wasn't even embarrassed to be naked in front of this stranger.

"Here, drink this." Angie pushed a glass toward her.

"What is it?" El looked at it warily.

"Don't worry. It's just a mild sedative. Think of it as a cocktail."

"But it's only ten in the morning!"

"Honey, it will make you more comfortable and my job easier." She shrugged. "Your boss suggested it."

That galvanized El into action. She drank the liquid quickly. It had a medicinal taste.

Angie seated her in the reclining chair. El became alarmed when she began strapping her wrists and ankles down. "What are you doing? Why do I need these?"

"Relax, doll. I just want to make sure you don't jerk. I don't want to hurt you."

"Please! I don't like this!" El wished she'd taken the whipping with Jack's belt. "What are you going to do? Please tell me!"

"We're going to do a Brazilian wax and then we're going to install some very nice pieces of body jewelry."

El tried to get up. She felt suddenly woozy. "No, I refuse! Tell Mr. Sawyer I'll take the spanking!"

"Too late, honey." Her voice seemed to come from far away. El tried to struggle, but her arms and legs were increasingly unresponsive. Her mind remained alert, but her body seemed to belong to someone else. It reminded her of the feeling she got when she smoked pot. She giggled.

"That's the spirit," she heard Angie's voice from a distance.

El watched with detached amusement as Angie adjusted the chair, separating her legs up and apart. She remembered being on her back on Jack's desk, like a Christmas turkey, while he shaved her. She giggled again.

It was fun to watch the stylist work. Angie scooted up

between her legs and examined her coarse stubble. "Not sure we have enough to work with," El heard her say, "but we'll give it a go. You can always come back for additional treatments."

She painted her mound and sides with a thick, sticky wax. It felt warm and good. Angie then laid thin strips of cloth over it and left them on a long time until the wax hardened thoroughly. El stared between her legs as if she were watching a nature show.

When Angie began yanking the strips off, El felt a sting, but otherwise it didn't hurt much. She could see as the strips came off that there was some hair stuck to the undersides.

"That's better," Angie said when she was finished. El felt her rubbing all around her pussy. She wished she'd rub her clit. "You still have some hairs that were too short to grab, but if you don't shave for three or four days, you can come back and we'll take care of those."

The experience really wasn't so bad. Was she done? No, she recalled, Jack had wanted something else. In place of a punishment. What could that be?

She watched, detached, as Angie went to the door and left for a few minutes. When she returned, another woman accompanied her. El felt exposed with her legs still up and apart like this, but it seemed more comical than embarrassing. She giggled and tried to wiggle her body at the new girl but her motor control was weak.

Angie came and stood by El's head. "This is Claire. She's the piercer."

Piercer? Did that mean what she thought it meant? Suddenly, this didn't seem so funny. "Whaaa?" she said, her voice slurring. "I doan wanna."

"Shush, just relax. You won't feel a thing. Claire's really quite good at this."

El watched as Claire rolled her chair up between her legs. Angie adjusted the neck brace to tip El's head up a bit more. She wanted her to see what was being done to her. Did Jack tell her to do that? Was that part of her punishment?

Claire took a tube of salve and rubbed some into the mound above El's slit. It felt soothing. Soon she grew numb down there. Claire pinched the fold of flesh right above her clit experimentally. With her other hand, she began rubbing her clit gently with her thumb, causing it to rise to greet her. El tried to fight the feeling, but she was helpless. If she'd just keep it up for another couple of minutes...

Claire looked up at El. "I'm going to put a gold ring down here."

Her orgasm retreated. El shook her head and pulled at her bonds.

"It's okay," the woman said. "I'm not going to pierce your clit—that's way too painful and doesn't provide the desired result." She held up a small gold ring, about the diameter of a pinkie ring, thin at the top and a thicker band at the bottom. "This is going to go through the skin just above the clit. The bottom part, which you can see is heavier, will bounce against your clit with every step—that is, if you don't wear underwear, which I'm told you don't." She patted El's upper thigh, just inches from her throbbing pussy. "This is a good thing, El, you'll see. A lot of women do this to keep them in a near-constant state of stimulation."

El thought about that for a second. Claire made it sound pretty good. "It woon hurr'? "

She laughed. "No, it won't hurt. It's going to feel woooonderful."

El relaxed a little then and watched her work. Claire carefully measured where the upper part of the ring should be hung in order to let the bottom part hit just the right spot on her clit. She made a tiny dot on El's skin and pinched it, drawing it away from the sensitive nerves underneath.

With a piercing tool, Claire punched a thin hole through a fold of flesh. El felt only a pinch. Working quickly, Claire pulled back the prong and threaded the ring through. She wiped up the blood and daubed the area with a healing salve. "There. That wasn't so bad, was it?"

El looked down and admired the gold band. It shone against her bronze skin. Her clit already had swelled from its touch. "It's bootiful," she managed.

Claire brought out another tool, one that was plugged into the wall. "Now normally, these are made to be easily removed. But Jack asked if I would solder it permanently." She caught El's surprised expression. "Oh, it's really not permanent. If you ever want it off, you can come to any good piercing studio and they'll remove it."

The soldiering iron hissed and there was a brief feeling of heat and then it was over. Claire brought over a mirror and tipped it up so El could see. The ring lay right at the edge of her pussy, so the bottom part hung over onto the slit. She could see her clit, poking out just under the edge of the shiny gold ring.

"Can I try id?" Her voice was becoming less slurred now.

"Not quite yet. Just a couple more things."

El looked around in alarm. *Now what?* She had her answer when Claire moved her chair up to El's chest and hit the lever to sink her down several inches. "No!"

"Oh, yes. Jack insisted." Without pause, Claire began rubbing some salve into her nipples, causing them to come to full attention. Soon they grew numb as well. "This won't take but a second." She set the piercing tool over the base of the left nipple and squeezed the lever. To El, it felt as if someone pinched her nipple—uncomfortable, but not as painful as she had expected.

Claire expertly threaded in a gold ring. It was about the same size as the one between her legs, but it was of uniform thickness. Claire cleaned up the area and daubed on some salve. She brought over the soldiering iron and made the ring permanent. She scooted the chair to the other size and in another two minutes, El had a matching pair of nipple rings.

"They are very pretty," she had to admit.

"These are both twenty-four carat gold—the best—so you shouldn't have any trouble with them. We'll give you some of this salve to take home. It'll help prevent infection and speed healing."

They unfastened El and let her sit up. She still felt woozy from the sedative.

"Are you still dizzy?"

"A little. Mostly, I feel ... happy, giddy."

"Good. We don't always use that stuff. Some women just prefer we use a local anesthetic. But Jack thought you'd be more comfortable with it."

How nice of him, she thought bitterly. Now she was marked as a true slut. Which is exactly what Jack wanted. Her jewelry would remind her every day just what her role is. As if she didn't already feel that way.

They helped her up and let her dress. El had to be careful pulling the top on. Her nipples tingled. At the counter, Angie gave her a tube of ointment. Angie went out to fetch Raphael, who helped her into the car. He got into the back seat with her.

"Let me see."

Once again, El found herself stripping. Raphael whistled

when he saw the jewelry. "*Madre di dios*! That's a good look for you, chica."

She gave him a thin smile. "Thank you."

"You make me horny again. Make me cum while I play with your new jewelry."

Although she still felt lightheaded, she was afraid to complain. She opened his pants and let his cock spring free. She brought her mouth to it and began to suckle him. She had learned quite a bit in the last two days at how to tease a man's seed from him quickly, so she used all her newfound talents to bring the driver off.

When he came, she held his cock deep in her throat, sucking down his spunk until he softened.

"Oh, mi chica! You getting pretty good at that!" He zipped up and stepped out, then got in behind the wheel. El didn't bother putting her clothes back on. She sat in the center of the seat, legs apart, while Raphael leered at her from the mirror as he drove.

She wasn't sure how she really felt about all this. In retrospect, the piercings were a lot less painful than a whipping would have been. And yet now she was marked. The only thing worse would be if Jack had ordered a tattoo. She hoped it would never come to that. Didn't he promise he'd do nothing permanent? Yeah, she thought, I can have these removed—and I will just as soon as Jack releases me.

Still, they do look pretty, don't they? She fingered the gold bands. *Twenty-four carat, didn't she say?*

When they arrived at the plant, El dressed again. She didn't really want to—she'd shown her body enough around the plant that nearly everyone had seen her. But she was shy about her new jewelry. It shouted 'slut!' to her and it no doubt would to everyone else.

It turned out to be a temporary reprieve.

As she walked across the lot, she noticed how the heavier ring tickled her clit. She could feel herself becoming aroused already. She knew she was producing more fluid and her pussy swelled with her hot blood. She couldn't imagine walking around like this all day.

No sooner had she entered the hall than a worker asked her to flash him. Gritting her teeth, she raised her top and the man's eyes nearly popped out of her head.

"Gooll-ly! Woodja look at that! She's got nipple rings now!"

Another man rushed out of a nearby office. "Wow! Those are great! Got any more anyplace?" He wiggled his eyebrows.

El sighed and lifted up her skirt. The men couldn't believe what they were seeing. They jabbered excitedly, calling others over to see her. El felt flushed, dizzy. She leaned against the wall and let them crowd close, touching her, tugging at the rings, feeling her breasts and her wet pussy. She was so aroused that she couldn't stop them. In her mind's eye, she saw herself on her desk, legs spread, while the men came at her, big cocks in hand. She didn't even care about getting credit, she only cared about getting fucked. Her clothes fell to the floor.

Chapter 11

Jack rescued her. He came out to see what the commotion was and sent everyone back to work. They obeyed reluctantly. He ordered El into his office.

"Looks like the secret is out," he said cheerily. "I guess there's no hiding what you are now."

"Yes, sir," she said, her head down. She knelt naked at his side, her pussy still aflame. *God, would somebody please fuck me!*

"Tell me all about it," he ordered, fondling the rings in her nipples and pussy. She felt no embarrassment, only desire.

El recounted her visit to the salon in rote detail, trying to concentrate while Jack played with her. The rings really did make a difference in how stimulated she felt.

"You're doing really well, El. I mean it. I'm very pleased." He entered her new totals into the computer.

El paid little attention. Her clit screamed at her to provide some relief and she was sure Jack could smell her sexual heat. She wanted to touch herself, rub her clit. She could come in a second if he would allow it. If possible, she felt even more aroused than on her first day, when Jack had teased her before sending Bob in to fuck her. She'd had her most powerful orgasm then, but she suspected she could have a bigger one now.

He tugged on a nipple ring, nearly sending her over the edge. "Please," she whispered.

"What was that?"

"Please, master."

"What's wrong? Am I making you horny?"

"Yesss." The word escaped from her like the air let out of a balloon.

He reached down and flipped up the bottom ring, letting it fall down on her engorged clit. She jumped slightly. Her blood boiled.

"Good. We have a busy day ahead. At ten-fifteen, Bob's returning."

Her heart leapt. Bob! Big, long, sexy Bob! She knew he would give her the orgasm she craved. Her face lit up.

"And at eleven-thirty," he continued, "we're meeting a realtor at your house. You're going to convince him to shave a few percentage points off his commission, so you can pay me more money toward your debt."

She could only nod, trying hard to hold back her orgasm.

"Don't worry about any details, the realtor and I will handle all of that. All you need to do is concentrate on your pussy."

There was no problem with that. She could think of nothing else. Suddenly, he pulled away, leaving her on the edge. Her eyes flew open.

"Bob'll be here any minute. Why don't you greet him at your desk. *Don't* touch your pussy. I don't want you to explode until his cock is firmly seated inside you."

Shaking, she stood up. She looked at her clothes, piled by the door, but she didn't think she could muster up the energy to put them on again.

"Don't bother with those," Jack called. "He'll be here any minute."

Feeling relief, El went out into her office. She paid no attention to the corridor or the people walking by. They've already seen her naked. She sat on the chair, hearing the squishy sounds of her pussy pressing against the vinyl seat. She wiggled experimentally, thinking maybe if she kept that up, she could come. But that would make Jack mad and she didn't want that.

El sat there, hands folded in front of her while people walked by, stopped and stared. Gloria just glared as she speed-walked past her door. Ralph came in with Duane and they tried to strike up a conversation, but El knew they only wanted a closer look at her body and the new rings.

Just having them look at her increased her sexual tension. She wouldn't have stopped them if they grabbed her, tossed her on the desk and had their way with her.

The intercom crackled to life. "Duane, Ralph, please return to work. We're waiting for a client."

The two men looked around guiltily. "The office is wired," El explained. Her legs were wide apart under the desk. She nearly put her hand on her pussy when she heard Jack's voice, but remembered not to.

The men left quickly. Word got around because soon the lookie-loos had drifted away. El waited, feeling her pussy leaking onto the chair.

Finally Bob's bulk appeared at the glass door. He looked in and his eyes bulged. He came in quickly, closing the door behind him and tried to shield her from view.

"What's this?"

"We've been expecting you, Mr. Orley," she said, her pussy tingling anew. "Jack is in his office if you'd like to go right in."

"But-but, what about you? What's all this?"

"Jack had me fitted with some jewelry. He says I look better this way."

"But you're naked, right here in front of everybody!"

"Yes. I got tired of putting on and taking off my clothes all the time."

Bob nodded his head like a puppet. "Um, okay. I'll go in now." At the door, he turned. "You coming?"

"Yes, sir." She got up to follow him, but he insisted she go first. She felt his hand on her bottom as she stepped through the door. She liked his touch and wiggled her ass appreciatively for him. She thought she should go kneel by Jack's desk, but Bob's big arm kept her close to him, rubbing her hot skin until she quivered like a tuning fork Her pussy leaked down both thighs and she welcomed it. The odor of her own need lay heavy on the air.

The men greeted each other like old friends and immediately began speaking in double entendres. Bob told Jack he had the contract "just about nailed," but "something came up at the last minute." El could see the bulge in his pants.

Jack told him he could use his office to "check those figures," while he went out for a tour of the plant. Once Jack had gone, Bob wasted no time in grabbing El and pushing her back on the desk. She was an eager participant. He unbuckled his pants and she reached out to feel his hard cock, like a bar of steel.

Bob began playing with her new jewelry and for the first time, El was glad she had it. The tugging and pulling caused her to go mad with sexual desire. She grabbed Bob's cock and pulled it toward her gaping, sloppy wet slit. He jammed it into her in one smooth motion and El's head exploded in such an earth-shattering orgasm that her brain short-circuited momentarily. When she came to, she heard someone screaming, "MY GOD, MY GOD!" and realized it was her.

Bob wasn't nearly done. He began to stroke her with his big cock as only he knew how to do. She had another orgasm, nearly as powerful as the first. When his cock began to erupt a few seconds later, and she felt the powerful throbbing deep within her, El had her third climax. She hugged the big man close to her, tears streaming down her face, her mouth open to gulp a lungful of air.

The sensations eased. Bob pushed up and looked down at her. "You are dee-licious," he said. "I'll bet they heard that all over the building."

El felt no embarrassment. She didn't care—she had had her long-delayed orgasm, and that was all the mattered. He pulled out. She knew her fluids were spilling all over Jack's desk. She thought she probably ought to clean that up before he returned.

"Tell Jack he's got a deal—as long as you'll be around to 'service' the contract."

El didn't want to tell him that her duties were temporary. "I'll tell him." He started to buckle up his pants. "Bob ... Mr. Orley."

He smiled. "You can call me Bob."

"Bob—that was ...incredible. You know that, don't you."

"Well, it was certainly good for me. You're a pistol, El, a real pistol."

He left, waving at her as he went out the door. El rolled over and got up. Her muscles ached—she must've pulled something during that first 8.0 orgasm. As soon as she stood up, she felt the fluids gush out of her slit. Chagrined, she squeezed her legs together and waddled to the bathroom.

She realized it had never occurred to her to ask Bob to use a condom. She had been far too horny for that. She doubted it mattered—Bob seemed healthy. But she'd have to be more careful.

She sat on the toilet and let the excess fluids leak out. Without thinking, she reached down and let some drip onto her fingers, then brought them to her lips to taste the salty mixture. El used a washcloth to clean up, being careful around the rings. She should put some salve on the wounds, she decided. Her tube of ointment was still on her desk.

She came out and saw that Jack had not yet returned. El used the damp cloth to clean up the mess they'd left on his desk. She went to her office, still naked, and sat directly on the wet stain she'd left before. Somehow, she didn't feel right cleaning it up first—not unless Jack said it was okay. The seat was cooling to her hot pussy.

She reached for her ointment. As she was dabbing it on, she caught sight of several people drifting by outside, stopping to peer in at her again. This can't be helping productivity, she mused.

She waited patiently, unconcerned about her nudity, until the intercom buzzed. She touched herself and answered it. "Yes, master?"

"It's almost time to go. Come in."

"Yes, sir."

She rose and went to the door. It pleased her that she didn't have to stop and strip off her clothes again. She knelt. "How may I be of service, master?"

"Tell me all about it."

El couldn't stop smiling as she described her orgasms, Bob's pleasure, and the contract she'd helped land. All the while, Jack fingered her jewelry, causing the heat to rise in her yet again. She thought he might fuck her before they left, but he didn't. He seemed to want her on edge.

"You didn't use a condom?"

"No, sir. There, um, wasn't time."

He laughed and told her to get dressed. Her clothes seemed tight and restrictive. In the car, she opened herself for him and let his fingers dance over her damp pussy, occasionally tugging at the ring above. It made her squirm in her seat.

Jack dropped her off at her house, and handed her the cell phone, telling her to call him when she needed a ride. The realtor's car was already parked out front. He was waiting on the porch. He came down, greeting her like a long-lost relative. El knew he was eager for a commission, but she could tell he was interested in her as well.

His name was Robert Abernathy, which brought a flicker of a smile to El's face—looks like she'll be fucking two Bobs today. This Bob was completely different—he was of average height, slender, and handsome in a prep boy kind of way. He couldn't be more than thirty-five.

They toured the house. It wasn't a big house, so it didn't take long. El managed to flirt with Bob as they walked through the rooms, at one point brushing one of her breasts against his upper arm. El told Bob about the first and second mortgages, and some other debts that had piled up while Bill had been unemployed.

"All the furniture's going to be sold or put into storage in the next few days, I think," El said. She'd have to ask Mr. Sawyer. "I should be out of here within a week."

"Well, I don't think you're going to clear much from this place," Bob was saying, "but it will be good for your credit rating to get out from under it."

"You know, I've had a lot of difficulties lately. My husband left me, I've ... been having some trouble at work and I nearly lost my job—is there any way you could trim your commission for me?" She batted her eyes at him.

He grimaced. "Uh, I don't know. You know, six percent is standard in our industry, and we all adhere to it, so if you're thinking you can get five-and-a-half or five percent in a bidding war, you probably won't find someone. And if you do, they'll be beginners or incompetents."

It was a well-rehearsed lie, but El figured many sellers bought it. But she had already done the math. "The problem is, Bob, you'll get more out of this house than I will, after I split everything with my husband."

"Well, I don't know what we can do about that," he said suggestively. El knew he was interested, but she was waiting for her to make the first move.

She decided not to beat around the bush, so to speak. "I'll tell you what," she approached him and put one hand on his shoulder, "if you cut your commission by a percent, I'll let you fuck me once a day for the next two months. And if you cut two percent off, you can fuck me once a day for the next five months."

Bob's eyes grew wide. El could see him thinking, running the numbers. It was a fair deal. "You mean, like, anytime? Like right now?"

She nodded, then stepped back and pulled her top off. When he saw the rings, his cock swelled in his pants, forcing him to tug on his belt to give it more room. "You've got nipple rings," he said stupidly.

"Yes, I just got them today. You like?"

"Uh huh," his head bounced up and down. His eyes never left her breasts.

"There's more to see—and experience. But let's decide, shall we?" She moved in close until her ringed nipples were rubbing across his Brooks Brothers shirt.

"Uh, how do I know this is on the level? How do I know you won't go back on your word later?"

"I always honor my commitments," she breathed into his ear, running her hands through his carefully combed hair. "Besides, if I failed in my duties, you could call my boss, Jack Sawyer."

"You mean, he knows about this?"

"Mr. Sawyer knows everything about me," she said simply.

"He, uh, won't get involved in the, you know…"

"The sex?" She laughed. "No. He'll leave that to me. But he'll make sure I follow through."

"That's a strange working arrangement you have there."

"I suppose it is." She stepped back. "So, what's it going to be—or do I have to call another realtor?"

"Uh, no! Don't do that. I'll take it. I mean, I'll take the two-month deal, for one percent off."

She came back into his arms. "Tell you what, Bob. After two months, when you will have wished you'd gone for the other deal, I'll let you fuck me anytime after that for, um, seventy-five bucks a lay." She knew she'd be getting credit for two-fifty from Jack.

She could see him calculating the figures in his head. "But, that's a lot more than I'll be paying under our deal!"

"Well, then take the better deal. If you don't, I know you'll regret it later."

He thought about it while El stroked his hard cock. "All right! All right! You win. Two percent off and I can have you any time over the next five months."

"No more than once a day, okay?"

He nodded.

"Great." She hooked her thumbs into her skirt and slid it down her thighs. Bob's mouth dropped open when he saw the ring through her skin, just above her slit.

"Good god!"

"It makes me horny all the time, Bob," she said, taking his hand and letting him touch it. "Do you want to start right away? Because I'm so horny I can't stand it."

His head bobbed up and down. He unbuckled his pants and let them fall to his ankles. He pushed her back onto the couch and thrust into her without any foreplay. El didn't need any—she was always ready. She lolled back and let him have her. It felt so right to be fucking a stranger in the house she had shared with Bill. She had gotten into this mess because of him and now she was fucking him out of her system, right on the couch they used to share.

Bob came quickly, apparently overwhelmed by her charms. El squeezed her legs around him, enjoying the sensation of his cock throbbing inside her. After a minute, he pulled away and grinned. "You understand I really am going to fuck you every day, don't you?"

El thought if he comes that fast every time, it won't matter a bit. She could take ten minutes out to fuck him while she's getting ready for work. "Sure," she said. "You just have to call me first so I can fit you in."

"Fit me in? You said anytime."

"Well, yes, but you aren't the only one I'm beholden to."

He opened his mouth, then closed it again. "You mean, if I just show up, I might run into someone else?"

"Yeah. That doesn't bother you, does it?"

"Uh, no, I guess... Wait. Yes, that does bother me. Who are all these other guys? You know, I could catch something here."

For the second time that day, El realized she hadn't made her lover wear a condom. What was she thinking? Bob was right. "All of the men are healthy and respectable. I'm not a street hooker." She shrugged. "But from now on, you should probably bring some condoms. I normally make my lovers wear condoms, but something about you just made me forget."

The flattery pleased him. "Well, all right then."

"Well, I've got to get back to work." She pulled out the cellphone and dialed Jack's number. "Hello, Mr. Sawyer? It's me. I'm all done here."

"Good. How did it go?"

"Fine. We came to an arrangement about the commission."

El rubbed her clit with her free hand while she chatted, completely unaware that Bob was staring at her all the time. When she hung up, she caught his expression. "What?"

"You were masturbating while you talked to your boss."

"Oh, that. Yes, he orders me to do that."

"He orders you to?"

"Yes."

"Do you do anything he orders you to do?"

"Pretty much." She didn't want to get into a philosophical discussion about her limits. They seemed to be expanding all the time anyway.

"What if I ordered you to do something?"

El smiled. "You can only order me to fuck you, once a day for the next five months. That's all." She dressed and headed for the door.

"Wait, I have one more question."

"Yes?" She turned, her hand on the knob of the house that used to be home.

"Where will you live, after the house is sold?"

"Oh. I'll be moving in with Mr. Sawyer. He'll probably be handling all the arrangements, the moving, the sale, you know."

"You'll be living with him? But, won't that affect our deal? I mean, won't he object?"

"Object? Hell, this was his idea! No, it won't matter. He's not going to watch. That's not his thing."

She left Bob standing there shaking his head and went out to wait for her master.

Chapter 12

As she had expected, El got a call from Roger, the straight-laced equipment-maker. She was sitting at her desk, naked, of course, her pussy satiated for the time being from a new client—John or Steve—she couldn't really remember. After a bit of small talk, Roger offered to sit with her and "counsel" her the following night, and she readily accepted.

Jack told her to wear something sexy, but not slutty—at least for now. Fortunately, he'd kept most of her old clothes, just for this purpose. She put on a white (virginal) blouse and a knee-length tan skirt. She asked about underwear, but Jack didn't think it would be necessary.

They met at Roger's church, which was deserted except for a Bible study group in one room. Roger took her into a spare office on the other side of the church "so they wouldn't be disturbed." They sat opposite each other, knees nearly touching.

They talked for a time about El's difficult childhood. She hadn't gotten enough affection, she told him, sniffling into a tissue. She let Roger touch her whenever he wanted, under the guise of consoling her when she described a particularly difficult moment in her life. She was a good actress and needed a lot of consoling.

When Roger "accidentally" brushed one of her breasts as he reached to hug her, El grabbed his hand and pressed it against her. Roger seemed surprised, and started to pull away, but then he felt the nipple ring. He stopped and asked her why she did that to herself.

"It makes me feel sexy and worthy of a man's love," she told him. When she saw the unasked question on his lips, she added, "I could show it to you, if it's not too sinful for you to bear."

"Oh, no, my child," he replied, a little too eagerly. "Nothing you do under the eyes of God is sinful if you don't have lust or hate in your heart."

El doubted Roger had no lust in his heart. She unfastened her blouse and let one breast peek through. Roger had stared at it a long time before he reached out and touched the ring, carefully. El could see the nipple swell to its full length. He tugged it gently, causing El to tingle all over.

"You're not wearing a bra," he said. "Why not?"

El almost told him that Mr. Sawyer doesn't let her, but caught herself in time. "They're too confining, especially with the rings."

"So you have a matching set, then?" Clearly, he wanted El to show him her other breast, and she obliged. When both breasts emerged from her blouse, his breath flowed into his lungs like someone coming out of the ocean after a long dive. He placed his hands on her breasts like they were gifts from God. Which, in fact, they were. Then El leaned in close.

"There's one more," she whispered and from his expression, she knew right away she had him.

He covered it well. He feigned ignorance of such things, pretending that she must have been talking about a navel piercing. When she said the words "clit ring" his eyes widened and she could almost hear a choir of angels in the background.

"I've never seen such a thing," he said softly. El believed him.

"Would you like to see one?"

"Well, I wouldn't … I mean, uh…" he stammered.

"No, it's all right. I feel very comfortable with you." She pulled her skirt up and he goggled when he spotted her smooth pussy and shiny ring. She looked down and noticed her slit was expanding and filling with fluids.

"You don't wear underwear?"

"No, it interferes with my ring. It has to hang down like this to work."

He asked why she needed it and she explained that because she had felt abandoned in her youth, that sex gave her back that feeling of closeness. And the clit ring was a substitute for sex because she didn't have a man in her life. This was technically true—she had several.

"So if you had a man, would you remove it?"

"I don't know, Roger. It makes me feel so sexy all the time, I don't think my man would want me to, do you?"

"Er, may I touch it?"

"Of course." She spread her legs apart.

He slid to the edge of his chair and brought one finger carefully to the bottom edge of the ring, trying not to touch her skin. But his finger bumped her clit, which was standing at full attention, as usual. When she jerked, he pulled back. "Did I hurt you?"

"Oh, no. It just makes me really … horny." Sitting there with her breasts spilling out of her blouse, and her skirt pulled up, she cooed: "Am I a sinner, Roger?"

He stammered, working hard to placate her. "No, sex is not a sin, my child. It's God's greatest gift to us. And the wearing of jewelry is not a sin, per se. I think, however, that God would prefer you simply had sex the regular way than walk around with, um, devices, you see."

"And if a lonely girl has no one? Then what should she do?"

"Uh, well, I don't know," he said, staring at her charms. "Prayer, of course."

Ellen flipped down her skirt in disgust. Roger hurried on, "In your case, however, perhaps a substitute might be in order. Someone with experience, who had your best interests in mind, you know. Someone you wouldn't fall in love with because you are waiting for your true love to appear."

El smiled. "Where could I find someone like that, Roger?"

"Er, I'd be happy to counsel you, until you found a man your own age."

And that became their term for it: Counseling. He didn't even take off his clothes. He just unzipped his pants and fucked her, hard and fast, on the couch in the office. When he came, he shouted, "Glory, Hallelujah!" Rather than laugh at him, she shouted, "Oh God!"

The next day, Roger signed a contract with Jack, adding another ten percent to Sawyer's slice of business.

After that, El made weekly trips to Roger's church for "counseling," which consisted of nothing more than several "Glory, Hallelujahs!" and "Oh Gods!" by both parties. El found his religious fever only added to his stamina. Not once did he ask her about birth control and not once did she ask him to use a condom.

Chapter 13

Life became a blur to El over the next few weeks. She no longer had to think about anything—every decision was made for her: Spread your legs, sign these papers for your house, suck this man's cock, show me your tits, let me play with your rings. Throughout, her mind was distracted by the constant stimulation of her clit.

She abandoned her clothes for the most part. They proved to be in the way. El kept a short, silk robe in her office that she used whenever Jack had a new customer visiting. He didn't want to shock them right off the bat. He needn't have worried, however, for customers began coming to Sawyer Metalworking *because* of El, not just because Jack's plant produced quality equipment.

Jack moved her into his house, but she didn't sleep with him and she rarely fucked him there. He preferred to use her at the office. She stayed in a small bedroom on the ground floor, near the kitchen. Probably at one time it had been the maid's quarters. She had her own bathroom and her own entrance, the back door off the kitchen that Jack insisted she use at all times.

She entertained her "guests" that way as well. Bob, the realtor, came by nearly every day, as promised. Most of the time, he scheduled himself at seven-fifteen for a quick fuck before work. He'd knock on the back door and El would let him in, naked, and reach down to feel his hard cock. They'd fuck in her bed, or, if it was warm enough, he'd take her in the backyard, as they both enjoyed outdoor sex. He'd fuck her on the lawn or bent over the picnic table.

Bob continued to ejaculate quickly, giving El plenty of time to shower and get ready for work. He brought his own condoms, but El had gotten fucked so many times without them that she no longer thought about protection, although she continued to take her birth control pills.

When it was time to go to work, she'd exit the back door and wait by the garage until Jack came out. If it was cold, she'd stand inside the back door until he honked. Then she'd get in and spread her legs and let Jack fondle her on the way to work.

To avoid being arrested for having a nude woman with him, Jack had the side windows tinted. Now, only oncoming drivers might catch a fleeting glimpse of her breasts. Few probably believed what they saw.

At the plant, there always seemed to be a crowd waiting for his car. Jack would jump out and walk ahead of El, and the crowd would follow along with her, watching her breasts bounce with each step. For El, these little trips only accentuated the quivering buzz in her clit caused by the heavy gold ring.

The crowd knew better than to bother her too much, as Jack was quite strict about wasting time staring at El when they could be working. He'd had to lower the boom on Ralph, threatening to fire him if he kept coming into El's office to fondle her. After word got out, workers realized that she was there to be seen and to entertain the top performers, but she wasn't a toy for general amusement. Still, the novelty of her nudity never quite wore off.

Jack sent her back to the salon to get another bikini wax, so her cunt was smooth and shiny at all times. He also had one more piece of jewelry installed: A gold pin in her navel that spelled out "slut" in small letters. She now wore false eyelashes along with her heavy makeup. Jack also ordered that her hair be cut short into a cute pageboy. When she looked in a mirror, she seemed like a completely different person.

As the weeks passed, El tried to keep up with the rate of her debt reduction, but the numbers that used to make sense to her no longer did. She couldn't believe she was getting dumber and chalked it up to the increased blood flow to her sex organs. There's something about being in a constant state of arousal that pushed all other thoughts out of her head.

As a further incentive to the workers, Jack told her to walk around the plant floor naked every day at ten-thirty and four-thirty, so both shifts could see her. They'd line up, clapping and cheering as she walked around. Although no touching was allowed, the bouncing of her rings kept her on edge. By the time she returned from her walks, she couldn't wait for someone to fuck her. Fortunately, it seemed Jack usually had someone waiting for her.

The day shift won their contest with the night shift, much to Tom's dismay. Scotty walked around with a big grin on his face long before he accepted his award. Since he had gone first with El, he graciously let all the others go ahead of him. This time, El remembered to ask the men to use condoms. After all, there were eleven of them in a row. Jack didn't want to tie up his office, so the men brought a small bed into the tool shop and set her up there, behind closed doors. It took most of the day to satisfy everyone.

When it came Darlene's turn, El told her she'd be happy to service her, but she might need a little direction. Darlene laughed and responded: "Just do to me what you like done to you." El didn't quite get it until Darlene pulled out a strap-on dildo that she'd brought from home.

"But then, why don't you like men?" El had asked, truly curious.

"Oh, I like men just fine, it's just that they don't like me much," the heavy-set woman had replied. "So I find lesbians are just as good or even better."

El understood. When Darlene took off her clothes, El made a point of telling her how nice her pussy looked. The woman kept her hair neatly trimmed, so El wouldn't have a mouthful to dodge. She dove in, using the techniques she had encouraged the men in her life to use and soon brought Darlene to a delightful orgasm. Then she strapped on the dildo and pounded her from behind. Darlene bucked like a horse and El was exhausted when the woman finally came again.

Chapter 14

El sat in her office, naked as usual, and waited for someone to tell her what to do. People passing by in the corridor hardly gave a glance at the slender slut now. She kept her legs spread under the desk and hoped Jack would call her in soon.

After installing a third camera, mounted over the glass door, pointed down at El, Jack had kindly sent the closed circuit pictures of her to the lunch room monitor, so workers could see slutty El at any time. She didn't mind, as it kept people from fondling her too much in the hallways.

It was hard for her to remember her life as a CFO. She'd been so busy these past few months that those old memories had been pushed out of her mind. She didn't mind being told what to do—it simplified her life.

The intercom buzzed. She answered it immediately, knowing at the same time that anyone in the lunchroom could see her fingers rubbing her pussy. The idea thrilled her.

"Yes, master?"

"Come in, El."

She rose at once and came into his office. Jack was alone. She padded over to his desk and kneeled down. "How may I—"

"El," he interrupted, "you've done it."

El was confused. "Done what, sir?" For a minute she thought she was in trouble, although it had been months since Jack had spanked her.

Jack turned the monitor toward her. She tried to make

sense of the numbers. "You've paid off all your debt—Two hundred, seventy thousand dollars. Principal, plus interest. What do you think about that?"

El was confused. "I'm paid up? That's good, huh?" She tried to remember why she had owed that much money. Oh, yes, she had stolen it from the company a long time ago.

"Yes, it means, if you'd like, you can leave us now. Go be a CFO at another company. I'll give you a good recommendation."

She shook her head, trying to clear it. Did he want her to leave? Did she want her former life back? It seemed so remote. She liked her life here. She didn't have to think about anything and she got to have so many tremendous orgasms she couldn't imagine putting an end to them.

"Do I have to, master?"

He took her by her arms and drew her to him. "Of course not, El. It's just that I promised you I'd keep accurate records and I have. You've now paid for all the money you stole—and you've helped bring in new business. We're expanding the plant because of your hard work."

El couldn't understand why Jack didn't just tell her what to do. "What should I do, master?"

Jack sighed and eased her down to her knees. "I'm not sure I can make this decision for you. Do what's in your heart. You could go and get a fresh start, far away from here. But I can tell you, that if you stay, I think we can triple our net income."

El nodded as if she understood, but the numbers meant little to her. She had come to think of the factory workers as family. She enjoyed their attention, their friendliness, their constant strokings to keep her stimulated. She needed her stimulation now. The idea that she'd have to leave it all behind was impossible to imagine.

She hugged Jack's legs. "Please don't make me go, master."

Jack took her into his arms and let her sit on his lap. She felt safe again. "You don't have to go, slut. You can stay here with us forever. Look," he said, pointing to her smooth mound right above her clit ring, "if you'd like, I could have the company logo tattooed right here, showing that you'll always be part of our team." He raised his fingers to the navel pin. "And I think these letters are too small. How would you like a larger pin?"

She looked up at him, her eyes shining. "Oh, yes, master!" She hugged him around his neck.

"There's more, El. As part of the expansion, I'm thinking about building you an apartment, so you can be here all the time. Would you like that?"

"Oh, yes, master!" Then a thought flashed across her overly stimulated brain. "But I also like staying at your house. I like it when you call me up to fuck me. Would you still fuck me if I lived here?"

"Oh, yes, my pet. In fact, everyone would fuck you, all the time. You'd have more friends than ever!"

"Bob too?" She meant big Bob, not the scrawny, quick-draw realtor who had been banished as soon as his time had run out.

"Oh, yes. Bob and Roger and John and all the rest. All our clients. They will come by day and night to keep you happy."

"Oh, master, that'd be great!" El's fears evaporated. "When can I start?"

"Start? Why, you've started already. In fact, I'm naming you Employee of the Month again! Now, get up on that desk!"

El clapped her hands and got into position.

Chapter 15

Andy Grogan sat across from Jack, holding the latest quarterly figures. "I can't believe that you've pulled it off, Jack. When my sister-in-law filled me in on your company, I thought I might be asking for trouble to accept the job. But you've made a believer out of me."

Jack smiled at his CFO. He'd been worried that Andy might turn out to be a prude like Gloria, but hiring him had been a stroke of genius. He had embraced Jack's exploitation of El, as long as it meant bigger profits.

"Thanks, Andy. You should know that I tried to let her go a few months ago. After all, at the time she'd brought in seven million dollars in new business. She's paid off her debt and then some. But she wouldn't go and she doesn't seem concerned about money. Isn't that funny?"

"I don't know how you did it, but I'd say, keep it up. By my calculations, Sawyer Metalworking is on track to net two-point-four million in profits this year."

"That's great, Andy. Before El, we'd have been lucky to net seven-hundred-thousand. This really puts Sawyer on the map."

Andy sat up and looked around, as if someone was listening. "Uh, Jack, do you think you could slip me in for a quickie? You know how it is, being married to Gloria's sister." He grimaced.

Jack turned to his computer. "No problem, amigo. Let me see what she's up to. Well, she's got her old friend Bob at ten, then Peter, followed by Scotty—he hit another production mark—Ernest, Richard, George, Mike and

Linda. Hmm. I could fit you in at five, if you're willing to take sloppy ninths. Maybe you'd prefer first thing in the morning, before she's all stretched out? Say nine?"

"Sounds great. If my wife calls, you'll make up some excuse for me?"

Jack waved his hand. "No problem. Anything to keep the engine of commerce rolling, right?"

They both laughed.

El stood by the front window of her apartment, looking out into the courtyard of the plant, while flipping her new, heavier gold ring up and down against her clit. It helped her pass the time until her next appointment. She needed the stimulation constantly now, like a smoker hooked on nicotine. Her clit stuck out all the time, demanding more of her attention yet Jack still forbade her to come on her own. But he didn't mind the ring flipping. He seemed to enjoy watching her play with her jewelry. The new ring was not only thicker and heavier, it had a small eyelet set at the bottom, into which Jack could put in a jewel, or a weight. It made a nice little thump on her engorged clit, sending shivers through her but never quite causing her to come.

She let her thumb rest against the tattoo on her mound, a sign of her devotion and attachment to her Sawyer family. They all had gathered around her table on the factory floor when the artist applied the bright logo. They applauded every line and color. They truly loved her.

She spotted Scotty walking by and waved to him. He waved back and flashed her a big grin. For a moment, she wondered if he would be coming in next. But he passed by and El settled down to wait some more. She didn't like these times, in between.

With her right hand busy, she brought her left hand up to finger the letters on the navel pin. She could spell out the word "SLUT" in one-half-inch letters, bringing a smile to her face. The name was interchangeable from El now. Her hand continued up her torso to the fine gold chain that now loosely connected her nipple rings. She tugged on the chain, feeling the resonance in both nipples. She giggled. The feeling echoed the one emanating from her clit. Jack had given her the chain on her one-year anniversary. Has she only been here a year? No, wait, she had another job before, what was it? She remembered a big office, lots of numbers. She shook her head.

She'd rather remember today. Already she'd had many nice people drop by to tell her how good she looked and how happy they were to see her. The men always had hard cocks for her to suck or fuck. She loved the taste of their seed. Even the women were very nice to her, although she often wished they'd use the strap-on on her once in a while. She took great delight in hearing them cry out when she pleasured them with her mouth. It made her feel as if she had done a good job. She had to thank Darlene for that. The kindly worker took El under her wing and taught her how to treat a woman.

Everybody was nice here at the plant and they really watched out for her. Even Ben, the night watchman, came by last evening to check on her, to make sure she was okay. She'd been asleep and woke to feel his hard cock lying along the crack of her ass, his arms around her. She knew it was him because only three people now had the key to her apartment: Sam, the day guard who stood outside and helped her keep her appointments, Ben, and, of course, Mr. Sawyer.

She also knew it was Ben because he always fucked her

in the ass. At the end of the day, when her pussy got a little sore, she liked to be able to switch over to the lesser-used passage. Not that she'd complain, of course.

Ben hadn't spoken to her—he often didn't during his visits. He simply retrieved the lubricant she kept in the nightstand and began to rub it on his cock. Then he had pressed his slippery tool into her sphincter. She had groaned and wiggled her ass to make it slide in more easily.

Once firmly seated, he had pulled halfway out and began pounding her in earnest. El remembered how her body had been jerked back and forth until he came in a rush. He had held her close for a minute, his fingers exploring her jewelry, but he didn't rub her to a climax. She didn't know why; it wasn't her place to ask. Then he had gotten up, taken a couple of tissues out of the box on the nightstand and left.

"Night, Ben," El had called after him, "See you tomorrow."

There were a few day visitors who liked her ass, but most seemed to prefer her pussy for some reason. Some liked to tie her up first, which meant Sam had to come in and untie her after they left. Somehow, he always knew when to do that. Naturally, if no one's looking, he often slipped his cock in for a quickie, but El didn't mind. After all, it's her job. And she's very good at it. Everybody tells her so.

BOOK TWO:

El Exposed

Chapter 1

El, dressed in her short blue silk robe that always tickled her nipples, waited in her office for Mr. Sawyer to signal her in. He was meeting with a new client and she had been summoned from her apartment behind the factory to help convince him that Sawyer Metalworking could offer more than the competition. El knew that Sawyer produced good quality materials; she was merely the icing on the cake. If a new client signed up, they got to spend some time with El. Some simply wanted to fuck her, others wanted a quick blow job. A few wanted to spank her, although Mr. Sawyer carefully monitored such activities so El wouldn't come to any real harm.

By now, this had become a routine function of her duties at the plant. She no longer thought it strange to spread her legs for a stranger or to have employees fondle her in the hallways. She was the office slut and had long ago lost any embarrassment or shame over her title.

El had put herself in this position—she couldn't blame Mr. Sawyer. She had stolen a great deal of money from the plant in her former position as chief financial officer and her boss had been ready to call the police. She had begged him not to, offering to pay him back. But she quickly realized that there would be only one way to pay him back—by using her sexual charms to help his business. It was a Hobson's choice, but it beat going to prison.

At first, it was embarrassing and degrading and El thought she had made a terrible mistake. But as the weeks went by and her internal barriers fell, she felt strangely liberated. It was as if a deeply hidden part of her had taken over. All she had to do was use her body. It became easy. And everyone was so nice to her.

Her hand rested on her thigh as she sat in her office chair, legs spread, ready to touch herself once Mr. Sawyer called her. She could hardly stand the waiting and she wasn't sure if she was more excited about seeing the new client, or hearing Jack's voice as she stroked her damp pussy.

The intercom buzzed. Her hand went immediately to her wet slit and rubbed even as her other hand picked up the phone. "Yes, sir?"

"Come in, El."

She rose and headed for the door, her pussy quivering in anticipation. Inside, she saw Mr. Sawyer sitting with a heavy-set man of about fifty. He had a shiny forehead that went halfway up his skull before meeting a fringe of red-gray hair. She hesitated before stripping off her robe, not sure if Mr. Sawyer wanted her to be naked right away or not. Fortunately, Jack noticed her discomfort.

"It's all right, El. Mr. Sisco has been told all about you."

She smiled and dropped her robe. Her jewelry glinted in the soft fluorescent lights. El approached Jack and dropped to her knees, making sure she spread her legs apart as she did. "How may I serve you, Master?"

Jack smiled. "El, I'd like you to meet Ernie Sisco, a potential new client of ours."

El knew her role whenever she met a "potential" client. She turned and gave him a big grin, then asked: "How can I help convince you that Sawyer is the best place for your business?"

Mr. Sisco didn't respond right away—he was too busy staring at El's bare pussy with the gold ring and the Sawyer logo right above it. His eyes rose slightly, taking in her

"SLUT" belly-button piercing, then continued up to her proud breasts and the matching gold rings in each nipple.

"Jee-sus!" He exclaimed, glancing at Jack. "You weren't kidding. She's a peach."

"She's all yours, once you sign with us. And I assure you, you won't be disappointed with the work we do. This is just to sweeten the deal, so to speak."

"She sure is sweet." Ernie had already begun to sweat heavily. He rubbed his upper lip, then took out a damp handkerchief and mopped his dome. "Boy, you drive a hard bargain. I can do anything I want with her?"

Jack's eyes narrowed. "Not anything. Just the regular stuff. We have to take good care of her, you understand."

"Oh, of course. Of course." Stains spread under each arm. The man was either very excited or very nervous. His eyes seemed to sink into his florid face.

El stared at him, a half-smile frozen on her face and imagined him laying on her, smearing her with his sweat, his sausage-like cock stabbing into her. She put the image out of her mind. This was her job and she was determined to do it well.

Sisco turned suddenly to Mr. Sawyer, thrusting out a beefy hand. "All right, Jack, I'll tell you what. I'll give you the auto parts business, once my contract with Minnesota expires. That's about twelve percent of my total revenues. We'll see how that goes, and then we'll decide on any future business."

Jack mulled it over. The auto parts deal was a good start, but he knew the Minnesota Manufacturing contract with Sisco didn't end for another six months. It seemed Sisco wanted something today for a promise tomorrow, and from experience, Jack knew how too often, those promises tended to disappear.

"Sure," he said, shaking his hand, "and I'll have El ready for you just as soon as the contract has been signed."

Ernie's hand froze in mid-shake. "You mean you won't let me partake in El's gifts until then?"

"Now what kind of businessman would I be if I did that? We both know that a lot can happen in six months."

Sisco's face darkened. "You don't trust me to honor any deal I make today?"

"This has nothing to do with honor and everything to do with the fact that Sawyer Metalworking is the best place for your business, whether El's involved or not. Consider her like an enticement—you can't expect to get the extra gift without the main purchase."

Sisco let go of Jack's hand and allowed his pudgy fingers to stroke El's breast for a second. No one said anything. Finally, he stood, adjusting his pants to conceal his erection. "I'll call you closer to when the contract expires," he said abruptly and left the office.

Jack said nothing for a long second after the door clicked closed behind the big man. Then he turned to El. "We'll never see him again."

El was not disappointed to hear that. "I'm sorry, Master—I hope I didn't scare him away."

"No, you did nothing wrong. He was just a schemer. He had heard about you through the grapevine and he'd thought he'd try to get something for nothing. I'm glad he failed. I'd hate to see him pawing you, frankly."

Me too, she thought. She could still feel his fingers on her breast and it made her feel a little dirty, if that was possible. As if reading her mind, Jack told her to go take a shower.

She jumped up and went into Mr. Sawyer's executive washroom. She stopped at the mirror to stare at her reflection. She had changed so much in the last two years, she hardly recognized herself. Instead of her shoulder-length black hair, she had a shaggy cut, streaked with reddish highlights. The tasteful makeup she had worn for years had been replaced by brighter accents around her eyes. Her lashes were long and her eyebrows trimmed. Below, her mouth was outlined by full red lipstick. Today, she wore her pearl earrings, but she also had a matching set of tiny penis ones she wore a couple of times a week.

Around her neck, she wore the penis necklace that Mr. Sawyer had given her a few months ago. She hardly ever took it off, unless he asked her to wear her "FUCK ME" necklace. She didn't like that one as much, simply because it was too obvious, but she had little say in what she wore — or didn't wear.

Her fingers moved down from the necklace to one of the gold rings through her nipples. She tugged at it and enjoyed the tingling sensation it gave her. She was constantly horny and she attributed it to the jewelry and to the way she was treated here. Rarely was she left alone. People were always coming up to touch her or ask to see her breasts or pussy. The robe helped immensely in displaying her body. Sometimes, she wouldn't even bother to wear it — she'd just stroll down the corridors naked and let everyone have their way with her.

No one fucked her, of course — that was strictly controlled by Mr. Sawyer. Six months earlier, he had fired one worker for violating his edict. Frank Jefferson had pulled El into the men's bathroom and tried to fuck her up against the tiled wall. El was prepared to let him, as she didn't want to be accused of being rude to any of the workers. At the same time, she warned him that Mr. Sawyer might be displeased. That didn't stop him. He unzipped his pants and has his hard cock out just inches from her well-used pussy when another worker came in and surprised them, causing Jefferson to back off. He zipped up quickly and left, leaving El standing there, half naked.

When Jack found out, he was furious and called the man into his office and dismissed him on the spot. El, in her office next door, couldn't help but overhear their angry voices through the door.

Jefferson, a bullying type, threatened to go to the police and "expose your sordid little racket," but Mr. Sawyer called his bluff and told him to go ahead—he'd file charges of attempted rape the same day. El wasn't sure if that was a smart move, considering her job, but it did seem to quiet Jefferson down. He left a short time later and there were no repercussions from his threats.

El realized she had been staring at herself too long, so she turned on the shower and allowed it to warm up. She wanted to wash off Mr. Sisco's sweat that lay like a slime across her right breast. She jumped in and washed herself quickly. Getting out, she toweled dry, and then opened the door to let the steam out.

Mr. Sawyer was sitting at his desk, working. El smiled at that—she loved watching him work. He motioned her over and she scampered out to kneel by his side, within easy reach. He stroked her breasts and tugged at her nipple rings. She found herself getting very wet and she hoped he would fuck her today. He rarely did any more. That was one part of her new job that disappointed her. She loved to lie on her master's desk and feel him pounding away at her pussy, his big cock sliding in and grinding against her clit before he'd pull out again. It was during those times that she felt truly loved by Mr. Sawyer. Or maybe it was the power he exhibited. She felt drawn to him and would do just about anything he asked of her.

He stopped fondling her just as she was about to climax and said: "I'm not sure Sisco's business would be worth it if it meant having his greasy hands on your body."

El thought she might just come right then. God, she adored this man! She hadn't wanted to tell him her real feelings about Sisco, but it was clear he felt it too.

"T-thank you, Master."

He nodded, then reached down between her legs and found her to be dripping wet, as usual. "God, you're a horny slut, aren't you? Don't tell me you were looking forward to having that fat man on you?"

"No, Master," she said, trying to keep the shudder out of her voice. "But I would've if you had asked me to."

"Then why are you so wet? Are you just like this all the time now?"

El wanted to say, *No, it's because I want you to fuck me*, but instead, she said, "I don't know. Maybe."

His hand fondled her gold ring, allowing it to drop onto her clit. El closed her eyes and found herself right on the edge of an orgasm. "Please, sir. If you keep that up, I'll come."

He stopped and she wished he hadn't. She found herself vibrating, ready to explode at the next touch or even kind word.

"Well, we can't waste that, now can we?" She heard him flipping through the pages of his "El Book" as he called it. "I don't see anyone scheduled for another two hours. How did this happen? How did you end up with so much free time?" His voice had a teasing inflection.

"Sisco, sir," she reminded him, coming down a bit from her high. "You thought he might take longer."

"Of course, how could I forget?" He paused and asked, "So, do you think I should allow you to come?"

El opened her eyes and beseeched him. "Whatever you want to do, Master."

"OK," he relented. "Get up on the desk and spread your legs."

Excitedly, she jumped up and started to lie back. He stopped her. "No, up on your knees. I want to watch you masturbate."

El tried to hide her disappointment. She'd much rather have his hard cock than her fingers. Nevertheless, she obeyed him, getting into position, her wide-spread cunt just a few inches from his face. She put her hand on it and waited for him to give her final permission. When he nodded, she began to rub herself quickly. She threw her head back and guttural noises rose from her throat.

Because she was always on edge, thanks to the constant stimulation, El came quickly. But it wasn't the satisfying climax she had come to expect from many of her lovers. She hoped Mr. Sawyer might take pity on her and give her a quick fucking, but he merely told her to suck him off. She dropped down to the rug between his legs and freed his semi-erect cock. Within seconds, she had him hard and, within minutes, she was rewarded with a tongue bath of his sperm. She swallowed eagerly, his essence like cream to her.

Afterward, Jack sent her back to her office to await the next client. El hoped this one would want to fuck her. She needed constant stimulation. Idly, she flipped her clit ring, allowing it to bounce off her sensitive pussy. She was so close to coming again, she decided to stop—Mr. Sawyer would be very upset if she came by herself. And it wasn't like she could hide it—her pussy was constantly on display in the coffee room.

Chapter 2

Gloria seethed. It was one thing to have this slut parade around half-dressed or even, god forbid, naked, but it was quite something else to have to see the woman's private parts displayed where she could hardly avoid seeing them! How could Jack ruin a perfectly good coffee room?

The human resources supervisor kept her eyes averted from the triple screens—one on the left, showing El at her desk, her bare tits hanging out of her robe for all to see, another on the right focused on the now-empty chair in her factory apartment where El often sat, waiting for her next customer. It was the third screen, right in the middle, that made Gloria see red. The under the desk shot that displayed the slut's wide-spread pussy, her hand always hovering nearby. Whenever the phone rang, her hand dipped down into her wetness and a cheer would go up from the coffee room. It was disgusting!

Gloria had kept her mouth shut for nearly two years now, but she was reaching her limit. If it hadn't been for her brother-in-law getting the job of CFO, she would've turned them all in long ago. Still, she felt trapped. She couldn't very well turn them in now, could she? Andy was just as culpable. Her sister would suffer the consequences of having her husband arrested or laid off.

So she seethed. Gloria walked into her office in a bad mood. Whenever she encountered El in the hallway, her depression increased. The way the men all gathered around her! Deep down, Gloria felt a twinge of envy—no one ever wanted to see her naked! Her sister Sarah had gotten all the looks in her family. Gloria was the heavy-set, doughy-faced girl who never had a date in high school. Her one date in college had been a disaster when she discovered he had been acting on a dare. She had nearly killed him with her purse.

Gloria felt she had to do something to solve her ethical dilemma or she'd go mad. That morning, she found the answer from Jack himself. Gloria had noted that El's "activity chart" had recently been posted on the company website, behind a password, so everyone could see when she was busy. But that's all they could see. Each hour of the day and early evening were listed and if Jack had her scheduled, a red "X" filled the box. Gloria guessed that Jack had to have names in there, protected by another password, no doubt.

She hadn't been able to take her suspicions further until a few days later, when Jack took El out to meet a client off-site. She decided to take a chance and see if her suspicions were correct. Using a flimsy excuse that she needed a file from Jack's office, she entered the empty suite and sat at his computer. His log-on screen came up. Gloria was nervous, but determined. She tried several different combinations, with no luck. Fortunately, Jack had not set it up so she would be locked out after three tries. She could conceivably try unlimited combinations—if she had that kind of time.

Frustrated by that whore, Gloria typed in "ELSLUT" and hit enter. Password Accepted, the screen read. She had done it! The screen cleared and his home page came up. She quickly riffled through the folders until she found the schedule. When she opened it, she could see each box now had a name neatly typed in. She gasped at some of them—how could so many people be in on this conspiracy? It was as if she were the only sane person at Sawyer Metalworking!

Then one name, down early on Friday morning, made her blood run cold. And it sealed Jack's fate in a heartbeat: Andy Grogan. Her brother-in-law. Fucking this slut on the side!

All her frustrations melted away, replaced by rage. She had to act now. She wasn't going to sit by and let her sister be two-timed by this despicable cad! With that slut! And after she had gotten him the job! The bastard!

She signed off the program and left the office. Gloria wanted to call the police right away. Seeing Jack hauled away in handcuffs, that slut right behind him would make her day. But she knew instinctively that she wouldn't be believed. If someone had told her what was going on here, she wouldn't believe it either, unless she had seen it with her own eyes. Gloria had to have proof. It wouldn't have to be much—just an example of El's slutty behavior and how everyone condones it should be enough to get the slow wheels of justice turning.

At lunch, she went to an appliance store and purchased a small, digital video recorder. It was expensive, but Gloria had been paid very well over the last couple of years and she delighted in spending some of it to bring about the downfall of this modern-day Sodom. No, that wasn't quite it. She was more like Sampson, pushing down the pillars, bringing the roof down on herself as well as others. There might never be another job that paid as well as this one, but it no longer mattered. She was determined to put a stop to this disgusting, illegal behavior.

It was all too easy to film El—once the slut entered a corridor, no one paid the slightest attention to Gloria. She could almost hide the recorder in the palm of her hand as she filmed the action. El, walking toward her, dressed in her nasty blue robe, stopped every couple of feet at someone's command to raise her hem to display her bare pussy or open it to show off her obscene breasts. Hands came at her from all directions to fondle her or to swipe the fluid from her slit. There were cat-calls and hoots—it was terrible.

El, on this occasion, was on her way to get coffee. It was easy for Gloria to hang back and film over the heads of the crowd around the door. Someone requested El bend over to receive a spanking for some imagined infraction. El wiggled her ass for the crowd—and the camera—as one of the workers gave her a few slaps, leaving red marks on her well-used ass.

"That's the spirit!" A man shouted. "Now turn around and show us your cunt again!"

And El obeyed. She always did what the workers wanted—except fuck them, of course. Jack was her pimp. Gloria wished she could capture the interplay between the two of them on camera. That would be the nail in their coffins! As it was, she felt she had enough. She left work early and drove down to the nearest police station and marched in.

"I'd like to speak to a detective in the sex crimes department," she told the startled desk sergeant. He looked her up and down, as if he couldn't believe someone would want to rape her, and said, "Sure, lady. If you'll have a seat over there, I'll have someone come up."

He made a call as Gloria seethed some more, tired of being treated like some kind of sexual leper. She had many fine qualities. If men had just given her a chance, she could've shown them what a wonderful wife she could've become. But men were all interested in superficialities. She never stood a chance against the Ellens of the world. Just because she didn't have a body like El's didn't mean—

Her thoughts were interrupted by two people

approaching her, a man and a woman. The man was tall, middle-aged, with tired eyes that probably had seen too much. His hair formed a graying fringe around a balding head. The woman was shorter than Gloria, thin, with short-cropped red hair. The woman smiled and spoke first.

"Hello. I'm Detective Bishop and this is Detective Granski. How can we help?"

Gloria stood. "Hello, I'm Gloria Cooper and I work at Sawyer Metalworking. There's some illegal sexual activity that's going on there that you should be aware of."

They glanced at each other and Gloria could immediately see the disbelief in their eyes, as if they were thinking, "Another busy-body." She would show them! Then they nodded in unison toward her and asked her to accompany them to an interview room, so they could "discuss this in private." The silent Granski trailed along behind, making her uneasy. Was she really doing the right thing? Did anyone really care what went on at the plant?

Once inside the room, however, all she had to do was show the tape and explain why El acted this way, and the detectives became believers. The embezzlement, the deal with Sawyer, the activities of workers and clients alike, all came pouring out. The detectives were clearly stunned.

"All this has been happening for two years?" Granski finally spoke.

Gloria nodded.

"And you're only reporting it now?" Bishop put in, making Gloria's stomach twist in knots.

"Well, I was trapped too, for a while. You see, my brother-in-law works at the plant in El's old position of CFO. If I turned them in, he'd lose his job—we all would, probably. I couldn't do that to my sister."

"Then why now?" Bishop leaned in.

The truth erupted from Gloria before she could stop herself. "Because that slut is fucking my brother-in-law!"

Both detectives leaned back, nodding, eyebrows raised in unison. Gloria thought she saw the male detective struggling to hide a grin.

"Very well, if you could leave your camera here for a couple of days, we'll need to download this evidence," Granski said. "This is going to take a few days to put together. You can return to work tomorrow if you like, or you can call in sick—it's up to you. But under no circumstances should you tell anyone about this, including your sister."

Gloria agreed, relieved that, at last, her long nightmare would soon be over. And that Jack's would be just beginning.

Chapter 3

Three days later, El was across town, under a conference table, sucking on one of four cocks that were thrusting out from four sets of slacks. A fifth set, still zipped up, belonged to Mr. Sawyer and he was leading the discussion among the executives of yet another potential client. El had forgotten the name already. They all ran together in her mind anyway. What was important was how well she did her job. Right now, she concentrated on sucking and licking this man's cock until he squirted into her mouth. She didn't even remember what his face looked like. When she had come into the room, dressed in her business suit, she caught a brief glimpse of the four men, but she quickly had been ordered under the table. Now her suit coat was unbuttoned and her short skirt hiked up to her hips as she worked to satisfy another client. The man's hands reached down to stroke a bare breast and tug at her nipple ring.

The man's thighs began to stiffen and El knew he was close. Suddenly she felt a hot stream of his spunk jet into the back of her throat and she swallowed it quickly. She cleaned the softening member with care and tucked it back into his pants. El zipped him up carefully and moved to the next one.

Later, in the car on the way back to the office, Mr. Sawyer rubbed her naked pussy and told her how much business the new clients would be bringing to the factory. El didn't really listen, she simply enjoyed the sensation of his fingers playing with her clit, tugging at her ring.

"I'm so proud of you, El! We're going to have to expand the plant again! I'm thinking of giving you a bigger apartment—would you like that?

"Whatever you want, sir."

He nodded, his eyes on the road. His fingers were beginning to tease a climax out of her and El found it hard to concentrate on his words. She closed her eyes and rode the sensations, drifting higher and higher toward an orgasm.

Suddenly, Jack's fingers pulled away and he muttered, "What the fuck?"

El opened her eyes to see the parking lot filled with police cars. There were two gathered near the front door, along with two dark, unmarked cars, and another patrol car was parked at the rear of the lot.

"What the hell is going on?" He said, then turned to El. "I'm going around the block; you fix your clothes!" He drove around, giving El a chance to button up her business suit and pull down her skirt. When she was ready her boss drove into the lot. He pulled up near the front door. Jack got out, ignoring El, and demanded of the first cop he saw: "What's going on here?"

The officer, a young man with a crew cut, eyed him suspiciously. "Are you Jack Sawyer?"

"Yes, yes I am. I own this business. I demand to know what's going on!"

The cop turned and signaled to a plain-clothed man standing by the entrance, standing next to a short woman with red hair. They hurried over.

"Jack Sawyer?" One asked. He was tall, with tired eyes.

"Yes, yes! Dammit, tell me what's going on!'"

The first detective jerked his head at his partner. She went around to the passenger side of the car. "And this, I assume, is Ellen Sanchez?"

Jack began to pale. "Yes. That's her."

"Mr. Sawyer, my name is Detective Granski and this is Detective Bishop. We're from the sex crimes division. We're placing you and Ms. Sanchez under arrest for prostitution, pandering and other assorted sex crimes. You have the right to remain silent..."

Before the man could grab his arm, Jack leaned down and said to El: "Don't say anything to the police." The detective jerked him upright and slapped the handcuffs on his wrists.

Bishop opened the door and helped El out. She looked bewildered. "Mr. Sawyer?" She asked, looking for guidance.

"It's all right, El. I'll call my lawyer."

El tried to be brave, but when the detective placed handcuffs on her and began reading her her rights, she began to cry. It was as if all the work she had done in the last two years to avoid being arrested for embezzlement had gone for naught. She watched as Mr. Sawyer was handcuffed as well. They were separated and put in the back of two police cars. El watched as another young man in a dark sports coat came out of the building carrying some papers. He stopped and talked to the other detectives. The tall one jerked his thumb over his shoulder toward the cars where she and Mr. Sawyer had been taken.

The man smiled and nodded. More police officers came out of the building, carrying computers and more papers. Then Gloria came out, smiling, accompanied by a blonde woman of medium height wearing a dark pants suit and a tan overcoat. The blonde dressed very well, El noted, and wondered if she was another detective.

Two officers got into the cars holding Mr. Sawyer and El and they drove off separately. "Where are you taking me?"

She asked, pulling against her tight handcuffs. The man said nothing. She sighed and sat back, fighting the tears in her eyes. She recalled what they had said about prostitution, but she wasn't sure why they didn't say embezzlement. Perhaps they are just waiting to get them downtown to formally charge her. She tried not to think about it. Just leave it up to Mr. Sawyer; he knows best what to do.

Jack knew his business would be hurt by the arrest and the resulting publicity. He had expected something like this could happen, but the longer it had gone on, the less it seemed possible. No one had raised a fuss before—why now? He wondered who had turned him in. Perhaps a client or a former employee. Or maybe Sisco? No matter. He had a good lawyer on retainer and he would help get him out of this.

Perhaps he should've insisted El leave once she had paid up, six months ago. But shit, she was so aroused all the time, so willing to continue to do what she was told! She was like the perfect woman—all sex drive and no brains. He smiled to himself, then caught the eyes of the officer in the rear-view mirror and turned away, chagrined.

This was no laughing matter. The cop pulled up behind the station that seemed to be full of media vans. Shit! No doubt the cops had alerted them. He wanted to hide his face, but the officer gave him no chance—he was hauled out and duck-walked toward the door. Microphones were thrust at him from the assembled back of reporters. Questions flew at him.

"Mr. Sawyer! Is it true you kept a sex slave at work?"

"Did she use sex to win new clients?"

"How many sex slaves do you have?"

He ignored them and they reached the back door. Just before they went inside, the crowd suddenly turned as one.

"There! Is that her? Is that the slave?"

"Come on!"

The crowd hurried over to the other car. Jack caught a glimpse of a frightened El in the back seat before the door shut behind him.

"I want a lawyer," he said to the cop, who just grunted. He was taken down a dull green corridor past a bull pen full of metal desks to an interview room. The room was about eight feet by ten feet and had a wall-length mirror on the side opposite the door. He knew there would be people behind the one-way glass, watching him.

The officer sat him in a chair and started to leave. "Hey," Jack shouted after him. "What about my cuffs? Aren't you going to remove them?"

The cop just shook his head and closed the door. Jack sat there for a few minutes, wondering what was happening to El. Though he had exploited her badly, he still cared about her. He knew she would be terrified by all this.

After what seemed like an hour, but was probably no more than fifteen minutes, the door opened and two people walked in—the tall detective from the plant, followed by the short red-head. His heart fell when he thought of all the evidence they must now have.

"Mr. Sawyer? Remember us? I'm Detective Granski and this is Detective Bishop. We'd like to ask you a few questions."

"No," he said at once. "I want my attorney."

"If you insist," Bishop said, coming close and perching on the edge of the table with one thigh. For one brief moment, Jack pictured her kneeling by his desk, naked.

He pushed the thought away. "But it might be better if we could just clear this up informally."

Jack snorted. "You must think I'm an idiot. I invoke my rights to remain silent until provided with my attorney. If you'll give me my one phone call, I'll call him."

They glanced at each other and the older man shrugged. "OK, tough guy. Have it your way. But things will go harder for you now."

They left.

Down the hall, in Interview Room 2, El sat terrified, tears rolling down her cheeks. Her wrists remained cuffed, preventing her from wiping her nose or fixing her makeup. *Mr. Sawyer's going to be mad*, she thought.

The door opened suddenly, and it startled her. She nearly fell out of her chair. The red-head she'd seen at the plant came over and steadied her. The larger man just stood there, staring at her.

"Are you OK?" the woman asked.

"No. I'm scared. I want to see Mr. Sawyer."

"He's busy right now. But you can talk to us. My name is Bishop and this is Detective Granski."

She shook her head. "M-Mr. Sawyer said not to."

The big man laughed. "Mr. Sawyer is in a lot of trouble. He'll probably go to jail for a long time. You'd better think about what's going to happen to you."

El looked over at the redhead, trying to find a friendly face. Bishop smiled. "Look, we don't want you to suffer any more than you already have. We just want to understand what went on at that plant. Can you fill us in?"

El knew better than to fall for that. If she told them, her embezzlement would be revealed. And she knew that those charges were far more serious than a few sex crimes in which she had willingly participated.

"I don't want to talk right now. I want to see Mr. Sawyer."

"You can't see him," Granski said harshly, causing more tears to flow from El's eyes.

"Listen—" Bishop began. Suddenly, the door burst open and a blonde woman strode in. "Bishop, Granski—why is that woman still in handcuffs?"

The detectives turned around as one. "Well, if it isn't our illustrious ADA," Granski said. "Why shouldn't she be in handcuffs?"

"Because that's not the way the state treats its star witness," she said. She came closer, extending a hand that she placed on El's right shoulder. "Please take them off so we can have a proper chat."

Granski goggled. "Star witness? We have a complaining witness already! And we have a half-dozen charges against her!"

"That's how you see it. I see her as a victim."

Granski opened his mouth and closed it again, then shrugged and shook his head. He slumped back against the wall. Bishop removed the cuffs. "There, that's better," the blonde woman said as El rubbed her wrists, then wiped her nose with the back of a hand.

The blonde pulled a tissue out of her purse and handed it over. "Try this." She waited while El got herself in better shape, then she said, "I'm Diane Franklin, the assistant district attorney for the county. I would like to talk to you about the ordeal you've been in for the last couple of years."

El stared at her. The "ordeal" she described was of her own choosing—if she revealed anything, this woman could put her away for embezzlement. She shook her head. "I want to talk to Mr. Sawyer."

"That's what she's been saying to us," Bishop put in. "It's like he's got some sort of hold over her."

"He does." She looked at the detectives. "Would you mind if I spoke to her alone?"

Granski shrugged again and the two detectives left.

Franklin sat down across the table from El. She put her hands over El's. "I know how this all started. We already have one witness. I know that you've been trapped into doing all sorts of things against your will. I've been authorized to give you immunity from prosecution for any embezzlement you may have done in exchange for your testimony against Jack Sawyer."

Chapter 4

"It's a good deal, I'd take it," her attorney told her. Betty Montrose was a public defender who specialized in sex cases and she had jumped all over this one with both feet. They were meeting in a small room just down the hall from ADA Franklin's office in the county courthouse.

When Jack Sawyer's lawyer had heard that the DA was offering El a deal, he tried to get the court to authorize his firm to handle her defense as well, an effort that was quickly shot down as a blatant conflict of interest. Because El had no money of her own until the complex finances set up by Jack could be straightened out, El's case had fallen to the public defender's office. Montrose saw it as an opportunity not only for her career, but for the cause of women everywhere.

She was a tall, broad-shouldered woman with dark, unkempt hair who took no crap from anyone. Her looks and manner had gotten her the nickname "Moose," which she pretended to dislike but had been secretly flattered. If you got in her way, the story went, she'd trample all over you. She knew for a fact that Diane Franklin had nearly busted a gasket when she heard Moose had the case.

"You've been brutally exploited and any crimes you may have committed before are being waived, provided you testify against Jack Sawyer," Montrose continued. "That means, the embezzlement never happened, as far as the DA is concerned. They consider the crimes Jack committed are far worse than the ones you allegedly did."

El couldn't believe her ears. The embezzlement never

happened? She was confused. "How could that be? I only got into this because what I did was so wrong. I knew it, he knew it—he had me trapped."

"Right. He did. He should've called the police. Making you do..." she wrinkled her nose, "... certain sexual things in exchange for your alleged debt was wrong. Now he's in deep shit and you're going to come out OK."

"What will happen to me?"

"You mean, after you testify?" Moose shrugged. "I don't know." She withheld a grimace when she thought of the circus El's life could become once she was free: Talk show offers, jokes, book deals—maybe a movie might even be made about her life. "I'm not sure you could work in your former profession—uh, I mean, CFO, not, you know, sex slave." She added quickly when she saw El's confused expression.

"Oh, that." El nodded. She knew she had once been an accountant, but she didn't feel she could go back to that now. All she wanted to do was experience orgasms and do what Mr. Sawyer told her to do. It made her life simple.

Betty leaned down and lifted El's chin up. "I'd like to know, between lawyer and client—meaning this will go no further—what *you'd* like to do, after this is over."

"I don't know." She couldn't think that far ahead. Her mind remained focused on what she was supposed to do in court. Testify against Mr. Sawyer, she had said. What did that mean, exactly? Would Mr. Sawyer go to jail?

"Ms. Montrose?"

"Call me Betty, dear."

"What am I supposed to say, in court?"

"You just tell the truth, that's all. Tell the court what happened and what Jack made you do."

"You mean, I'm supposed to tell about the embezzlement? It was a lot of money." She felt deep shame about it.

"Yes. That will explain why you agreed to become Jack's sex slave in the beginning. That was illegal coercion in itself. But later, when he showed you that you'd paid off your debt, plus interest, that's when the jury will really sympathize with your predicament. I doubt they'll sympathize with Jack."

"But I don't want to hurt him!"

"After all he's done to you, you still want to protect him?"

"He's been good to me." She shifted her legs, feeling the gold ring rub against her pussy underneath her suit. She wished she could stand up and walk around, to let the ring do its magic on her clit.

"I think you'll find you're mistaken," Betty said. She looked at her watch. "Look, Franklin is waiting for us. Can I tell her you'll accept the deal? As your lawyer, I urge you to do it."

El didn't know what to do. She didn't want to hurt Jack, but the chance to escape punishment for the theft seemed too good to be true. She also didn't want to make her lawyer angry—the woman so wanted her to take the deal. She grimaced. "Okay."

"Good! Let's go tell her." She rose and El followed her out. Betty rapped on the window set in the door to the ADA's office and it opened at once.

Diane Franklin was seated behind her desk, but rose immediately when the two walked in. They swept past a young, dark, sharply dressed man that Betty knew to be Franklin's latest up-and-comer, Brian Something.

Diane said nothing, merely waved them to a small conference table. Brian Something—Cicetti, Moose remembered suddenly—stood by the wall as the rest sat.

"Well, what can I tell the DA?" Diane began.

"Providing that nothing Ellen Sanchez says in court will be used against her in any past alleged crimes, we'll take the deal."

Diane nodded and turned to El. "So you agree to testify without reservations?"

El looked at Betty, who nodded. "Okay," she said in a small voice. She wished Mr. Sawyer were here.

"Good!" Diane said, nodding. "All charges will be dropped, once you show up to testify. Meanwhile, you'll be released on your own recognizance pending Sawyer's trial."

"How long will that be, do you think?" Betty asked.

"I'd say two months."

"Will he be released on bail?"

"I'm not sure. We're recommending no bail, but the judge might see it differently."

"If he gets out, my client could be in danger."

"You really think so?" Diane raised an eyebrow.

"Better safe than sorry."

"No," El said at once. "He would never hurt me."

Betty turned to her. "How can you be sure, after what he's already done?"

"He hasn't hurt me. He's taken care of me."

Diane pursed her lips. She turned to Betty. "I can offer her some protection. We could put her up in a hotel, with a policewoman."

Betty nodded. "That will work for us. As you know, Ellen lived at the plant, or at Jack's house, so it's not like she has some place else to go."

She rose to leave, but Diane held up a hand. "I'd also like to have Ellen examined by a psychiatrist. We'd like to know what kind of witness we've got."

Betty nodded. "Very well. Who do you want to use?"

"We've had success with Gerald Butler. You know him?"

"Yes, I've heard of him. You set up the appointment and I'll have El there."

Chapter 5

Jack listened intently as his lawyer, Sam Keppel, outlined their strategy. They were sitting in a private room, just down the courtroom where Jack's preliminary hearing was about to begin. It was two days after his very public arrest. Jack had been kept in the county jail and he was anxious to get out.

"Besides Gloria, they've got Ellen as a primary witness, so no doubt they're going to lay it on thick about how you abused her. So we're going to counter with the egregious theft that you so kindly did not report to the authorities. The statute of limitations is still open on that charge, you know. I suggest –"

"No. I'm not going to file charges at this late date. Besides, she's paid off her debt to me." He paused, trying to organize his thoughts. "But I also think you might misjudge El. I don't think she'll sink me. To tell you the truth, I think she liked being ... uh, with me."

Keppel, a short man with a round, red face, stared in disbelief. "How can you say that? They've given her immunity! The DA is expecting her to sing like a canary."

"Oh, she'll tell the truth, all right, but I don't think she'll lay it on thick. Because, you see, I think I understood her."

"Yeah? What's that supposed to mean?"

"That she likes it. She likes being under control—as long as she's protected, you understand. I never pushed her too far or had her do things that were abhorrent. I just led her where she wanted to go."

"You led her where *she* wanted to go? Don't you mean where you wanted her to go?"

Jack grinned. "Well, sure, it was a dream come true for me—and my workers and clients. But El fell into it so readily, it was like there was another woman in there, waiting to get out. I just found the right key."

"The embezzlement."

"Yeah. Once she felt trapped—prison or sex, she chose sex so willingly that I think she found her true self in it. That's why she didn't want to leave once she'd paid me back."

"I'm not sure how we can use this in court."

"Just make sure we have lots of men on the jury, OK?"

A knock came at the door. A bailiff stuck his head in. "They're ready for you."

Jack followed his lawyer out of the room and immediately was bathed in the bright lights of cameras. Flashes went off in his face as he stared at the floor, trying to see where Sam was going. Questions flew at him, which he ignored. They were no different then the ones they'd asked before, except one, which caught him off guard.

"What's it like to have a sex slave?"

Jack stopped and stared at the man who had asked the question. He could sense envy in the man's voice and wondered if that feeling might extend to the jury. He could only hope so. Sam tugged at his sleeve, so he turned and walked quickly into the courtroom.

They sat at the left side table and Jack stole a glance at Diane Franklin and her second chair, Brian Cicetti. She was an attractive woman, but right now her face was set like stone, eyes dark and flashing her disgust at the CEO. She was really going to enjoy this, he knew.

"All rise."

He stood with Sam and watched the judge enter and take his seat. Judge Roy Liming was an old, heavy-set black man with white curly hair set close to his scalp. He'd been on the bench for twenty-three years and probably had seen just about every crime that could be committed. His wire-rimmed glasses surrounded world-weary eyes and every one of his decisions seemed to weigh in the deep lines of his face.

"You may be seated," the bailiff said.

The judge nodded to the clerk, who read from a document in front of her. "The People vs. Jack Sawyer. Compelling prostitution, theft of services, sexual imposition and sexual assault."

"How do you plead?" The judge asked by rote.

"Not guilty, your honor," Jack said quickly.

Diane was on her feet at once. "Your honor, we have a particularly heinous crime of sexual slavery here and we'd like to have the defendant remanded without bail."

Sam jumped up. "Your honor! My client has been an upstanding member of this community and an employer of more than one hundred workers for many years. This is his first brush with the law—"

"And what a doosey it is, counselor." The judge scanned the document before him.

"Your honor!"

Judge Liming held up a hand. "Not to worry, counselor." He turned to Diane. "Now, why are the People asking for no bail in this case?"

"We feel the state's witnesses could be in danger if the defendant is allowed to roam freely, your honor—"

"That's completely unnecessary! My client has no ill will toward any witness. In fact, I've heard that one of their witnesses is reluctant to even testify."

Diane seemed beside herself. "Your honor, we've had to put the witness under protection at a safe location at considerable expense. We feel that—"

"You don't feel a restraining order will be sufficient?"

"No, your honor. This man faces prison if he's found guilty. We feel he's capable of anything if he's allowed out pending trial."

"Your honor! Let's not impugn the defendant! He will obey the court's order."

The judge turned to Sam. "If I issue a restraining order, will you make sure your client honors it?"

"Of course, your honor! Mr. Sawyer has no intention—"

"Got it, counselor." He faced Diane. "Ms. Franklin, considering the charges, the state really has no basis for denying bail." He raised his gavel before she could speak. "The defendant will come no closer than one-thousand yards from any witnesses the DA names or face immediate arrest and forfeiture of bail. Bail is set at two-hundred-fifty thousand dollars." The gavel slammed down.

❧

El was escorted to the hotel by her lawyer and the young ADA, Cicetti. He told them that a policewoman would be meeting them there.

"Here we are," he said, arriving at Suite 266. "She'll be safe here." He unlocked the door and waved the two women inside.

El looked around at the room and thought it was not unlike her apartment. She frowned, realizing that she may never see her apartment again. They were standing in a two-room suite. The main room consisted of a couch, desk, TV, and a small kitchen area, separated by a door that led into a bedroom with a queen-sized bed. A small bath with shower lay behind another door near the closet.

"What do you think?"

"It will be fine," Betty answered for both of them. She put her purse and briefcase down on the desk and walked around, taking in the place. El followed her like a puppy. She felt lost without someone telling her what to do.

"We selected a room with a kitchen so you wouldn't have to eat out or have food brought up all the time," Cicetti said. "If you don't want to cook—"

"It will be fine," Betty said dismissively.

Cicetti got the hint. He looked at his watch. "The policewoman should be here any minute. You want me to wait with you?"

"That won't be necessary. I'll stay and get things squared away."

He nodded and left the two women alone. Betty locked and chained the door, then took Ellen by the hand and led her to the couch. "I need to talk to you about something Ellen. It's important."

El looked up, fear in her eyes. "Yes?"

"It's about the jewelry and the tattoo. I'd like to have them removed before the trial. Is that all right with you?"

"But why?"

Betty sighed. "Because those are all things Jack did to you against your will. They will need them as part of the prosecution exhibits."

"I like them," El said simply. She wanted to reach underneath and flip her heavy gold ring against her clit, but knew her attorney wouldn't like it. She hadn't had an orgasm in such a long time!

"I know you do. You can keep them for now, if you really want to. But I'll want to take you to a shop to have them removed soon. And," Betty grimaced. "I'm going to want to have some pictures taken of your tattoo. I'll make sure the photographer is careful not to show your, um, private parts. Okay?"

El nodded, wishing this ordeal was all over with so she could go back to her job at the plant. She wondered if Mr. Sawyer would be mad at her.

A knock sounded at the door. "That will be your policewoman," Betty said, moving toward the entry. "You wait here."

Betty checked through the peephole, then unlocked and unchained the door. A young policewoman with dark hair tied up in a bun under her cap stood there. "Hi. I'm Officer Reynolds. I've been sent –"

"We know. Come in."

The officer looked around, checking out the suite, making sure everything was secure. She went into the bedroom and checked out the bathroom before joining the two women in the outer room. Ignoring the lawyer, she sat down next to Ellen and put a hand on her forearm.

"Hi, I'm Officer Tami Reynolds. I'll be keeping an eye on you for a few weeks."

El smiled at her. She liked the woman immediately and she couldn't quite explain why. Perhaps it was her petite shape or her kindness toward her. "Okay," she said. She eyed the gun in its shiny black holster.

Moose stood up abruptly. "Well, I've got to get back. I have other clients I need to attend to. You'll be all right here, Ellen. I'll see you in the morning."

She left and El noted that Officer Reynolds securely locked the door behind her. They were alone. She waited to be told what to do.

"Well, are you hungry? Thirsty? We can have some supplies sent up."

El shook her head. Tears came to her eyes.

"What's wrong?" Tami came close and sat, her thigh touching El's.

"I'm scared. I don't want any of this. I just want to go home."

Tami put her arm around Ellen's shoulders and said, "It's all right. You'll be safe here—"

"Everybody says that!" El said with surprising heat. "Mr. Sawyer would never hurt me. He loves me, in his own way."

"Well, I don't know about that and it doesn't matter. I'm just here to make sure you testify at trial. If you're not in danger, that's great. We'll just talk and watch TV and have a nice time while we wait. Okay?"

El shrugged. She didn't want to say what was really on her mind. She just wanted to feel loved again, like she had with Mr. Sawyer.

Chapter 6

Tami, now dressed in civilian clothes, escorted Ellen to Dr. Butler's office and sat with her while they waited. It had been five days since El had been moved into the hotel and they were slowly becoming better friends.

"Don't worry, I hear Dr. Butler is a good guy. He'll treat you right," the policewoman told her. She smiled and patted El's hand.

El nodded nervously and whispered low, so the receptionist couldn't hear: "What if he thinks I'm crazy—will that affect what happens to me?"

"He won't! That's silly talk. Just talk to him and don't worry."

The receptionist looked up. "The doctor will see you now."

El stood. Tami squeezed her hand and nodded her encouragement. "I'll be right here when you come back out."

She went in through the oak door that the receptionist indicated and found herself in a large, comfortable room containing a couch and an upholstered chair positioned near two walls full of books. On the other side of the room was a large desk. Behind the desk, a man sat writing something in a journal. He was dressed in a very expensive suit and had on a red power tie. His hair was almost completely gray, although he didn't appear to be older than his mid-fifties. He looked up and stood.

"Hi. I'm Dr. Butler, Ms. Sanchez. Please have a seat and make yourself comfortable."

El went to the upholstered chair and sat. She squirmed uncomfortably as Tami had insisted she wear underwear. It had been so long since she'd worn them, they chaffed at her every move.

The doctor walked over to her. She could feel his power as he loomed over her. "Would you feel more comfortable on the couch? It's entirely up to you."

El felt she'd violated some patient-doctor protocol and immediately got up and reseated herself on the couch, her legs held tightly together.

The doctor took the chair. "I can see you're nervous. Please don't be. This is going to be painless, I can assure you."

El just nodded nervously and tried to smile. It came out cracked.

Butler looked at a clipboard and read some information there. He nodded to himself and smiled at El. "It says here, you're to be a witness in a trial coming up soon. How do you feel about that?"

"Terrified and worried."

"Why?"

"My boss is on trial. Mr. Sawyer has been good to me and I hate it that something I say might send him to prison."

"What might you say?"

El looked at him sharply and said nothing.

"Don't worry, Ellen. May I call you Ellen?" When she nodded, he continued. "I work for the DA in this case. So we're on the same side. However, due to doctor-patient privilege, I cannot and will not divulge any deep secrets you might tell me. I would only tell the prosecutors broad strokes about your personality, your state of mind and your possible reaction to being on the witness stand."

El nodded and asked, "But what about … the

embezzlement? They tell me it won't matter, but I'm so ashamed about it. How can I get up in front of all those people and admit that I stole all that money?"

"It will be hard, I'm sure. But it's the truth, isn't it? That's all they can ask of you, the truth. Once you tell it, your part is over. You can begin to put this behind you."

"But what will I do? I'm no good at doing anything right now." *Anything but sex*, she thought to herself. *I've become very good at that.*

"I'm sure opportunities will come forward. You just can't see them yet."

El shook her head. Unconsciously, she tugged at her clothes. The doctor observed her actions.

"Ellen?"

"Yes, doctor?"

"Are you uncomfortable?"

"Well, yes." She hitched her shoulders and looked embarrassed.

"Why? Am I making you uncomfortable?"

"Oh, no, Dr. Butler. I'm, um, well..."

"It's your clothes, isn't it?"

El seemed relieved that he said it, not her. "Yes. Frankly, I'm not used to wearing so many now."

"Really? Tell me about that."

"Mr. Sawyer always had me, um, undress whenever I came into his office. After a while, I got used to being, er, free."

"It's all right, Ellen. You can use the words."

"Naked. That's what I meant to say. He liked me naked." She stared at her knees, afraid to look up.

"And now, after two years of getting used to being naked, you feel uncomfortable in clothes, is that right?"

"Yes, sir. Especially underwear. I really don't like them any more."

"Why do you wear them now?"

"Ms. Franklin says I have to. She said I have to 'act right.' I'm not sure why I have to. But I do it because the policewoman watching me makes me."

Dr. Butler licked his lips. "Well, I'd like you to think of this office as an oasis, Ellen. A refuge from all the confusion out there, all the people telling you what to do. I'm trying to help you and learn more about you so that I can give you good advice. Do you understand what I'm saying?"

"Not really."

"I mean that inside this office, no one will know what goes on. Whether or not you wear underwear or even any clothes at all. That remains between you and me."

"Really?" El wanted to ditch her confining bra and pantyhose.

"Really. In fact, if you'd like to get more comfortable right now, I would encourage you to do so. Here, I'll turn my head."

El thought he was being so very polite about it. It didn't bother her to have men look at her. They've been looking at her naked body for months now. "I, um, don't mind if you look, doctor. It's okay."

So he looked while El unbuttoned her blouse and shrugged it off. She quickly unclasped her bra and let it drop to the floor, then massaged her breasts briefly to get some of the wrinkles out. She smiled at the doctor when she saw him staring at her, a slight tug at the corner of his mouth. Her nipples felt empty without her rings. Her attorney had had all her jewelry removed yesterday.

El put the blouse back on, but left the buttons unbuttoned as she stood. She turned sideways, feeling just a little self-conscious now. She wondered if the doctor was getting an erection and would that affect the quality of their session?

She pulled up her skirt and tugged her tight pantyhose down to her thighs, then sat back down and worked the material down each leg until she was finally freed of it. She knew the doctor could catch glimpses of her bare pussy and didn't care. For reasons she couldn't explain, it made her feel proud. She wished she still had her heavy gold ring above her clit. She wanted to feel that sensation of being on the edge all the time.

"Aaahhh, that feels good," she said, allowing her legs to splay apart, still covered by her skirt. Her breasts played peek-a-boo with the doctor's probing eyes.

"I'm glad," he said softly. "Now, let's continue." He acted like nothing was any different, but El could see his eyes had a gleam to them now. It made her feel proud that she could arouse this staid and professional man. She decided not to rebutton her blouse.

"Tell me how it made you feel, to do whatever Jack Sawyer told you to do."

"Hmm, it made me feel used and embarrassed, at first. But I had to do it. It was preferable to jail."

"And later?"

"Later, it became ... well, exciting in one way and routine in another. It was my job, after all. My new job, I mean. I guess I got used to it." She started to say something else, then stopped.

"What else?" He probed.

"I don't know, Dr. Butler. I'm not sure I can explain it."

"It would be helpful if you could try."

Ellen suddenly felt shy and she pulled her blouse together over her breasts. "It's hard, doctor. I only just met you." It wasn't the nudity that she worried about—it was revealing her reasons for becoming a slut. She had never really had to talk about them before. She only had to act.

"That's true. Trust is earned, I know. But look, you've already felt some rapport with me—otherwise, you wouldn't have felt comfortable enough to remove your undergarments, right?"

"I guess that's true."

"I certainly don't want to rush you. The county has authorized a few sessions with me, so if you need more time..."

"No," she said, making up her mind. "I need to say this, despite my reservations. I need to know if I'm, well, crazy."

Dr. Butler leaned back, nodding, saying nothing. He waited for Ellen to continue. The silence stretched on until Ellen couldn't stand it anymore.

"All right." She took a deep breath. "The reason I didn't object more was ... I liked it. Not all of it, you understand. But something in me was satisfied by being told what to do, when to do it. Not having to make any decisions. By using my body like I was this sexual goddess..." She blushed and looked down. "You must think I'm sick, huh?"

"No, not at all," the doctor said smoothly. "This is not uncommon among women. They are professional and confident on the outside, but on the inside, they are indecisive, afraid and searching for direction. You are not alone, young lady."

His words made her feel better and she breathed a sigh of relief. "Really? There are others like me?"

"Of course. Now, you have to protect yourself, you know. You can't give up all control or else you might get into some serious trouble."

"That's what was good about Mr. Sawyer. He protected me. He made sure that no one, um, had me unless he said it was okay."

"Had you? Do you mean, have intercourse with you?"

"Yes." She was embarrassed to admit it. Where had that come from?

"Did you protect yourself? Wear condoms?"

She frowned. "Mr. Sawyer always said I could, if I wanted to. I started to, at first, but after a while..." She shrugged.

"Didn't you worry about diseases?"

"I should've, I suppose. It just got to be so much trouble. I just trusted Mr. Sawyer."

The doctor seemed nonplussed. He leaned back and templed his fingers, tapping the pads together as he thought. His face remained impassive. He leaned forward again, his hands on his knees.

"Would you be willing to tell me about some of your experiences? It might help to understand your mental state."

"Um." She wondered where to begin.

The doctor sensed her discomfort. "How about this: Tell me about a typical day."

That was easier, she admitted. "Well, I wake up about seven and have a cup of coffee."

"This is in your apartment at the factory?"

"Yes. I shower and put on my robe and wait for my escort."

"Why do you need an escort?"

"Because it would take me too long to get to my office. Men, um, they stop me and ask me to do things."

"Such as?"

El looked at her shoes. "Like show my p-pussy or breasts to them. They would touch me."

Dr. Butler nodded. "Okay, so you get to your office. Then what?"

"I call on the intercom to let Jack know I'm there, and then I wait."

"Wait for an assignment?"

"Yes. He tells me what I'm supposed to do."

"And what do you do, for example?"

"Well, last week, one of the workers passed a production quota, so I was given to him for an hour."

"And you had intercourse?"

"Yes..." She paused.

"And what else?"

She looked up. "Do I have to say?"

"Why? Are you suddenly embarrassed?"

"Yes, I am. I shouldn't be, but I am."

"But you expressed no embarrassment while it was going on, did you?"

El had to think about that. "No, I guess I didn't. I didn't have to think about it. I just did it. Now, everybody's always asking me questions and Mr. Sawyer isn't around to help me. I feel a bit lost."

"It's perfectly understandable. You're changing, that's all. It's a good thing, I think."

"Really?"

"Yes. Now in this example, what else happened that you're embarrassed about?"

El stared at her shoes again. "He, um, spanked me ... and then he fucked me up the butt."

"And Jack said that was okay for him to do that?"

"Yes."

"Don't you see how abusive Jack was?"

El didn't want to tell the doctor that she enjoyed it. The spanking had merely warmed her up. Being fucked like that had made her feel owned, a sensation she experienced on a primal level.

"Jack would never let them hurt me."

"But you had to have sex with strangers. Tell me—would

you have had intercourse with this man if Jack hadn't told you to?"

"Probably not. He controlled all of that."

"And you just went along."

"Yes." El wasn't sure he would ever understand.

The doctor sighed again and sat back against his chair. He gazed at El for a long minute. Finally, he glanced at his watch.

"I'd like you to come back and see me again, OK? I think we have a lot more to talk about."

"Oh, is our time up?" She was disappointed—she had enjoyed slipping out of her confining underclothes and didn't relish the prospect of putting them back on again. Yet she knew Tami would spot the omission in a second if she didn't.

"We have a few more minutes. But I agree, you didn't get much time out of your tight underclothes. How about if you remove them sooner next time? Then you could have a whole hour free of them."

El flashed him a big grin. "Thank you, doctor."

They chatted for a few more minutes, then it was time for her to go. He watched as she struggled back into her underclothes and showed her to the door. "Have my secretary make another appointment for Thursday, all right?"

She nodded and left. Tami was sitting in the waiting room like a mother hen. She smiled at El, but there was concern in her eyes. El knew she wanted to ask her how it went, but dared not. It made her happy that she had at least some secrets from her bodyguard.

Chapter 7

The headlines were brutal: "Sex Slave Boosted Sawyer Profits," "Plant Really a Brothel?" "Sawyer Customers Say They're Shocked."

Jack put down the papers in disgust. "That's a good one—'Customers Shocked"—they weren't so shocked when they were getting their dicks wet." He shook his head. "Shit. Maybe I was wrong. Maybe they *are* going to fry me."

"Oh, I don't know," Sam replied. He had a cat-that-ate-the-canary look about him.

"Wait a minute. Just last week, you were worried and I was the calm one. You've certainly changed your tune. What do you know that I don't?"

"Nothing really. Just a feeling I'm getting about this case."

"Yeah? What kind of feeling?"

Sam looked at the ceiling and said. "Remember Sidney Biddle Barrows or Heidi Fleiss?"

"Yeah. So what? Didn't they serve some time?"

"Yes, but not much. The buzz surrounding those trials was one of amusement, not horror. They titillated the American consciousness. They got short sentences and they've gone on to success in other fields. In other words, America forgave them. And I see the same thing happening to you."

Jack was surprised, but pleased. "You really think so?"

Sam shrugged. "Like I say, it's just a feeling. We still have to put on a strong defense. But I'm more hopeful today than I was before."

"That's always good for a defendant to hear his lawyer say," he said dryly.

Sam laughed, then grew serious. "OK, you know we're going to play up the embezzlement big. I think that will help discredit Ellen and show that the sex was really her idea."

"I don't like that strategy." He couldn't explain to his attorney how much he cared for El, even if they now were on opposite sides of the case. By all rights, he should be looking forward to making her look bad. Yet his anger about her embezzlement had long been replaced by ... something else. He wasn't sure what yet. All he knew was, he didn't look forward to what his attorney might do to her on the stand.

"It's our best way of keeping you out of prison!" Sam said. "That video tape you took that first day is going to be a big help."

"You got it back from the police yet?"

"Yes. It's really too bad they found it. That would've been a great exhibit to spring on them during the trial. But now they're going to be prepared for it."

"Yeah, but there's nothing we can do about it. The police really took just about everything—the cameras, my computer, El's computer—they even spent a day in El's apartment, taking photos and looking for dirt."

"Oh, they have plenty of that." He paused. "Of course, Gloria will be a problem—we don't have anything with which to discredit her."

"I know. She's such a prude. I can't believe she turned on her own brother-in-law!"

Sam spoke sharply. "I hope you're not thinking of firing her?"

"No, not yet. I'm not stupid—I know how it would look. But I will, once I'm acquitted."

"How are things at the plant, anyway?"

"Not great. Five customers have cancelled their contracts and three of them El helped me win! The hypocrites. I guess they're just running for cover."

"Can't blame them. They're probably all afraid of their wives or customers themselves."

"Yeah." Jack shook his head ruefully. "I guess I should've known I was pushing my luck. But it just seemed to be going so smoothly, I hated to put a stop to it."

Sam looked at his watch. "Well, I know you want to get back to the plant. I'm going to be doing a little research here to see if I can't find some surprises for Franklin."

"Right." Jack stood. "I guess I'd better go face the gauntlet of reporters."

Jack left and drove back to work. He found he missed El already. He'd gotten used to having her around, waiting breathlessly for his every command. He knew he was just being a sexist pig, but boy, had it been fun while it lasted!

Tami sipped a cup of tea as she sat on the couch across from her charge, who was lounging in an upholstered chair reading a book. She couldn't help but stare—she found Ellen Sanchez fascinating. She'd never a met a woman who had so totally lost herself to sex. *Her mind must really be messed up. Thank god the county authorized more sessions with the shrink—this girl needs it.*

The first time she had seen Ellen naked—the woman was not shy about it—she'd been shocked by the jewelry she wore. Rings in her nipples and clit—and that tattoo! Outrageous! She'd heard that the poor girl had been made to wear a big "SLUT" pin in her belly button and some penis earrings as well. Thank god those had all been removed!

Tami wondered what it must've been like for Ellen to give up all control to others. To do whatever you are told. She knew Ellen loved Jack in her own way, so maybe that explained it. And from what she'd heard about the case, she suspected Jack wasn't quite the monster the prosecutor made him out to be. In her line of work, Tami had seen plenty of men who were abysmally cruel to women. Jack didn't seem to be that type. He was more of a manipulator. He took full advantage of the situation and had Ellen agreeing to everything. That was what confused Tami. How Ellen could still speak highly of Jack after all this. Maybe she just felt it was a fair deal—trade sex to atone for her embezzlement.

Tami had noticed right away how hard it was for Ellen to return to her normal life. She seemed to be happy doing Jack's bidding. Or anyone else's, for that matter. She had seen how Ellen responded to her lawyer—as if the Moose was just another dominant to be obeyed.

That was it, of course. Ellen was the prototypical submissive. She probably had repressed it when she was working her way up the corporate ladder, but when everything came crashing down around her, she reverted to her true nature. And Jack, being a natural dominant, was there to take control. Control she willingly gave up. To outsiders, it may appear that Ellen Sanchez had been woefully mistreated, but to her, this treatment was just what she subconsciously craved.

Tami felt a tingle in her loins as she recalled her own brush with the dominant/submissive lifestyle. She'd been a college freshman, away from home for the first time and open to new ideas. Her roommate, Linda, had been a natural dominant—and a lesbian. She wasn't a dyke, with big arms and a butch haircut—she had actually been attractive and slender, though taller than Tami. She wore her brown hair in a bun or a ponytail much of the time and she liked to wear jeans and tee-shirts. They'd become friends and although Linda didn't come on to her, Tami had allowed some of those thoughts to cross her mind. They had even talked about it a few times. Tami had been curious how Linda "became" gay, and Linda had to straighten her out that most are just born that way.

"Although a lot of people are bi," Linda had said, her eyes on Tami. She felt a quiver in her stomach and wondered if she might be offering to experiment. At the time, Tami wasn't sure how she felt about it, but she had been curious.

Linda was the first person to describe dominant and submissive behaviors to Tami. She had been quite naïve in those days. Linda had explained that just like some people are born gay, others are born to be submissive or dominant. They can repress the feelings, but they never go away. Tami wasn't sure which she was at the time. Linda helped her figure it out.

She took another sip of her tea, now growing lukewarm, and recalled how it had started. Linda had brought a girl back to the dorm room, thinking Tami was on a date at a basketball game.

"Oh, sorry," Linda had said when she saw Tami on her bed, reading. "I thought you were out."

Tami looked past her to see a small, shy Asian girl, with shaggy dark hair. "Rick showed up drunk, so I told him to take a hike." She suspected her presence was interrupting something. "Uh, I can leave, if you want me to."

Linda started to speak, then stopped. "No, that's okay. It's your room too." She turned to the girl, who she learned was also a freshman, although she looked younger. "Kim, this is Tami. Tami, Kim. Kim's in my sociology class."

They exchanged hellos. Tami noticed Kim seemed very shy and deferred to Linda. She wondered if her roommate had found a natural submissive. Tami felt awkward, being there, but had been burning with curiosity as to how Linda might handle things.

Linda wasted no time. "Kim, I need a shoulder rub. Come here." The order had been given softly, but with an edge to her voice. Kim jumped to obey, only pausing to look in Tami's direction.

"Don't mind her."

That voice! It had changed somehow. It made you want to obey her, Tami noticed. Had Linda told her to help, she probably would have. For the first time, Tami marveled at the power of the dominant.

Kim rubbed Linda's shoulders for a while on her bed. Tami turned back to her book and pretended to read, but she kept her ears open. If she turned her head slightly, she could still see them out of the corner of her eye.

"My shirt's in the way, please remove it," Linda said.

Tami glanced up and saw Kim pulling Linda's top off without hesitation. She resumed rubbing her roommate's shoulders. Tami returned her attention to her book.

"My bra is killing me; you can take that off too."

Tami couldn't help but look up as Kim unhooked Linda's bra and eased it off of her arms. Kim noticed Tami was watching her and bit her lip, but she didn't stop what she was doing. Tami, knowing that Linda had told Kim not to mind her roommate, dropped all pretense of reading and continued to watch the two women.

Kim massaged Linda's bare back and shoulders, but didn't touch her breasts, Tami noticed. It all seemed rather innocent, except that her roommate wasn't wearing her top. Why didn't she lie down and cover herself? Tami suspected this was all for her benefit, although she couldn't understand why. She had seen Linda naked many times since they had started living together, but it had always been inadvertent, such as when she was changing her clothes. This seemed rather blatant, so Tami suspected Linda wanted her to observe what was going on between her and Kim.

"I like it when you rub your nipples on my back," Linda suddenly announced and Kim's hands stopped moving. Her eyes moved over toward Tami and she seemed frozen, caught between her embarrassment and her urge to obey her dominant partner.

After two long seconds, Linda turned toward Tami and said, "Well?" over her shoulder. The edge to her voice broke the spell. Kim unbuttoned her blouse and slipped it from her shoulders. She wasn't wearing a bra and her breasts were rather small. A pink blush crept from her chest to her cheeks and Kim refused to look at Tami. Linda caught Tami's eye and winked at her, as if to say, "Watch this."

Kim moved closer and began to rub her nipples against Linda's back. There was absolutely no benefit in this to the backrub—that much was clear. It was simply a way for Linda to exert her power over the smaller, submissive girl. Although Kim was embarrassed and half-dressed, she couldn't help but obey.

Tami found it incredibly erotic. At the time, she hadn't decided if she was dominant or submissive, but there was no question that the sight before her was having a powerful effect on her. Her nipples hardened into points against her bra and her arousal made her panties wet. Tami felt her clit harden and thrust against her clothes and she had a sudden urge to strip that she resisted—for now.

Kim kept rubbing, her eyes focused on Linda. Her expression was one of helplessness, as if she couldn't stop what she was doing. Tami almost felt sorry for her. Almost. In addition to her embarrassment, Tami could tell that the girl was as turned on as she was. Her mouth hung open and her nipples were hard peaks at Linda's back.

She likes to be ordered about!

The knowledge hit Tami suddenly, almost causing her to gasp aloud. So this was what a submissive was. *I guess that means I'm not*, she told herself. She doubted she would strip down and do Linda's bidding. *Yet, if that's so, why am I so turned on?*

"Come around front and rub your nipples on mine," Linda ordered.

Kim caught Tami's eye and hesitated for just a second before moving into position. Tami never let her gaze waver. It seemed to embarrass and arouse them both. She imagined herself sitting there, ordering Kim around and found her own arousal increased. *I must be a dominant*, she mused.

As Kim rubbed her breasts up against Linda's larger ones, the roommate held the smaller girl by her upper arms, guiding her. Kim tried not to look at Tami now, concentrating on making Linda happy.

Tami couldn't help herself. Her hand crept down to her shorts and she pressed hard against her mound. She thought it might alleviate some of the pressure she felt, but it only made it worse. She began to rub herself, her eyes on the pair before her. Linda looked over and caught her red-handed and Tami pulled her hand away, embarrassed. Linda just smiled and gave a half-nod, as if to say, "It's all right."

Tami couldn't believe that she was falling under Linda's spell. Somehow, it helped that she had been given permission. Emboldened, she allowed her fingers to return and tease her clit.

"I can smell your arousal," Linda told Kim, who dropped her head to Linda's shoulder, afraid to catch Tami's eyes. "Don't be embarrassed, my pet. I'm aroused too. You're doing such a good job."

The girl's head came up and Tami saw a glimmer of pride on her face.

"Remove your shorts and let me see you." The words froze Kim again.

Oh, this was too much! Surely the girl would refuse and leave! Tami waited for Kim to grow angry. She couldn't tear herself away from the scene and felt Kim's eyes lock onto hers.

"Don't mind her, Kim." There was that edge again. It was a warning: *Don't cross me.*

Kim scooted to the edge of the bed and quickly yanked her shorts off, dropping them into an untidy pile on the floor. Tami was not surprised to see she wasn't wearing panties either—did Linda order her to walk around that way? Her slit was nearly hairless, with just a tiny line of hair right above her clit.

As soon as she was naked, Kim immediately climbed back into position, which allowed her to use her left thigh to hide her nudity. She resumed rubbing her nipples against Linda's, only now there seemed to be a sense of urgency about it.

"Did you fold your clothes?" Kim stopped moving again and held tight to Linda's arms. Her face looked up and beseeched the stronger girl. Linda said nothing else, just stared back at her until Kim's eyes lowered in defeat. She climbed out of bed, this time making no effort to hide herself from Tami's gaze. She picked up her shorts and neatly folded them, then placed them on the dresser. She returned to grab her top and folded it on top. Kim even took Linda's top and put it neatly away. When she turned, Tami could see her smooth round ass cheeks and found her own hand had begun to rub herself harder.

Then Linda said something that shocked Tami. "Kim, why don't you go over and help Tami remove her shorts? They seem to be in the way."

Tami's hand jerked away and she almost told Linda to stop it, this was too much. She was torn between wanting to leave the room and wanting to see if Kim would obey this outrageous request. Her mouth was half-open, ready to protest, but she held her tongue. Her curiosity overcame her displeasure.

Kim too had frozen in place, staring at Linda as if to ask, "Must I?" Linda's steely gaze gave her no option. Like a robot, she came toward Tami, her nakedness on full display. Tami could see the wetness around her pussy and her hardened nipples. Kim was as turned on as Tami was.

Tami said nothing as Kim knelt by the bed. Her hands grasped the sides of her shorts and the girl caught Tami's attention as if to ask permission for what she was about to do. Tami nodded very slightly, once, and Kim proceeded to pull down her shorts, leaving the young woman in her panties.

When Kim's hands returned to remove those, Tami came out of her spell and grabbed both of Kim's hands in hers. "Wait a minute," she said, looking up at Linda. "What about you?"

"Me? I'm already half-naked," she said, her large breasts proudly on display. "You're still wearing your top." She paused and smiled. "You want me to remove my shorts too? Would that make you feel better?"

Tami wasn't sure how to answer that. She didn't know if she wanted everyone to get naked. What might happen?

"I guess I just feel, um, like I'm an observer, not a participant," she finally said. *Therefore, I shouldn't be involved in your games*, she almost added.

"If you're here, you're a participant," Linda replied, using that firm voice that made Tami want to obey. The choice was clear. Leave, as you had offered to earlier, or stay and let what happens happen.

Tami said nothing, but removed her hands and lifted her ass, allowing Tami to slide her panties down her legs. She clutched the hem of her tee-shirt and tried to pull it down to cover her nakedness. Linda laughed.

"Kim, I think my roommate is shy. Come here and help me with my shorts—maybe we can make her feel less self-conscious."

Kim returned to her mistress and helped her remove her shorts and panties. Now that the girls were both naked, all pretenses were gone. Linda stretched out on the bed on her back and ordered Kim to lie on her. Linda kept her eyes on Tami as the Asian did as she was told.

"Go ahead and frig yourself—you know you want to," Linda said.

It was true, but all of her upbringing prevented her from moving. She sat and watched the scene before her. Linda finally smiled and turned her attention back to Kim, who was still clearly embarrassed. She made little mewing noises in her throat and averted her eyes from Tami.

"Oh, hush, my pet. If I don't care that Tami's watching, neither should you."

And that was that. Kim settled down and allowed Linda to kiss her lips. Linda's hands roamed over her slender body and Kim didn't object when they stroked her ass or dove in between her legs.

Tami couldn't help herself now. Her fingers returned to

her pussy and found she was sopping wet. She moved up to the bud of her clit and swirled the juices around, sending shock waves up into her stomach. Her eyes were recording the events in front of her as her fingers were translating those images into raw sexual gratification.

Linda stopped stroking and brought her hands up to Kim's shoulders. She pushed the girl down and Tami knew what she wanted. Kim tried to resist and Linda moved her hand down and slapped her hard on the ass. There were no more protests from Kim. She eased down and began licking and sucking on Linda's nipples.

Tami's mouth was half-open and her fingers were busy as she watched, fascinated. She could feel an orgasm approaching but wanted to make it last, so she slowed her movements.

Linda apparently had enough of Kim's attentions to her breasts, so she pushed her down again. Kim glanced over at Tami before she resigned herself to the inevitable. She slid down to between Linda's legs and started licking the nectar there.

It was too much for Tami. Her fingers became a blur and with a sudden intake of breath, she came hard, shuddering with the power of it. Her mouth rounded into a silent "O" and tears came to her eyes. She tried to be quiet, but a small yelp of emotion escaped her. Her orgasm was far more powerful than any she had ever experienced before.

Linda looked over, her face a mask of bliss. She didn't speak, only smiled and winked as if they now shared a secret. Not just about Kim, but about the power of dominants and the needs of submissives.

As Tami looked across the room at Ellen, she believed she understood more about the woman's inner needs. They made her more accepting of Sawyer's outrageous demands.

Had a woman like Linda been caught embezzling, there's no way Jack would've been able to convince her to become his sex slave. Ellen and Kim had a lot in common. Just as Linda controlled Kim, so did Jack control Ellen. And without his guidance and direction, Ellen feels lost, she realized.

There's a power vacuum in her life. That's why she seems so lost. She's just waiting for the next dominant to come along. Tami wondered if she could become that dominant. Or if she should. The idea excited her, even as it scared her.

Chapter 8

El came into Dr. Butler's inner office and closed the door firmly behind her.

"Hello, Ellen. Please come in and get comfortable." The doctor rose from behind his desk and came around to greet his patient.

She smiled thinly. She knew what he meant. She'd been coming here for two weeks now and they had quickly established a pattern. El would come in, remove her clothes, and lie on the couch. At first, it had seemed like her idea, but lately, the doctor had begun to demand more of her. She was hardly in a position to refuse.

She unbuttoned her blouse and shrugged it off her shoulders. Her bra followed quickly. She felt better and tried to ignore Dr. Butler's eyes boring into her breasts. *I should be used to this*, she told herself. Her skirt followed and her panties were soon added to the small pile of clothes.

El rolled her shoulders and stretched to work out all the kinks her tight clothes had caused her. Tami, of course, made her wear the undergarments. El was perfectly comfortable walking around without them.

The doctor came over to the couch and sat down next to her. His fingers began to roam over her body. This had become part of the pattern too. El wasn't sure how this was supposed to help her overcome her "ordeal," as everyone kept telling her, but it felt good, so she didn't complain.

It was rare for El to have a man take his time with her like this. Most men in the past two years just wanted to jump on and fuck her or order her to suck his cock. She had come to expect it. Jack had been one of the few who seemed to care whether she experienced pleasure and El thought that might explain why she still missed him, no matter what that prosecutor Franklin told her.

Dr. Butler's fingers stroked her breasts as he began asking questions about her childhood and her relationship with her mother and father. She tried to answer him as truthfully as she could, but her mind kept wandering. Her thoughts became clouded with her growing sexual desire.

"Did your father ever touch you like this?" he asked, his fingers tugging at her nipples.

"I...I don't remember," she gasped, feeling an electric connection between her nipples and her clit. But, of course, she did remember. The nights when he came to her room after her mother had fallen asleep. He had been gentle, loving. That had made all the difference. It had taken him months to work up to touching her pussy. By then she found she grew wet simply by being in his presence. She quivered whenever he patted her shoulder or touched her hair. When that magical night finally came, Ellen had been more than ready for him. It wasn't a rape, she told herself. It was a surrender.

"I see," the doctor said smoothly, his hands now leaving her breasts to trickle down to her bare mons. His fingers danced over the Sawyer logo and El knew she was very wet, thinking of her father.

"Tell me about the first time you, um, submitted to someone? Was it a lover? A friend? A girlfriend, perhaps?"

"Submitted?" El tried hard to concentrate on his words. "You mean, like made love to?"

"No, not quite, although one can submit to someone's sexual advances. It's clear that you are a submissive personality type, El—may I call you El? It fits you so well."

El nodded, not wanting the doctor to stop what he was doing. Her pussy leaked, her clit stood up at attention and her nipples were so hard they ached. She tried to bring up a memory for him, for she feared he might stop if she couldn't think of anything to say. She didn't feel comfortable yet talking about her father, so she reached back to recall a time when she "submitted" to someone.

"Oh, yes!" she cried out suddenly, remembering an occasion at the same time that the doctor's fingers touched her G-spot. Wisely, Dr. Butler eased up on his fondling, lest she climax before she could talk.

"It was when I was nineteen," she said, able to breathe more regularly now. "There was this boy, Roger..."

The doctor played with her, slowing down when her tale faltered and quickening when she was giving him details. Ellen learned right away to tell him everything.

"He was a jock, a demanding sort of young man. He asked me out and I was pleased, because being Latina, I didn't think he'd want to date me. He was a tall, blond, second-generation Swede, you see. Not that I think all white boys are prejudiced, you understand, but enough of them have been in my life that I didn't want to assume anything."

The doctor's fingers sped up, and Ellen took that as a sign that she should get to the point.

"Anyway, we went out and we had a good time. He was a gentleman. But he did things—like opening the car door, ordering my meal for me—that made me feel really special and cared for. I really liked it."

That's not all I like, she thought, as his left hand stroked her breasts while his right hand caressed her sex. "We went out again a couple of nights later and he, uh, 'requested' more of me. He wasn't demanding, but he was firm, you understand? He told me what to wear before he picked me up. He had me change my skirt into something shorter. I was happy to please him."

Ellen arched her back, on the verge of an orgasm. Dr. Butler immediately withdrew his hands. She hung there, desperate, but couldn't climb over the mountain without further stimulation. Her hand dropped down to her clit and the doctor grabbed it. She caught his eye and he merely shook his head.

"Please continue, El."

She nodded. She knew her orgasm depended on this story. She spoke more rapidly, trying to get it all out so she could climax. She desperately wanted his hands on her again. "So, uh, I found I really fit in to what Roger wanted in a woman. I guess I was submissive, but I didn't have a name for it at the time. To me, it was just sexy and, I don't know, I had this feeling of being protected somehow."

"When did you have sex with him?"

Ellen nodded, remembering. His fingers returned to just touch her. "It actually was on that second date. He kept pushing and I kept giving in. But I don't mean he was pushy or overbearing or anything like that. He just seemed to know that I was willing to go along, a little at a time, until I was doing things that I never expected I would."

"Such as?"

"Well, we went out to dinner again. Only in the parking lot, he told me to remove my panties and hand them to him. I was shocked! But he didn't say it in a mean way. His voice was light, almost teasing, yet it had a firmness to it. I'm probably not explaining it well. I just felt compelled to obey. It was like a game to me in a way."

His fingers parted her sopping wet labia and moved up and down, stopping just short of her clit. She tried to press her ass down farther into the couch to encourage him to touch her. She could come in an instant if he would only brush her clit. But he didn't and Ellen knew she had to continue her story.

"I was embarrassed, of course, but I did it anyway. I half-turned away from him as I reached under my skirt to pull them down and he didn't object. It was awkward, doing it in the car. When I finally got them off, he held his hand out and I put them in it. I was so embarrassed! I could see a big wet spot even in the dim parking lot. I looked away, afraid of what he might say. He said, 'Look at me,' and I did. He put the panties to his face and breathed deeply. He had big smile on his face. I smiled back and felt better. He wasn't repelled by my dirty panties."

"Dirty? You called them dirty. Why is that?"

"Uh, I don't know. I had leaked all over them, they seemed soiled to me."

"But that's just your natural lubricant. Do you feel dirty now?"

His fingers felt good. "No. Of course not. That was back when I was just a kid."

"Of course. Please continue."

"We went inside. I felt so exposed! My skirt only came halfway down my thighs and I felt like anyone could tell that I had no panties on."

"Did you feel ashamed?"

"No, not really. I was with Roger, so I felt he would protect me."

The doctor nodded thoughtfully. His fingers dug deeper into her pussy. She gasped and thought he would finally allow her to come, but he pulled out once again. She caught his eyes and knew he was waiting for her to continue.

"At the table, there was a tablecloth that draped over, so after I sat, I felt less exposed. Then he leaned over and told me to spread my legs! I almost refused, but the cloth covered me so I thought, 'What the heck.' I could feel the air on my damp pussy and it excited me so much! I knew I was going to fuck him that night."

"Did anything else happen during dinner?"

Ellen blushed. "Yes. After the meal, when the waiter brought the check, Roger pulled out my panties and left them on the table! I guess they were part of the tip, I don't know. But I felt as if everyone's eyes were on me as we left.

"We went back to his apartment that he shared with two other roommates. When we came in, I was ready to jump him, but his roommates were both there. I thought he'd just take me to his room. Instead, he had me sit on the couch and chat with everyone for a bit. But the couch was old and broken down, so I kinda sank into the cushions. I knew my pussy would be visible if my legs came apart, so I pressed my thighs together so hard I got a muscle cramp.

"Roger got me a drink and as he handed it to me, his other hand reached down and touched my knees, putting his hand in between them and wedging them apart. It was clear he didn't want me to keep my legs so tightly together, so I allowed them to come apart, just a bit. He smiled and nodded. I don't know why I did it—I guess I was under his spell or something."

"What did the roommates do?"

"They paid a lot closer attention to me! I felt very sexy. I was hot and wet and I was ready for just about anything. I just put myself in Roger's hands." She paused. "I guess I really was submissive."

"Did Roger make you show more of yourself to his roommates?"

"Not that night..."

The doctor raised an eyebrow. "But there were other nights?"

She hesitated. Dr. Butler immediately removed his hands. "Yes! There were other nights!"

"Let's go back to that night—you said he made love to you then?"

"Oh yes. After we had a beer and chatted—me with my legs open just enough to tease them—Roger took me into his room. He didn't even say anything, he just began taking off my clothes. I wasn't in any shape to refuse him! I wanted him bad! After we were naked, he laid me on the bed and entered me right away. I didn't mind because it was as if the whole night had been foreplay. I came about five times in a row."

"We're you noisy?"

Ellen ruefully nodded, her head cocked to one side. "Oh, yes. And the funny thing is, now that you mention it, when we were done and I sat up, I could see that Roger had left the door ajar! I'm sure his roommates heard everything!"

"Did that excite you?"

"Yes! And embarrassed me too. I was completely satiated by then, so I worried what they might think of me."

"On subsequent nights—you said you showed more to the roommates?"

"Yes. Roger made me. But he was right there, protecting me." When the doctor didn't say anything and his fingers stopped, Ellen knew he wanted more. "He made me show them my breasts, one time." The fingers returned briefly, then stopped again. "All right. I'll tell you all of it."

She spread her legs for him so he could touch her clit again. "Roger said it turned him on to show me off. He said his roommates were good guys and that they would protect me too. He didn't have me strip down or anything, but he'd make me flash them, all the time."

She blushed and shook her head. "Afterwards, he'd fuck

me and I'd scream. I had very powerful orgasms. He never closed the door! He'd encourage me to be loud. At first, I was shy, but later I got to like it. Once..." she stopped, as if too shy to continue. The doctor teased her by just touching her clit, then pulling back. "Once," she went on, "right after I had come and Roger was still inside me, I opened my eyes, I saw them at the door! Both roommates, just standing there! I tried to push Roger off, but he held me tight and began to stroke into me again. It felt so good! I found I no longer cared if they were watching and I can again, even harder."

"So did they watch you regularly after that?"

"Yes. But I wouldn't let them fuck me, even though I knew they wanted to."

"And Roger didn't make you?"

"No. I've always wondered what would've happened if he had."

The doctor sat back. "You enjoy having someone in control—I'm sure you must be aware of that. That's what a submissive is."

She immediately missed his fingers on her. "I...I guess so. But Mr. Sawyer wasn't like Roger—I mean, at first. Jack forced me to become his slut."

"I know. But not only did you ultimately like it, you *needed* it. That's why you stayed with him, later. Don't you see that?"

The impact of his statement caused El to try to sit up, but Dr. Butler leaned toward her to press his hands down on her breasts, holding her in place. "Now, El, it's all right. I'm not trying to disturb you. I'm only trying to get you to see what you are. You must know by now that your subconscious used the excuse of being blackmailed to do what you really wanted to do."

One of the doctor's hands again drifted down to her pussy and lightly stroked it. Any arguments that El might've had disappeared. She needed this, she realized. Not just from Mr. Sawyer, but from all men. Even the strangers her boss introduced her to. Even her psychiatrist.

"I *am* a slut," she whispered.

"That's right. A submissive slut. You can't help yourself. You want this all the time. Admit it."

"Yes." His fingers brushed against her clit and she nearly came. She shuddered and grabbed his hand, meaning to press it against her cunt so she could climax, but the doctor pulled his hand away.

"Please, doctor! You said I needed it!"

"What you really want is my cock. Say it."

After so much teasing, Ellen didn't care how she came as long as she came. What's one more cock in her life? "I want your cock, doctor! Fuck me! Please!"

"Shhh! Not so loud. We wouldn't want your 'keeper' to hear you, now would we?"

El shook her head. "No, I'll be quiet. Please. Fuck me."

Dr. Butler unzipped his pants and pulled down his underwear. He didn't bother removing any clothes; he just freed his cock and climbed up over El. He used his knees to press her thighs apart. His rock-hard cock hovered just in front of her sopping pussy.

"It's okay to admit what you are. That's what psychiatry is all about—allowing you to be yourself," he said, allowing just the tip of his penis to touch her. She gasped and nodded. "So don't feel bad about yourself, okay? Just enjoy it."

With that, he plunged into her in one smooth motion. El gasped and came instantly. It was as if she had been waiting for days to climax. Her entire body shook and balls of light flashed before her eyes. She started to cry out, then bit hard on her lip to keep quiet. She feared Tami might come bursting in, probably armed. She might even shoot the good doctor.

She hung onto him as he pumped, climbing immediately into another orgasm. This one was only slightly less powerful than the first, but when Dr. Butler suddenly erupted inside of her, she felt a new wave of emotion sweep through her. She hugged him close, trying to prolong the moment, even as the doctor struggled to free himself from her. He finally pulled out and stood up.

"Do you feel better now, El?"

"Uh huh." She lay limp, like a puddle of humanity, without bones...except, something was different. It wasn't the same with Dr. Butler as it had been with Mr. Sawyer. By all rights, it should've been. He was strong, she was weak. He was in authority, she was subservient. Yet Mr. Sawyer had something special that this man did not. She couldn't explain it any better.

She watched as he straightened himself up, zipping up his pants and returning to his chair.

"I'm afraid that's all the time we have. I'll give you a few minutes to recover. I'd like to see you again on Thursday, all right?"

El nodded, pushing her doubts out of her mind for now. "All right, doctor."

Dr. Butler looked at his watch the moment El, once fully dressed, closed the office door behind her. Five till eleven, he noted. *I'm late.* He went to the rear door of his office and opened it. As he expected, Bernie, his bookie, was standing there. Behind him was a large man the doctor hadn't seen before. Without waiting for an invitation, the men pushed past the doctor.

"I hope you weren't eavesdropping," he said sternly.

"No," Bernie said, chewing on a toothpick he seemed to keep constantly in one corner of his mouth. "I didn't hear any whack-job secrets, if that's what you mean."

Oh, if you only knew, the doctor thought. "My patients aren't 'whack-jobs.' And I've told you before, I'd prefer you didn't come to my office."

"I don't care what you want. You owe me money, so I'm going to come and collect whenever and wherever I want. Unless you wanna make arrangements to pay me on time."

The doctor grimaced. His voice took on a pleading tone. "Look, Bernie. You know I'm good for it. Have I ever stiffed you?" He glanced up at the big man. "What's he for? You know you don't need muscle for me."

Bernie shrugged. "You say that, doc, but here we are, three days later and you still haven't paid me. You owe me twenty large. By tomorrow, it will be twenty-four."

"Twenty-four! Come on, Bernie! You can't demand that kind of interest! I...I just got caught a little short. I was surprised Denver didn't cover the spread—they're doing really well this year. And they were playing Cleveland, for god's sakes!"

Bernie held up a hand. "I'm not here to argue the merits of the bet. I want my twenty G's."

Dr. Butler's eyes again went to the big man. He licked his lips. "Uh, I don't have all of it right now..."

"How much you got?"

"Nine thousand." He went to his desk and pulled out an envelope. "I swear, I'll have the rest to you by, uh, tomorrow—Friday at the latest."

"Like I said, tomorrow you'll owe me twenty-four." He

grabbed the envelope and began thumbing through the bills inside. "So you'll owe me fifteen more."

"Hey, come on! I've been a good cust–" Butler shut up when the big man moved toward him threateningly. Bernie stopped the thug with one upraised hand.

"Not yet, Bubba. The doc's still a good customer, as he says. But you should know," he leveled his gaze at him, "that this is a business. Just like yours is a business. You don't let your patients stiff you, do you?"

Of course not, he thought. But he said, "I've been known to work with my patients..."

Bernie shook his head. "That's fine, if you want to run your business that way. I don't."

The doctor racked his brain, trying desperately to convince Bernie not to charge him fifteen thousand more. *Jesus!* He knew it would be a stretch to raise eleven—he might be able to get that in a week. *But fifteen! Shit! I'll never get ahead of this debt.*

An idea jumped into his mind and though he tried to reject it, he found his mouth opening anyway. "Wait! I know!" He glanced at the big man. "Uh, can we talk privately about something?"

Bernie shook his head. "Uh uh. You got something to say, you say it to the both of us. I've seen too many desperate gamblers try to get me alone in order to conk me on the head."

"Hey! I wouldn't do that!" The doctor would too, if he thought it would do any good. But he knew that would only get him into more trouble with Bernie's pals. "Uh, no, I was thinking..." He couldn't believe he was about to say. He was about to violate his doctor-patient privilege. "There's this patient of mine..."

Bernie's face twisted up in confusion. "What?"

"Wait! This is good. This girl—woman—who comes to see me. She's a nympho. How about if you come by Thursday and I'll let you fuck her...ah, in exchange for not charging the extra, er, interest."

Bernie laughed. "You actually see nymphos here? Jeez, maybe I'm in the wrong profession!" He laughed and Bubba laughed with him, a rumbling sound like thunder. "You think this broad's worth four G's interest? Come on, whatddaya take me for?"

"No, really, she's a knockout! And she'll fuck you silly!"

The bookie paused, his head cocked to his side. "No broad's worth four G's. I can get a great piece of ass for five hundred easily."

"Bring your friends!" The doctor blurted before he could catch himself. He saw Bubba's pig eyes grow wide and the muscle man actually smiled a thin little grin, like a knife had just sliced his face.

Bernie stared at him. "You'd actually give this broad over to us for fun and games, just to weasel out of four lousy grand?"

"Uh, no, you can't take her away. It would have to be here. She's, uh, got a bodyguard." Dr. Butler wished he'd never said anything now. He was just digging himself a deeper hole.

"A bodyguard! What the hell for?"

"Uh, she's a witness in a trial."

The side of Bernie's face crinkled up in the semblance of a smile. "Maybe she's gonna testify against some friends of mine, huh? Maybe she might be worth more to me than a fuck, right?"

"No, no! It's a sex trial. No, uh, professionals involved. You don't even know the poor shmuck she's going to testify against."

"I know guys who run girls—I'll bet a pimp would pay good money to convince her not to spill her guts, huh?"

"No! She doesn't have a real pimp. I mean, she's been working for this one guy and he turned her out, but not on the streets..." *God, this was so hard to explain!*

Suddenly, Bernie snapped his fingers. "Hey, this wouldn't be that factory pimp job I've been reading about? The sex slave who embezzled?"

Dr. Butler's shoulders slumped in defeat. He had hoped Bernie wouldn't learn the details. "Yeah. That's it."

"You're seein' the girl? The sex slave?" Bernie smiled broadly now. "Well, that puts a whole different spin on things, doesn't it?" He sucked on his teeth. "But what about this bodyguard? It's a cop, right? That could be dangerous."

"The cop waits outside for her. As long as you're quiet, you can do just about anything...well, short of hurting her. I've already fucked her and she's a pistol, I can tell you. She's coming back on Thursday, same time."

Bernie pondered it for a minute. He took one glance at the grinning Bubba for him to make up his mind. "OK, I'll tell ya what, doc. You give me an hour with her—me and Bubba here and anyone else I wanna bring—and I'll waive the extra four Gs." He held up a hand. "Providing, of course, that you pay the remaining eleven grand by Thursday. Deal?"

The doctor grimaced. "By Thursday? Uh, I don't know..."

"Take it or leave it, doc. I'm giving up a lot for a little piece of ass, you know. The only reason I'm agreeing to it is, I like the idea of boinking someone kinda famous. I can read about her in the papers and laugh myself silly. That's worth four grand to me, but just barely."

Dr. Butler shook his head. "Okay. It's a deal. Be out back at ten a.m. Thursday. Wait for me to bring you in. And remember, no rough stuff!"

"Sure doc. Just don't forget to have my money or the deal's off."

Chapter 9

Tami loosened her shoulder harness and eased it off her shoulder. Damn that felt good! It was like wearing a second bra, only not as forgiving. The weight of her pistol made her want to walk lopsided and she couldn't wait to take it off every evening. She was grateful her lieutenant told her to dress in plain clothes, but at least with the uniform, she could wear the gun on a wide belt. She had a clip-on holster, but found it didn't really fit with her suits.

Unlike most female officers, Tami carried the five-shot Smith & Wesson Model 360, the Airlite .357 magnum. It was a smaller gun—a so-called "ladies" gun, yet it had real stopping power. She didn't want to be pumping bullets into some big ape who was charging her, hoping he'd stop before she ran out of bullets. One or two shots from a .357 would stop a charging lion.

She put the gun in the cabinet by the door, so it would be ready whenever someone knocked. Later, she'd move it into the bedroom when she went to sleep. On patrol, she often carried a back-up gun, a compact .38, but decided the fewer guns in this apartment, the better. Not that she was worried about Ellen grabbing it to harm her, but she might use it to harm herself. She didn't seem overly depressed. Tami was just being cautious.

"Can you make us some tea?"

Ellen nodded. She jumped up to put on the teakettle. Tami just watched her, a half-grin on her face. *The girl loves to wait on me!* They've been together now for three weeks, and Tami had observed how she deferred to her about everything—what TV shows to watch, what to have for dinner—everything. It hadn't been hard to achieve, either.

It would be so easy to treat her like Linda treated Kim, she mused. Only her fear that she might get caught prevented her from taking advantage of the situation—so far. She worried that Ellen might report her to the lieutenant. She had to be sure Ellen was completely under her control.

It was difficult not to push harder—she was really curious how it might play out. Ever since that year in college, Tami had wondered if she could be a dominant like Linda. She recalled how she was often submissive around Linda—not in a sexual way, but in other ways. But she also loved seeing Linda with other submissives. It was as if she lived vicariously through her roommate. Now, ten years later, she had her own submissive just waiting for her command. If only she could keep her mouth shut...

"Ellen."

Ellen turned, hitching her shoulders in a way that told Tami she didn't like the bra straps cutting into her. Up until now, Tami had ignored the childish display. But it gave her ideas.

"I know your underwear is bothering you. And I'd like to let you just wear what you want—or don't want—but I'm afraid if Franklin finds out, she'll tell my lieutenant that I'm not doing a good job."

Ellen looked hopeful. She recognized Tami was willing to discuss it. "How would she find out? I mean, if I always have it on when I'm around her?"

"Well, it might slip during your discussions with her. You two do spend a lot of time, going over your testimony."

The woman shook her head. "I would never violate your trust."

"Really? If I let you take off your underwear while here in this room, you'd keep it a secret?"

"Oh, yes! I've gotten used to not wearing it. In fact, I don't like clothes much any more."

Tami nodded. "I suppose I could allow you to get out of your clothes as well. You know you'd have to obey me when I told you to put them back on."

"Oh, yes, Tami!"

"Call me ma'am." Tami didn't know why she said that— it was something she remembered Linda doing.

"Yes, ma'am."

Tami pushed her a little further. "That goes for anything I say."

Ellen smiled broadly. "Oh, yes, ma'am! Of course!"

"And you couldn't tell anyone. Not Franklin or even Sawyer. It would have to be our secret."

Ellen nodded her head vigorously. "I promise."

"All right. While the teapot's heating, you may remove your clothes."

"Thank you!" She came over and gave Tami a quick hug. Tami grabbed her and held her close for a second longer, then let her go. Ellen started to head for the bedroom when Tami's voice stopped her.

"I didn't say you should leave the room." Tami held her breath. She waited for Ellen to refuse and if she had, Tami would've pretended she had just been kidding. But Ellen paused and turned to face the officer. Her hands went to her blouse and she unbuttoned it slowly, almost suggestively.

Her blouse came open and Ellen shrugged it off, leaving her breasts encased in the lacy white bra. Her hands went around behind her and Tami said, "Stop. Let me do that for you."

Ellen stared at Tami as the officer approached. She turned to give Tami better access to her bra clasp. Tami unhooked it and watched as Ellen shrugged and let it fall to the floor. She turned, her breasts just inches away from Tami's.

"Now the skirt and panties," Tami said. "I'm sure you can do those by yourself."

Ellen nodded. She unfastened her skirt and let it fall. She wore pantyhose over her underwear and Tami knew she hated to put them on every morning. But Franklin had insisted.

Ellen peeled the pantyhose and panties down to her thighs and sat down on a nearby chair to remove them from her legs. All of her jewelry was gone, locked up safely in the ADA's office, pending the trial. Tami noticed how the woman's slit was still bare and wasn't sure if she shaved regularly or if Jack had something done more permanent. Probably a wax job of some sort, she guessed. It surprised her how turned on she was getting and not just because she had lesbian feelings—no, this was more about power. She had control over another human being. She knew this girl would do just about anything she asked of her.

It would be easy to order Ellen to lick her cunt and Tami felt her own juices flow at the thought. Or maybe my asshole, she thought and smiled wickedly.

Ellen stood up again, completely nude. "Do you want me to get my robe?"

There. She was already asking permission, just as she had done with Jack. "No. Don't bother. I know you like to walk around naked." The teakettle whistled.

Ellen smiled and returned to the kitchen. She reached up overhead to grab the teabags and Tami could see the way her butt cheeks clenched with the effort. They looked good enough to spank, Tami thought, and another memory flooded back.

Linda had brought home another submissive. God

knows where she found them all. She must've had radar for that kind of personality trait. This one was a thin blond named Susie, with lank hair and small breasts. Her one redeeming feature was her perfect, heart-shaped ass. Linda used to order Susie to remove her shorts immediately upon entering the room and display her ass for the pleasure of both Linda and Tami. She made her keep her tee-shirt on, "to hide those disgusting breasts," she'd tell the embarrassed girl. Tami knew it was simply a way of keeping her off-balance.

But just watching that ass wasn't enough for Linda. She had to put her hands on it too. She'd rub it and slap it and make Susie bend over so she could get a "better look," as she was always saying. At first, when she slapped it, it was just playfully, like saying, "Job well done!" Later, Linda began finding reasons to punish her. They couldn't make a lot of noise in the dorm room, so Susie's spankings were far more arousing than painful. Tami could remember how wet the girl got. Linda would always run her fingers along her slit and comment at how slutty Susie was. The girl would get so red, Tami thought she might faint. But she knew Susie was highly aroused by the treatment. Who wouldn't be?

She looked at Ellen's nicely shaped ass and wondered if Jack had spanked it. She would guess he did. It was so spankable! "Ellen."

Ellen turned, teabags in hand. "Yes, ma'am?"

"Did Jack ever spank you?"

Ellen's face grew red. "Uh, yes, ma'am."

"Why? We're you bad?"

"Sometimes. Sometimes he did it just because he liked it."

"Did you like it?"

She turned away and fumbled with the cups. "Well..."

"It's all right. You can tell me. I'll keep your secrets if you'll keep mine."

Ellen nodded and turned back, smiling shyly. "Yes, I did. I mean, up to a point. Sometimes, he would hurt me. When I deserved it, of course."

"How did you deserve it?"

"Oh, I don't know. There were different reasons. Sometimes I wouldn't, uh, rub myself when he called me on the intercom."

Tami had heard about this from Franklin, who had said it with a sneer on her lip. But Tami had been fascinated.

"Or one time he let a worker spank me because I was rude to him in the hall."

"Did it make you obey better?"

"Yes. I learned my lessons."

"You have a very spankable ass, do you know that?"

Ellen looked over her shoulder, trying to see herself. "No, I didn't."

"I would like to spank it myself. And I will, if you don't do what I say."

"Oh, I will, I promise, ma'am." But El couldn't stop from wiggling her butt, as if the idea excited her. Tami picked up on it right away.

"Are you wiggling your ass at me?"

"Uh, no ma'am. I wasn't aware I was doing anything." The ass just twitched now.

"You're still doing it! You'd better come over here. I won't take this kind of disrespect." Her voice teased Ellen with mock anger.

"Yes, ma'am." She came over and stood next to Tami's chair, her head hung low.

"Turn around."

Ellen did and Tami immediately stroked her wonderful

cheeks. They were so soft and smooth. She couldn't believe she was doing this, and yet, she couldn't stop herself. Another opportunity like this may never come along in her lifetime.

She gave the skin a light slap and Ellen twitched in response. She struck her again, harder and Ellen sucked in a breath.

"Are you enjoying this?"

"Uh, well... er..."

"You are, aren't you? I guess I'm not doing it right. Maybe I should do it harder." She slapped the right cheek again, smartly, leaving a red handprint this time. Ellen rocked on her heels.

"Ow!"

"Good. It should hurt. It's not supposed to be enjoyable."

"But why are you punishing me? What have I done?"

Tami frowned. She was right. That Ellen twitched her ass at her was no reason to punish her. Tami wondered what Linda would've said in this situation. "It doesn't matter. I'm doing this because I want to. That's a good enough reason."

Ellen nodded and Tami smiled at how easily the woman accepted her dominance over her. She was beginning to see just why Jack Sawyer kept her around, even after she paid off her debt. The woman was a perfect submissive.

Tami decided to stop, before she got herself in deeper. She slapped Ellen's rump again, lightly and told her to go pour the tea. Ellen scampered off, rubbing her ass with one hand as she did.

Tami knew, watching her, that they were going to be experimenting a lot in the next few weeks. She just couldn't help herself.

Chapter 10

Diane Franklin considered herself a scrapper. Tall, good-looking, smart and well-dressed, she was the prototypical ADA. She had risen fast in the ranks since she'd first come on board, right out of law school eight years ago. This would be her most visible trial to date. She would love to slam dunk Jack Sawyer and send a message to men everywhere: You can't treat women like shit.

Diane lived to stick it to men, put them in their place. They thought themselves so superior, making more money than women, being stronger than women and not being subjected to the constant barrage of hormones that woman had to endure. Ha! she thought. I'd like to see a man give birth! They'd be a whimpering mess, begging for drugs. Not that Diane had given birth yet. She didn't have time for babies right now. Maybe later. But when the time came, she wouldn't whimper. She wouldn't even need a man around. She'd just have herself artificially inseminated and be done with the entire gender.

Unless, of course, she had a boy.

She put the thought out of her mind. It wasn't important now. What was important was the case of the People vs. Jack Sawyer. Diane almost rubbed her hands together in glee. This was going to be so much fun! She envisioned herself, standing on the courthouse steps, facing the crowd of reporters. Her face would be on the evening news every night for two or three months! This could pave her way to the D.A.'s corner office, if that weasel Montgomery would ever retire.

There was a polite knock on the opaque glass door of her office.

"Come!"

The door popped open and Brian Cecciti's head came in. "Uh, Diane, Sanchez and her attorney are here."

"Good. Send them in."

Betty and Ellen walked in, followed by Cecciti. The four gathered around a small conference table, just as they had done so many times before. Diane could tell from Ellen's face that the witness was not looking forward to going over her testimony yet again. Still, it had to be done. She didn't want any mistakes.

"Ellen, I know you probably think we've done this to death, but it's important. You have to be careful on the stand. I won't be there to help you when the defense attorney is questioning you. You'll have to know what to say on your own."

"I thought I was just supposed to tell the truth."

"From the mouths of babes," Betty said dryly.

Diane blushed and glanced over at Brian just in time to see him smirk. "Yes, you are supposed to tell the truth, Ellen, but the truth, said in the wrong way, might let the defendant walk. Now you wouldn't want that, would you?"

Ellen didn't say anything for a few seconds. Diane sharpened her gaze. "Remember, Ellen—you have a free ride on the embezzlement, provided you help us. I would hate to see you fail to live up to your end of the bargain."

The threat worked. Ellen glanced over at Betty, who nodded. Ellen shook her head, "No, we wouldn't want Mr. Sawyer to walk."

"Good! That's so much better! Now, let's go over some key questions. Brian here will pretend to be Sawyer's defense attorney. I'll be me and I'll make objections when

I can, but I'm limited by the rules of the court. You should be prepared for whatever he asks."

Diane noted that Ellen gave a soft sigh before she settled in, her face a mask. The ADA worried that Ellen's heart clearly wasn't in this.

Across town, Sam Keppel was grilling Jack on his testimony. He had debated keeping Jack off the stand, but his client insisted. Sam had to agree that Jack's testimony could help explain the tape of Ellen's agreeing to her new duties. Yet he worried about what Franklin might come up with. Jack was vulnerable, that much was clear. So he put himself in Franklin's head and tried to think of questions she might ask on cross.

"Okay. Why, after Ellen paid off her debt to you, did you keep her around?"

"She didn't want to leave," Jack said. "I offered to write a letter of recommendation and to provide her with a small stipend, but she wanted to stay."

"And you didn't insist?"

"No, I didn't."

"Why not? You had to know that what you were doing was highly illegal."

"So is embezzlement," he said quickly.

Sam shook his head. "No, Jack. That borders on sarcasm. That never goes over well with a jury. Besides, this is after the debt was paid, so it's like the embezzlement never happened. I think you'll want to emphasize that Ellen had come to like what she was doing. We want to make her out to be a real sex maniac, okay?"

Jack sighed. "I hate to do that to her. She's really a sweetheart, despite the theft. I worry what this trial is going to do to her."

"You should be worried what it's going to do to you, Jack. You could be spending the next twenty years in jail."

"All right, all right. Let's get on with it."

Sam got back into his DA character. "Why didn't you force her to stop what she was doing and leave?"

"She didn't want to go. She said she liked it there."

"Really? She actually enjoyed having sex with strangers?"

"Yes—as long as I strictly controlled it. I never put her in a bad situation or endangered her life."

"What about disease? Did you protect her against disease?"

"I told her to use condoms. That was part of the deal I made with her, originally."

"Yet the court now knows that she often did NOT wear condoms, thus putting herself at risk. You call this protecting her?"

"She's a big girl, she could take care of herself."

Sam put his head in his hands. "No, Jack, jeez. That comes across as so uncaring. Remember, she was under your spell. Or thumb. She had to do what you told her to do or else she'd get turned over to the cops, right?"

"Right. I don't want to come across as still angry at her. I mean, she really helped me out. I'm far better off now than I was before she stole from me."

"That's right. Keep that in mind. Let the jury know that you're doing this reluctantly, telling them what a slut she is. That's why she stayed and that's why she skipped wearing condoms, even though you suggested it."

"Right." Jack shook his head. "This is going to be tougher than I thought."

Chapter 11

Dr. Butler was sweating as he awaited his ten o'clock appointment with Ellen. *Jeez, how could I have gotten myself into this?* He nervously fingered the fat envelope in his suitcoat pocket. Eleven thousand dollars, just as Bernie had demanded. He had raided his pension fund—and paid a withdrawal penalty—to come up with the cash. The fund was already sorely depleted by earlier failed bets. He knew, from his own training, that he needed help. But he couldn't bear to go to another psychiatrist and admit his problem. He hoped he was about to experience "shock therapy" that would cure him of his gambling. Making Ellen have sex with these men was beyond crazy. His entire career, indeed, his entire freedom, rested on how the next hour would go.

The two thugs had already showed up and they'd brought along a friend. Bernie hadn't introduced him. He was a sallow man with a bad complexion. When he grinned, Butler noticed he had one tooth missing in front. The doctor had managed to convince Bernie and his pals to wait outside in the rear corridor until he could explain things to Ellen. But he had to leave the door ajar so they could hear everything. He had violated so many canons of his profession he doubted there were any left.

The intercom buzzed and his secretary announced that Ellen was here. For a brief moment, he considered asking the female officer to come in as well, which would certainly spoil the party for Bernie. But that would cost him an extra four grand and make Bernie very angry. No telling what the bookie might do.

"Send her in," he intoned and wiped off his face with his handkerchief.

The door opened and Ellen walked in. She smiled and immediately began removing her clothes. Dr. Butler stood and came around to help her, taking her clothes from her. He began to speak in a quiet voice.

"Listen carefully to me, Ellen. Today marks a very special day in your therapy," he lied smoothly. "I want to see how you reacted when Jack told you to have sex with a strange man. Or men," he added quickly. "Often a trained psychiatrist can learn things by having his patient relive certain experiences."

Ellen looked confused. "What? You want me to ... um, have sex with someone?" She looked around. "Who? And why, again?"

"To test your reactions," he said again. "From what you've told me, it became almost second nature to you. That's quite an achievement, you realize. To have subsumed your own needs so completely for Sawyer."

"Well, yes, that was for him. I owed him. I'm not sure—"

Bernie chose that moment to barge in from the unlocked back door, closely followed by Bubba and the stranger. "Well, here I am, doc, just as you asked. You said you needed our help in something?" Ellen shrank back behind Dr. Butler, her eyes wide.

"Uh, yes. Ber—I mean, Barney, this is Ellen. Ellen, Barney. And this is, uh..."

"George," the big man rumbled, giving Ellen a leering smile.

"Ralph," the sallow man said, an evil grin on his face.

"Barney and, uh, George and Ralph are going to help me. I mean, help you, recreate your visit with a client...or more."

"I don't understand."

"I explained it, Ellen." He turned around and gripped her firmly by her upper arms. "I realize this may seem unorthodox to you, but I assure you it will help us get to the root of your problems. You see, we have limited time and, uh, this method has been known to achieve results much more quickly."

"Results?" Ellen tried to cover herself with her hands while the doctor tried to show the men all her charms.

Ellen was flabbergasted. For the first time in months, she actually felt embarrassed to be naked in front of strangers. Whenever she had entered Mr. Sawyer's office, she felt proud to show off her body because he was there. She trusted her boss. Dr. Butler wasn't Mr. Sawyer, but she had felt safe in his office. Now she was confused. Was she supposed to be doing this? Wasn't Dr. Butler supposed to cure her of her problem? Or at least help her to understand it?

"I don't understand," she said again softly.

"There's nothing to worry about. I have condoms." He fetched them from his desk drawer.

The man named Barney scowled. "What the hell is this? You didn't say nothing about no raincoats."

"It's for the protection of my client."

"I ain't got no VD," Barney insisted.

"If it will keep Ellen from becoming upset, what's the harm?" he said urgently, tipping his head at the closed door to the reception. "You wouldn't want her to become agitated, would you?"

Barney's lip curled, but he said nothing else. Finally, he nodded and accepted a foil-wrapped package from the doctor. George followed suit. Ralph took one, and tossed it into the trash can by the doctor's desk. Butler stared at him but said nothing.

Ellen had almost been forgotten in the brief exchange. She still looked worried. "I don't... I'm not..."

"Hush, now. You want to get better, don't you?"

She nodded.

"Well then, you have to trust me. I know what I'm doing."

Ellen started to speak, but the decision appeared to have been made for her. She seemed to shrink as she kept her hands over her breasts and pussy.

❧

The doctor worried that he might be causing her to withdraw. He wondered why she was so ready to do Sawyer's bidding, but would suddenly balk when her psychiatrist—another dominate male in her life—would ask the same thing of her.

Barney spoke up, breaking his train of thought. "Hey, you're not going to watch or anything, are ya? I don't need an audience."

The doctor's temper flared. "You've got Ralph and Bub–, I mean, George here—or are they here just to help you put it in?"

"Careful, doc," Barney warned. He looked from the doctor to his bodyguard, then Ralph, and back again. He shrugged. "Maybe you could all leave for a little while."

"No," Dr. Butler said. "The deal is, I need to be here to monitor Ellen. If I'm not here and she suddenly cried out, why, who knows what might happen." He jerked his head toward the door again, just to make sure Bernie got the message.

"All right, all right. But I want you the rest of youse way in the back. I don't work well with an audience."

George smiled. He spoke for the first time since

they arrived. "Who says you get to go first?" His voice rumbled.

"Yeah?" Ralph put in.

Barney's eyes widened. "I'm the man who is owed the money! You're here out of my good graces."

"Whaddya say we flip for it?" George suggested.

"Or rock, paper, scissors," Ralph added.

"Get real. You guys get sloppy seconds or none at all."

Ellen didn't follow the conversation. What was all this about money? With Mr. Sawyer, money had been important, sure, but why was the doctor concerned about it?

She eyed the big man called George and wondered if his cock was proportional to his body. She shivered when she thought of the heavy man lying on her. She thought back to when Mr. Sawyer had ordered to fuck a fat man and tried to put her mind in that place. She remembered Bob Orr, the large man who turned out to be a great lover. Perhaps this George would be like him.

She was more worried about the two weaselly men. The tall one and the greasy one with the bad tooth. Why would the doctor use them to help in her therapy? They looked like criminals. The shorter man looked as if he hadn't shaved in days. She knew her breasts and face would be scratched up by it. Why couldn't the man shave at least?

She fought her fears and tried to calm herself. This was just another duty to be performed, same as all the others. She had enjoyed the attention so much, why worry about these guys? Okay, so they weren't as clean and nice as Mr. Sawyer's clients and employees, but they probably had their redeeming qualities.

Barney jerked his thumb over his shoulder. "You guys,

head over by the back door. I need some room." He approached Ellen, who shrunk back. "Hey, now, little one. Don't be scared. I'm not going to hurt you." He looked over his shoulder. "Am I, doc?"

"Uh, no. Ellen, trust me, everything will be all right. Just do what you do best, all right?"

She nodded. Barney led her to the couch and made her lie down. He kissed her cheek and Ellen could feel his scratchy beard. She shivered. He soon grew tired of her face and move down to her nipples. He licked and sucked, taking her tender nipples into his mouth and sucking them. Sometimes he was too rough and he pulled too hard. She began to squirm.

"Oh, you like this, huh, slut?" He cooed.

"No, you're doing it too hard, you're hurting me."

"Come on, you like it, you know you do."

She tried to relax and accept her role. Barney soon moved down to her slit. He played with her clit roughly. "Goll, will you look at this," he said, staring at the Sawyer Metalworking logo tattooed on her mound. "You must be one sick chick to let them do that to you."

Sick chick? Mr. Sawyer had never called her a sick chick. Dr. Butler never had either. Why was this man insulting her so? Didn't he know she had been coerced into using her body for Jack? She had come to like it, that was true, but only because Mr. Sawyer was so careful with her.

"Doctor—" she began, trying to free herself from underneath the man's body. He grabbed her arms and held her down.

"Oh no, you don't, you little slut. You put out for the doc, now you put out for me."

He told her that!? Wasn't that confidential? What was going on here? "Doctor! Help! I don't want to do this!"

The man was strong. He held her down as he reached down and unzipped his pants. His hard cock sprung free. Ellen looked around for the doctor, and spotted him across the room, just watching. "Doctor!"

He took a step forward and stopped. His face was a mask of worry and indecision. He tugged at his tie.

Barney pushed her legs apart and climbed over her. Ellen could feel his erection press against her slit. She wasn't wet yet and he didn't seem to want to give her time to become aroused. "Wait," she said. "Wait."

He didn't wait. The tip of his cock speared her, spreading her labia apart and scraping her skin. She began to struggle, fighting panic. Barney's face darkened. "Hey, you bitch! Stop it!" He raised one hand as if to slap her.

"Doctor!"

Ellen's raised voice galvanized Dr. Butler into action. He raced over and pulled the bookie from his patient.

"What the hell...?"

"Get off of her! The deal's off!"

"Hey! It's too late now!"

George came over and grabbed the doctor by his arms and pulled him away from the smaller man.

"No! Stop! I'll pay you the four grand!"

Everything froze for a moment: Barney, standing over the naked Ellen, his softening cock sticking out of his pants; George, his meaty hands still tightly gripped around the doctor's arms; Ralph, standing a few feet away, the hard bulge of his cock visible in his pants; and Dr. Butler, his face white, his lips set. And Ellen, a shocked look of understanding slowly spreading over her face.

There came a knock at the door. "Doctor? Everything all right in there?" The door rattled. Dr. Butler thanked the stars that he'd had the presence of mind to lock it earlier.

Only the eyes of the four men moved—they flitted from one to another before the doctor suddenly shrugged free of George's grip and turned toward the door.

"Yes, *officer*, everything's fine..." he said through the closed door. "We're just having a bit of a breakthrough."

"I'd like to talk to Ellen," the voice insisted.

The doctor turned back to the men and jerked his head toward the door. Barney pointed at him and whispered, "Four grand," then zipped up his pants as if in emphasis. "Tomorrow." He tossed the unused condom, still in its wrapper, at the doctor as he and George headed for the back door.

"All right," Dr. Butler said to the door, snatching up Ellen's clothes and tossing them to her. "I'll be right there." To Ellen, he hissed, "Get dressed! Quickly!"

Ellen paused. "Why? Tami's seen me naked before."

"Uh, I don't want her to see you naked here—she might get the wrong idea," he whispered.

Ellen nodded and began getting dressed, but her mind was working, putting together the pieces.

The doctor leaned down to pick up the condom, slipping it into his pocket. He walked to the door and pretended to fumble with the lock. "Hang on, the door seems to be stuck." He looked over his shoulder to see Ellen buttoning her blouse, then pulling up her skirt. There was no time to put on underwear. She tossed it behind his desk. He opened up the door and peeked his head out.

"What is it, officer? We're right in the middle of a breakthrough here."

"I heard shouting—and it sounded like there were others in there. I want to see Ellen, make sure she's all right."

"Of course she's all right," the doctor took one last glance and saw that Ellen was presentable. "Come in, see for yourself."

She pushed past the doctor and strode to Ellen's side. "Are you all right? Are you upset?"

Ellen gathered herself. She exchanged a long, even look with the doctor and saw his eyes pleading with her. She turned to Tami. "Everything's fine, ma'am."

"I heard voices. Was there someone else here?" Her eyes roamed the room, settling on the back door. "Did someone just leave?"

Ellen took a deep breath. "No. That was just the doctor, pretending he was Jack Sawyer. It was part of the therapy."

The doctor's eyes closed in relief, then opened again when Tami turned toward him. "I don't know what kind of therapy you're doing here, but I don't like it. I plan to report this to Franklin."

"Of course," he said, his face a professional mask. "You do what you think is best. I'm sure that you, as a law enforcement professional, know far more about how psychoanalysis works than I do." He paused. "Especially through a closed door. I'm sure you'll give an accurate description of what went on here."

His words caused Tami to flinch. Doubt crept into her face. "You may be the expert, but I know when something's hinky."

"Hinky? Is that going to be your professional description of our session today?"

Tami's face grew red. She turned to Ellen. "Would you like to stay or go?"

Ellen eyes focused on the doctor's as she thought about her options. He dropped his gaze and glanced at his watch. "We still have, um, a half-hour, if Ellen would like to continue..."

Ellen thought about it. She wanted nothing more than to get out of here and never return. She now knew she had been used and why. But she didn't think she could leave without confronting the doctor.

"I'd like to stay a few more minutes," she finally said. "I'll be all right."

Tami's eyes narrowed. She turned her suspicious gaze to Dr. Butler. "Are you sure?" she said, clearly still talking to Ellen.

"I'm sure. I won't be long."

Tami waited another beat, then nodded and moved toward the door. She paused there, one hand on it, then turned and said softly, "Be careful, doc." She left, shutting the door quietly behind her.

For a few seconds, neither the doctor nor Ellen spoke. Each seemed to be waiting for the other one. Finally, Dr. Butler, nervously rubbing his hands together, said, "I hope my, uh, treatment didn't upset you too much."

"You bastard!" Ellen pitched her voice low, but her anger was clear. "That wasn't therapy and you know it. That was a debt being repaid. What was it for—drugs or gambling?"

"Uh, it wasn't like that..."

"Bullshit!" For the first time in months, Ellen felt her anger return. Her mind was no longer occupied with sex and submission. "Those thugs had something over you and if you don't tell me right now, I'm going to tell Officer Reynolds everything!"

"Do you think she'd believe you?"

Ellen scoffed. "You saw her face. She's very suspicious. I'm sure, if I went downtown and looked at mugshots, I'd be able to identify 'Barney,' 'George' and 'Ralph,' even if those aren't their real names."

Dr. Butler opened his mouth, then closed it. He began to worry the edge of his bottom lip as he thought things through. Finally, he held up his hands. "Okay, okay, don't do that." He grimaced. "I owed him for a bet I made."

"He's your bookie?" She shook her head and turned away.

"Ellen, please understand, I was desperate! They were going to ruin me!"

"You fail to realize, doctor, that I could ruin you too." Just like that, the tables had turned. Ellen was now the one with the power. The power to destroy.

Butler stared at her. "But, you did such things for Sawyer, you never threatened to ruin him."

She laughed out loud. "There is a world of difference between you and him. I'm surprised you thought you could get away with it."

His face twisted, as if in pain. "Ellen, when you came to me, your mind was very confused. You seemed consumed by sex—and by Jack Sawyer. You seemed to under his spell despite all he's done to you. You are a classic submissive personality. I...I thought maybe you would go along if I displayed similar dominate personality traits. You'd automatically obey, just as you've been doing for him. It was just going to be for this one time..."

Ellen just shook her head. There wasn't any way to explain herself to him. Much of what he said was true—except for the part about mindlessly obeying any dominant personality.

The doctor rushed on, trying to sway her. "But look at you! You've bounced back! You're probably much more like you were before Jack caught you embezzling!" He rose to his feet and came toward her, beseechingly. "You've become a stronger woman already. Doesn't that count for something?"

Ellen stared at him for a long moment. He was right—and he was wrong. The near-rape proved one thing to Ellen: that she only wanted to be a slut under the right set of circumstances and only for the right "master." And Dr. Butler wasn't him.

She moved toward the door. "I think we're through here, doctor. If you want me to keep quiet about what went on here, I want you to do whatever you can to weaken Franklin's case against Jack."

"What? Why would you want to do that?"

"Because I'm responsible for his predicament. And you know it. I hope he gets off."

Chapter 12

El felt out of sorts back at the apartment. Used and abused. Tami picked up on it right away.

"Hey, what's wrong? You okay?"

"Yeah," El said at once, not wanting to share her experience with the creepy Dr. Butler. She wished Jack were around to comfort her. "Just a little tired."

"Here, sit down. Let me rub your shoulders. You look tense."

El sat on a kitchen chair. She made no objection as Tami moved behind her and began to massage her shoulders, easing the tense muscles there. It felt nice, for a change, to have someone wait on her. She'd been so focused on everyone else's pleasure, she rarely had time for her own. Of course, she had brought that on herself, she knew. She had to pay the piper.

She groaned, low in her throat, as Tami's fingers dug in. Her tight muscles gave way and a warmth spread throughout her chest.

"Wait," Tami said. "Let me get some cream. Don't move."

El sat, her eyes closed, until the officer returned. She leaned over El's shoulder and told her to take off her top. El obeyed. She had put her bra back on before she had left the doctor's office, so she didn't feel exposed. But she wished she could take it off, but she had to wait for Tami to give her permission.

Tami surprised her by unsnapping the back without telling her. "Here, let me get rid of this. I don't want your bra straps to get in the way."

El let the bra fall away and leaned forward slightly so Tami could apply the lotion to her shoulders and upper back. Then the policewoman began to knead her flesh once again, drawing moans of pleasure from El. For several long minutes she expertly dug away El's tension until all her troubles seemed to melt away.

Tami's hands pulled away for a moment and El thought she was done. But a few seconds later, the hands returned and she was grateful. Then, suddenly, El felt something strange on her shoulder blades. It couldn't be her hands—they were still on her shoulders. They felt like fingers... She realized what they were with a start—nipples!

She half turned to see Tami had removed her top and bra and was rubbing her nipples lightly against her back. She started to speak, but Tami said, "Shhhh. It's okay. Just relax." And she did. It was easy to obey when she was receiving such pleasure. She didn't mind when the nipples returned, pressing harder this time, rubbing back and forth across her back. Her own nipples grew hard and she imagined them rubbing together.

Tami leaned in and nuzzled El's cheek. El was flattered and a little surprised. Wasn't she supposed to be protecting her? What would the ADA think?

"Tami," she began.

"Shhh," the officer said again. "You know you like this. Don't worry—this will be our little secret, okay?"

El nodded her head slightly. It did feel very good. And she'd made love to several women as part of her duties. But they had all been demanding, selfish. Tami was being so nice to her. It couldn't hurt to be nice in return, could it?

So she didn't object when Tami came around and sat on her lap, legs on either side, so they could press their breasts together. Tami kept massaging her shoulders from the front, but soon her hands moved down to touch her breasts. God, it felt good! It had been months since someone had been this gentle with her.

El felt a little shudder of heat, like a tiny orgasm, that flowed from her nipples to her pussy. She knew she was getting wet and got even wetter when Tami leaned in and nuzzled her cheek next to hers.

"You are so beautiful, you know that?" Tami whispered in her ear.

El didn't know what to say. So she brought her hands up to touch Tami's breasts. The woman's nipples were hard points, just like hers.

Tami pulled away and stood up. "Come on. I can't give you a proper backrub unless you're lying down."

El knew a lot more than that would happen and the thought excited her. She knew this wouldn't be a one-way session, where she gave all the pleasure. They went into the bedroom and Tami pulled down the covers. El started to get in, but Tami stopped her.

"No, you don't need these," she said, unzipping her skirt and letting it fall to the ground. Her hands returned to remove her panties. El just stood there, not objecting at all as she was stripped naked.

"What about you?"

Tami nodded and let the rest of her clothes fall away. It was the first time El had seen the woman naked. She had a firm body, a little thicker than El's, no doubt due to the exercise a police officer gets on the job. Her nipples were hard, her breasts firm. El glanced down to see the furry mound covering her pussy and wished it were trimmed, like hers.

Tami seemed to read her thoughts. "What? Too hairy?"

"No, it's fine. Really."

"You're just being nice. I know I've let it go. You don't have to worry about such things when you rarely date anyone."

"Why not?" El thought an attractive woman like Tami would have plenty of attention.

"Because I don't want to date cops—too close to home and they make lousy husbands. And I don't get to meet many 'regular people.' So I just don't do anything."

"I'm sorry to hear that. You're a very attractive woman." She paused. "Are you gay?"

Tami laughed. "Well, I'm standing here naked with another naked woman, about to give her a backrub and who knows what else. So I guess you'd have to say I'm at least bi. I hope you're okay with this. If you're not, speak up now."

El smiled. No one had ever asked her what she thought before. "I'm okay with it. You're so nice."

Tami made El lie face down and used more lotion to massage her back, moving down to the golden globes of her ass. El laid perfectly still, every muscle loose, as Tami worked on her. When she reached her upper thighs, El felt another little shiver go through her and her legs came apart. Her pussy leaked.

Tami pulled El's legs apart as she worked on her thighs, her hands tantalizingly close to her pussy. El made a soft noise in her throat that essentially said, "Go ahead," and Tami allowed one finger to run up along the slit. It was immediately covered in wetness. El's legs fell apart a little more. Now two of Tami's fingers rubbed along the slit and El shuddered again.

El expected the woman would rub her to a quick orgasm, but Tami surprised her by moving away from her hot core and began rubbing her thighs, then her calves. El was in heaven, being stimulated far beyond anything she had felt in the last several months. Only when she was being fucked by Jack had she experienced this level of arousal.

Tami rubbed her feet now, using the lotion to sooth her tender flesh. El felt like she was floating away. Then her feet were dropped back on the bed and El waited for Tami's fingers to return to her wet slit. *Please,* she thought. *Please.*

The fingers didn't return. Finally, El looked up over her shoulder to see Tami grinning at her. "What?"

"I want some too. If I let you come, you'll be useless."

El laughed. "You're right. I'd be a puddle of goo and probably fall asleep. What do you want me to do?"

Tami cocked her head to the side. "Everything," she whispered.

El turned over and opened her arms. Tami fell into her embrace.

Chapter 13

Ellen came into Moose's office and shut the door behind her, leaving Tami out in the hallway, as usual. She stood up tall as she could, straightened her shoulders and smiled at her attorney.

"Wow," Betty Montrose said at once. "You look ... different. More assured. That Dr. Butler must be doing you some good."

Ellen nearly snorted with derision. She moved to the desk and sat down in one of the two empty chairs in front. She took a deep breath. "I want you to tell the DA that I'm not going to testify against Jack."

"What?! What are you talking about?" She stood up, her eyes wide. "We have a deal!"

"I know. If she wants to file charges against me for the embezzlement, she can go ahead. Meanwhile, I want you to contact Jack's attorney and tell him I'll testify for the defense."

Moose shook her head. "I don't get it. Why would you do that?"

"Because Jack isn't to blame for what happened, not really. It was me."

"You're nuts if you think they're going to drop the charges."

Ellen shrugged. "Then we'll go to trial. I don't think the jury will convict him, do you?"

"I'm more worried about you. You could get fifteen years, if convicted."

"Maybe. But I don't think it will come to that."

"Why not?"

"Because we'll introduce evidence that the DA's psychiatrist used his treatment as an excuse to have sex with the troubled sex addict in the case."

Moose's jaw dropped and she sank back into her chair. "You're kidding."

"Nope."

"How did that happen?"

Ellen laughed. "I think that's obvious. I seemed to be the perfect victim. I'm a natural submissive, you know."

"But–" Betty shook her head. "Wait. Let's go back. You say Sawyer's not to blame? After what he did to you?"

"Let's just say, I've found out a lot about myself in the last few weeks. I figured out why I stayed with Jack, why I allowed him to control me."

"And why is that?"

"Because I needed it. I can't explain it any better than that."

Betty leaned back in her chair. "You needed it? How could you?"

"Some women are just..." she shrugged. "...that way. Jack allowed me to uncover that part of me."

"You sound as if you love the bastard."

"I do, in my own crazy way. But I wouldn't expect you to understand it."

"What will you do, if Franklin goes along with this? I mean, afterwards? Surely you wouldn't go back to Sawyer and pick up where you left off."

Ellen shook her head. "I'm not that naïve. I think that chapter is over."

Betty didn't speak for several seconds. Finally, she let out a sigh. "Okay, I'll make the proposal. But Franklin's probably not going to budge unless she hears about Butler. That okay with you?"

"Sure. I hope the bastard loses his license."

"If she's forced to drop this case, she'll be coming after you, you know."

"That's all right. If it comes to that, let her." Ellen kept her eyes steady on hers so she'd know she meant it. "But I have the feeling Jack won't want to testify."

Moose nodded. "Okay. I'll go see her."

Ellen got up and paused at the door. "One more thing."

"Yeah?"

"I want my jewelry back." She left, enjoying Betty's open-mouthed expression.

Tami fell in behind her as she headed toward the elevator. "What's up? You okay? You seem distracted."

"I'm fine, Tami. Let's go back to the hotel."

The next morning, Betty walked into Diane's office and sat down across from the ADA, her face smug, her eyes shining.

"So what's so damned important? I've got a trial to prepare for. We open in two weeks."

"I've come to tell you that Ellen has decided not to testify against Sawyer."

"What?" Diane was incredulous.

"In fact, we'd recommend that you drop the charges against Sawyer. Tell the press the evidence didn't stand up."

Diane jumped to her feet. "Are you nuts! He's a sexual deviant! We're not going to let him off! Besides, the press would have a general coronary." Her eyes narrowed. "Why wouldn't she testify? If there's no trial, she's up for an embezzlement charge."

"I know that. I'd prefer that you let that go as well."

Diane shook her head. "You must be smoking something. It's never going to happen."

"If you go ahead with this, I have evidence that will make your office look ridiculous. You'll be the laughing stock of the town. Think you could get a conviction then?"

"What? What have you got?"

"Seems your shrink decided to take advantage of my very confused and sexually troubled client. Not only did he have sex with her in his office, but he attempted to bring in other men to fuck her." She used the crude word on purpose and saw that it had the effect she'd sought.

The blood drained from Diane's face. Two red spots appeared on her cheeks. "Nooo," she whispered.

"Yes. And I can prove it—if I'm forced to. The officer heard the commotion and can swear that she heard someone besides the doctor and Ellen in the room. And I'm sure we can find the gentlemen in question—one of them was the doctor's bookie."

Diane dropped her head down and rubbed her forehead with one hand. "Jesus."

Betty waited until Diane recovered. She actually felt sorry for the tough ADA. She knew this would be a big career setback for her.

When Diane could gather her thoughts, she asked, "Even if this was all true, what does it have to do with Ellen's testimony? Why wouldn't she want to see Sawyer get what's coming to him?"

"Ellen feels partially responsible for what happened with Jack. She, uh, was not totally acting out of duress."

"So you're saying, she liked it?"

Betty shrugged. "Something like that. She doesn't want Jack prosecuted and I don't want my client to face jail for theft. Besides, I doubt Jack would testify anyway. He's been paid in full."

"Crimes have been committed." Diane was just stalling. She tried to come up with some way out. She was in a no-win situation and she hated it. At least if she knew what she was up against, she'd have a chance to save face. "We'd be hard-pressed to try to explain this away. I don't even have any idea what I would tell my boss."

"Well, you can give him Butler. That might help."

Diane nodded dully. They both knew it was a small consolation prize, but it was all she had.

Chapter 14

"She did *what?*"

"It's true," Sam said. "El's attorney asked Franklin to drop the charges against you. Said she had some blockbuster she was going to reveal at trial if she didn't. Diane is ready to spit fire she's so mad."

"What does El have?"

They were meeting in Sam's office on a sunny day in September. The trial, which had consumed the two men for weeks, now suddenly seemed in doubt. Sam slid open the middle drawer of his desk and leaned back, putting his number eleven shoes up on the improvised footrest.

"I don't know. Moose won't say, of course. You have any idea?"

Jack shook his head. "No." He stared off into space. "I'm surprised. I never thought El would go out of her way to save me. I guess I was wrong."

"Whatever you have between you, I can't understand, but she clearly has feelings for you."

"Yeah, I guess so. I'm a little surprised."

"My guess is, you have some feelings for her, too."

"Yeah. I do. Who wouldn't? She's a good-looking woman. But I was blinded by my rage at first. Mostly, I liked seeing her in a subservient position, doing my bidding."

Jack rubbed his chin and scowled. "Do you know what the shrink said about her?"

"Diane hasn't given me the report yet. She said something about getting a new shrink. I don't know the full story over there yet. Of course, if the charges are dropped, it's moot anyway." Sam put his feet down with a clunk and leaned over the desktop blotter, a stubby finger pointed at Jack. "You know, this makes sense in a strange sort of way. Remember what I said to you a couple of weeks ago? That this trial titillated the populace, rather than repelled them?"

"Yeah? I'm not sure I follow."

"Well, maybe that's why the case is falling apart. Maybe it's not just El, but maybe Diane's hearing through the grapevine that people don't really want to see you in prison for doing something every red-blooded American male would love to do. Remember, you said it—and you were right—all we'd need is to have some good men impaneled and we'd wind up with a hung jury."

"Yeah, but if that happened, the DA would probably refile, don't you think?"

"Maybe. They're in a no-win situation no matter what happens. If they forge ahead with a trial, Moose will uncover her big secret and..." he shrugged. "...it might work, it might not. Knowing her, she's got something good. If it doesn't work, we still can appeal to the men on the jury to let you off. Then the DA faces the impossible choice of refilling and going through the whole thing all over again, or dropping the charges and looking like they can't stop crime in the city."

"What do you think they'll do?"

"Oh, I expect a phone call, any minute now." He gave a broad grin. "They're going to offer a plea bargain."

"What kind of plea bargain?"

"The best kind. They know you'll reject anything that involves prison, right? So they have to offer you a misdemeanor deal. Maybe sexual imposition. Give you a fine and some probation."

"You think that will be enough for Franklin to save face?"

Sam laughed. "No, but that's her problem. It's the best she can do."

Jack drove back to the factory, his mind swirling with possibilities. He was confused by El's actions. He had to admit that he missed her. He just hadn't known, up until this moment, that she missed him as well. How could that be? He hardly ever fucked her anymore. He made her have sex with other men and parade about the shop half-naked. She was a sex object, that was all. Wasn't she? *And yet, she went to bat for me. She doesn't want to testify. She must feel she shares the blame for what happened to her.*

His mind drifted back to the beginning of their unusual relationship, back when he had first hired her. There had been other candidates—men—who were more qualified. Ellen was certainly competent, but he had to admit, there was something more. He had been attracted to her. He liked the idea of having her around. It wasn't consciously sexual—she was married, after all. Yet there was some flirting there. He had been very careful, of course, not to tease her if she didn't respond. But she did respond. She had enjoyed the attention. They went no further than some gentle, verbal banter.

Yes, Jack came to learn that Ellen's marriage wasn't perfect. Far from it, in fact. He made sure not to interfere or to tempt her. Whenever the subject of her marriage to Bill came up, he had remained silent. Perhaps she was sounding him out, trying to see how he might react if she were single again. Was she interested in him as well? If so, why embezzle from someone you supposedly cared about?

No, there was something else going on, something he clearly didn't understand. She sabotaged her own career— for what? A chance to make Jack furious at her? A chance to ruin her marriage? And her reputation? To go to prison?

Was it all because El was driven to be a subservient sex slave? It seemed impossible.

He pulled into the parking lot. There seemed to be more media trucks today. Did they get word of the deal or is it just because the trial's about to open?

He got out of the car and was immediately surrounded by the gaggle of reporters. Despite the crush, he felt more in control now than he had over the last six weeks. Questions flew at him.

"Jack! What's your strategy for the trial?"

"Have you talked to Ellen lately?"

"What's happening to your business as a result of all this?"

He smiled and shook his head. "Come on, guys, you know I can't talk about it."

A short, intense reporter from the local paper pushed forward and said in a low voice, "Is it true that the case is falling apart? That the DA is backtracking?"

Jack couldn't disguise his startled expression. "Where— where did you hear that?"

The reporter jumped in. "So it's true? What's happening? Can you tell us?"

The other journalists stopped and stared at the dark-haired man. Then they started in on him, as if he were the celebrity.

"Whattya got, Steve?"

"Yeah, what's this about? Where did you hear this from?"

Steve shook his head at the crowd. "Forget it. You guys need to do your own work." He turned back to Jack. "Come on, Mr. Sawyer, I know you've heard something."

"I can only say that my attorney and I are busy preparing for the trial, which we fully expect to open next Monday.

If the DA has something different to say, you should ask Franklin."

He pushed through the group and entered the building. He spotted Gloria in the hall and tried not to grimace. With the case in doubt, he'd soon be free to do as he pleased. Gloria was not long for this place.

She spotted him almost at the same time and scurried away, as if he might come after her with a tire iron. That's twice that female employees have turned on him, he mused. He got revenge on one by turning her into a sex slave and he will get revenge on the other by firing her. He went into his office.

The call came an hour later. He had been looking over the projections and was in a very bad mood, seeing how Sawyer Manufacturing had lost fully thirty-one percent of last year's business. He had already laid off ten employees, but it appeared he'd have to lay off at least ten more to keep the finances on an even keel. The business was far less fun to manage than it had been last year.

When the phone rang, he half-expected it to be another customer, canceling another order. Instead, he heard the voice of his attorney on the line.

"Jack? Great news! Franklin just called. They're folding up like a cheap tent in a windstorm. She's ready to offer you a reduced charge with probation and a two-thousand dollar fine."

"What's the charge?"

"Second degree sexual imposition. Normally, it carries a six- to nine-month prison term, but she's agreed to waive that. Probation would be for two years. It's a great deal, Jack."

Jack almost felt disappointed. He had been burning with curiosity about what blockbuster Ellen would have revealed at trial. Now he might never know. Plus, he'd have a record, even if it was only a misdemeanor. On the positive side, it might allow him to save his business.

"You think I should take it?"

"Take it? Of course you're going to take it! You understand that under the original charges, you faced twenty years?"

"I know. Okay, it sounds good." He paused. "But—what happens to Ellen?"

"Ellen? Oh, they dropped the embezzlement charges against her as well. She's free to go. I suppose she'll leave town, try to live this down. I mean, wouldn't you?"

"Yeah." Jack felt a pang deep inside and wondered if he'd ever get to see her again.

"You don't sound thrilled."

"Oh, I am," Jack recovered quickly. "It's just, you know, all so sudden. I'm still processing it."

"Well, get over it. Diane's going to give a press conference in an hour to announce the deal. I have to call her back and give her our decision."

"Yeah, go ahead. I'll take it."

Jack stayed in his office for the next hour, trying to concentrate on his work. He turned the TV on and kept the sound down so he wouldn't miss the announcement. When it came, it all seemed so surreal, as if they were talking about someone else.

Diane Franklin stood up before the huge crowd of reporters and announced the plea bargain. She tried to put a positive spin on things, but the reporters weren't buying it. They were going to be deprived of the best trial in a decade and they demanded to know why. Diane fielded the questions as best she could, but she was clearly flustered and frustrated. When she left the podium, it was more of an escape from the brutal questioning than a dignified retreat.

Jack turned the sound down when the reporter faced the camera to give her summary. He didn't want to hear any more. He knew the crowd outside would grow and he'd have to fight his way through it. He thought about where he might go from here. Should he stick it out and be the butt of jokes in the community for the next decade? Or should he sell out, buy a sailboat and disappear? He smiled ruefully. As pleasing as that idea sounded, he knew he had to stick around for his probationary period. After that, he could run away, if he was so inclined.

The phone rang. He picked up, expecting Sam. "Jack?" The soft, lilting voice made his heart pound.

"El ... Ellen?" He couldn't believe it.

"Yes, it's me."

"Does your attorney know you're calling?"

"No, she'd have a fit, I'm sure." She breathed lightly into the phone and Jack could picture her perfectly in his mind. "I assume you saw the press conference."

"Yes, yes I did. And I understand you helped destroy the DA's case against me. I think I owe you a thanks—and an apology."

"An apology? For what?"

"For what? For, you know, making you do all those things."

"Jack, I think we should talk. Can we meet somewhere, sometime?"

"Why, sure. I have to check with Sam—"

"No, don't. I mean, please don't. The attorneys will tell us it's a horrible idea."

"Well, sure. I mean, the criminal part of the case is over, but I have been convicted, so I expect you'll be suing me next."

She spoke firmly. "I won't sue you, Jack."

He was taken aback. "Why not? I probably would, if I were you."

"Jack, in the last six months, how much have I earned, you know, according to our little deal?"

Jack called up the spreadsheet on his computer and said, "Looks like a little more than one hundred thousand."

"And you've said that's mine, right?"

"Right. I won't cheat you, Ellen."

"I know, Jack. If you sent that over to my attorney, that would satisfy me as far as any lawsuit goes. I'll have her draw up some paperwork."

Jack was stunned. "Well, sure. Thanks."

There was an awkward pause. Then she said, "I know you've got a lot to think about and to do in the next week or so. Why don't I call you back, here, later on? If you want to talk, we can meet. If you don't, we won't."

"Uh, okay. Sure." Jack didn't want to tell her he missed her. That he thought about her all the time.

Chapter 15

"I feel like a secret agent," Jack said as he slipped off his raincoat and slid into the darkened booth across from Ellen. He no longer thought of her as "El"—that name and what it represented had been burned out of him during the weeks of intense publicity following his arrest. They were meeting at Yancy's, a restaurant thirty miles outside of town. Both had taken care to shake off anyone who might be following them, but it was mere precaution.

In the two weeks following the press conference, life for Jack had returned to a near-semblance of normalcy. The press had disappeared from his parking lot and moved on to a new scandal—a local psychiatrist was being investigated for having sex with a nameless patient. Jack's customers had begun to drift back, although every man expressed disappointment that El was no longer available. Jack believed many felt guilty for publicly yanking their business when privately they had enjoyed El's charms.

"Hi, Jack."

The sound of his first name, coming from Ellen, startled him. She had called him "Mr. Sawyer" for months, years even, and now she seemed to have regained her old CFO persona.

"Can I buy you a drink?" Jack looked around for the waiter.

"I'm all right," Ellen said, holding up her glass of white wine. "I got here a little early."

The waiter approached. "I'll have a martini, on the rocks," he told him. The waiter vanished.

"This is a surprise, I have to admit. I figured you'd be really angry at me."

"Yes, I should be, shouldn't I? But I'm not. Do you have any idea why?"

"Uh, no, not really." Jack thought maybe Ellen was so caught up with remorse over the embezzlement that being his sex slave made sense somehow, but that seemed a weak reason following his arrest.

The waiter returned to place a cold martini in front of Jack. It gave Ellen time to take a deep breath.

"Well..."

Jack took a sip of his drink and waited.

"I'm not sure how this is going to sound to you."

"Try me. I promise to keep an open mind."

"OK." Her dark eyes fastened on Jack's. "You probably know that you couldn't have gotten me to do those things if... well, if I didn't agree to them. I mean, I could've chosen prison. Or I could've had you arrested after a short time and maybe even gotten a lighter sentence myself."

"As I recall, prison terrified you."

"Yes, yes it did. But there was more going on."

Jack raised an eyebrow but didn't speak. He knew this to be true, but he'd never fully been able to explain it. He hoped Ellen could.

Ellen blushed. "I know this sounds strange, out in the light of day to be saying this, but... Jack, I needed to become your... um, slut." She turned an even brighter shade of red and looked away.

"Oh, please don't be embarrassed. I suspected something like that."

"It was actually my crooked shrink who got me to see the light. He helped me to understand why I'm so easily used."

"Listen, I'm sorry about—"

"No, don't be. It showed me, um, my proclivities. But only for the right man."

Jack raised both eyebrows. He put his drink back on the table, his eyes never leaving Ellen's.

Ellen put her palms out. "Jack, I don't expect anything to come of this. I just thought you should know. I, uh, liked being your... well, under your control. It satisfied some deep inner desire I must've had since childhood or something." She laughed lightly. "I don't pretend to know exactly why I'm this way. It probably has something to do with my father, or some of my early boyfriends." She didn't explain further and although Jack was curious, he decided not to press it. "My shrink even suggested that I subconsciously sabotaged my marriage and my job, in order to start my life over in a different way. I'm not sure I can recommend going about it the way I did, but..."

"So you don't hate me?"

"No, Jack. Do you hate me?"

"No! Of course not."

"I did embezzle quite a bit of money from you."

"Yes." He seemed embarrassed. "I was paid in full. The anger's gone."

"Good." Ellen took another sip of her drink. "You showed me a side of myself that's both terrifying and exciting. I lived the life I guess I always wanted to. To be a complete sex object, to be desired by many men, to be told what to do, without thinking about it." She shook her head. "I think I've almost gotten it out of my system. Almost."

"So you kind of miss it?" Jack couldn't believe what he was hearing.

"Well, if you think I'd like to report to work Monday as your company slave, no. I don't miss it that much. But

I do miss part of it. The abandonment of all responsibility. Awaiting your orders. Doing your bidding. It's somehow quite freeing, you know."

Jack shook his head. "No, I don't know." He chose his next words carefully. "So, what are you going to do now? For a job, I mean?"

"I don't know. If I had my way, I'd be a kept woman to some rich man. Just lie about the pool all day and eat bon-bons."

"And be his, um, slut?"

Ellen tipped her head. "That's the sixty-four-thousand-dollar question, isn't it? For most men, no, I don't think so. But for the right man, yes, I would."

Jack was stunned, but he covered it well. "How do you go about finding the right man?" He really wanted to ask, *Would you want to stay with me?*

"I don't. I guess I just have to hope he finds me." Her eyes locked on to his.

"No you don't." Now it was his turn to blush. "I mean, you don't have to find him. You've already found him."

"Oh, Jack, that's nice to hear and all, but I think we have too much baggage between us, don't you?"

"Maybe. All I know is, I've missed you these past few months. I was almost looking forward to the trial so I could see you again. How strange is that?"

She smiled and the room seemed to brighten. "I missed you too, Jack."

"Really? I figured you'd be gleefully planning your testimony, plotting your revenge."

"No, even from the start, when Franklin made me that offer I couldn't refuse, I didn't want to go through with it. Consciously, I was appalled by my behavior, but subconsciously, I knew I had myself to blame. I didn't want to see you go to prison any more than me."

Jack took another sip and finally asked the question that had been on his mind since his attorney had told him the case was imploding. "So, tell me, Ellen, what was the big secret that caused the D.A. to back down?"

She smiled again. "Maybe that should be my little secret."

He reached across the table and touched her forearm. He felt a sudden rush of emotion, almost like electric sparks. "I could always command you to tell me."

She placed her free hand on top of his. "Well, if you put it that way, I guess I'll have to." She paused for effect. "You know that when I was taken from your factory, I was still a bit, um, addled. I had sex on the brain, thanks to you and that damn jewelry. People picked up on that. The shrink the DA hired to evaluate me screwed me instead. I was so eager to please and lost that I substituted them for you, I guess. Someone told me to do something and I did it."

"So that's the shrink I've been reading about! You were the patient? And you threatened to testify to that in court?" Jack couldn't believe it.

"Yes."

Jack sat back, stunned. His martini sat forgotten on the table. "Now I understand things better. About why the cases fell apart, I mean."

"The DA wanted to try me for the embezzlement, but I told my attorney that I doubted you'd testify against me. Was I right?"

He nodded. "You bet. I couldn't've gone through with it."

They each sipped their drinks, thinking about their close calls.

Jack asked suddenly, "Do you have a place to stay?"

"Since the trial was dismissed, I've been living at the

hotel. Tami—the officer—is gone, but the management checks on me. My attorney expects my finances will be straightened out soon."

"Yes. I sent over a check to your lawyer last week. I'm surprised you haven't gotten it by now."

"Oh, I guess there are a lot of expenses they have to take out." She sighed. "They're treating me like a child, you know. Like I don't have a brain in my head."

"Just make sure no one steals from you. You should have enough to live on for a while before you have to worry about working."

"Yeah. Thanks for that, Jack."

"Hell, you earned it." Jack noticed that her hand was still resting on his and he thought about all the anger he had directed her way over the last two years. All the pain he had put her through. And yet, she's still here, forgiving him.

"I'm not sure I can let you go," he said, blurting out the truth.

"I'm not I'm sure I'm the submissive little slut I was before," she responded and there it was. If they were to get together, it would have to be on her terms.

"You got it all out of your system?"

She tipped her head. "Mostly."

"But there's part of you that still needs it, right?"

"I don't know. I'm still processing all that."

Jack understood her reluctance to talk about her future. "What will you do next? Will you stick around?"

"Just until the check clears. Then, I don't know."

Jack gave her a half-grin. "You really have this all figured out, huh?"

She laughed. The sound was pleasing to his ears. "OK. I admit it—I'm a mess. I'm confused, I'm embarrassed and

I feel remorse. Right now, I think the best thing to do is to leave town and try to start again somewhere else."

"I'm sorry to hear that, but I understand." He shrugged. "I'd leave too, if I didn't have to stick around for this probation."

Silence descended over the pair. There seemed little else to say.

Finally, Jack finished off his drink and placed it carefully down in front of him. His eyes locked onto hers. "Will I ever see you again?"

"I don't know. I'm not trying to be coy, I just simply don't know what's going to happen next. I have people offering me book deals, guest spots on news shows—but I don't want to exploit myself for financial gain." She laughed. "How ironic is that?"

Half of Jack's face crinkled in response. "I'm really going to miss you, Ellen."

"And, I'm sure, in my own way, I'll miss you too."

They stood, suddenly awkward with each other.

"You know where to reach me, if you ever want to talk or drop me a line."

"I know."

"Well, 'bye."

"Goodbye, Jack." She reached up suddenly and kissed him on the cheek, then pulled back, tears in her eyes. Jack reached up and touched his skin and felt that same electricity there.

"Are you sure we want to do this?"

"I don't know. If it's a mistake, I'll know it, later."

He nodded. "I'll walk you out." He tossed a couple of bills on the table and followed her to the door. Outside, the sun had just dipped under the horizon, casting a red-orange glow across the sky. It seemed a magical moment.

He stood, shifting from foot to foot as Ellen unlocked her car. "Goodbye, again. Call me sometime." Her hands were on the door frame. He placed his hands over hers.

She looked into his eyes. "Goodbye, Jack." And she slipped her hands free and drove off. Jack watched her go, his heart sinking.

Chapter 16

The next two years passed slowly for Jack. Ellen, as she had planned, left town almost immediately and he hadn't heard from her since. He concentrated on rebuilding his business, but quickly found his heart wasn't in it. Nevertheless, he went through the motions, all the while secretly planning to sell the business as soon as his probation was up. With new clients replacing some of those who had bailed out, he figured the operation was worth about ten million, of which he owned seventy-five percent. After taxes and expenses, he'd probably clear six million. A nice bit of change—but would it be enough? What would he do? He'd been wrestling with that question for months.

Six months before he was completely free of the justice system, Jack put out feelers to his competitors and soon had two firm offers. One company offered twelve million, but they planned to simply take Jack's customers and close down the plant, making all the equipment in Mexico and China, where labor costs were far cheaper. He didn't want to do that to his employees, although he was realistic enough to know that the day would come. He accepted the second offer, for nine-point-five million, on the promise that they would keep the plant intact for at least two more years. It was the best deal he could make.

When he went to his probation officer for the last time, he was semi-rich and at loose ends. He shook the officer's hand and said he was leaving town.

"Where will you go?"

"I don't know," he said. "Somewhere away from here."

"A fresh start, eh? That's probably good. Just stay away from loose women." He tried to make a joke, but it made Jack instantly angry. He covered it well.

"Yeah. Well, gotta go." He left the office and walked to his car. He could've found Ellen—after all, she had been on his payroll, so he knew her Social Security number. Any private eye could've found her. But he had held off. She could've called him at any time. Clearly, she doesn't want to be found. He ought to be content to leave it alone.

He drove home. The house was up for sale and most of his furniture had already been sold or put into storage. He kept a bed, a couch, a television and a stereo. There was nothing to hold him here, yet he wasn't sure where he wanted to go.

When he pulled into the driveway, he was surprised to see a man standing on his porch. He got out warily, thinking it was a creditor or a salesman.

"Can I help you?" he asked, a bit sharply.

"Are you Jack Sawyer?"

His heart sank. A process server, he imagined. "Yes, yes I am."

The man approached with an envelope. "This is for you. Would you sign here?"

Jack looked at the envelope, but it had no return address. He signed hurriedly, his curiosity burning. The man thanked him and left. Jack stood on the porch, the letter heavy in his hands. He waited until the man drove away, then, with hands shaking, opened it.

Dear Jack,
I know I should've written before now. I always meant to, but something stopped me. I thought perhaps it would be best if I just disappeared and let you live your life. I

would find somebody else and life would go on as it should. But I've kept in touch with my attorney, Betty Montrose, and she informed me that you were selling the business and leaving town yourself. She also said you have remained single. I felt I had to write and tell you what's going on in my life.

I needed this two years, Jack. I needed to figure out who I was and what I wanted. I went about as far away as I could, even began using my middle name and tried to start again. As Maria Sanchez, I'm anonymous, which is just the way I wanted it. No one here knows my past. I'm working part-time and being very frugal with the money I "earned" from you.

But it's not working for me. Something is missing. Believe it or not, I miss you. I miss what we had, even though by all rights I shouldn't. I guess it's true what Dr. Butler said—that I can't escape who I am. If you read this and feel the same loss I do, then come visit me, once you sell your business. If you'd rather put the past behind you, then just tear up this letter and forget you received it.

Yours,
Ellen Maria Sanchez

Jack stared at the address printed at the bottom. She was more than a thousand miles away, but it didn't matter. His entire world shifted from despair and depression to elation. Now his life had direction. He couldn't predict what would happen, but at least he had a direction.

He started packing that night.

Jack stopped by the realtor's office two days later and told his agent the house was completely empty now; everything was in storage. He gave him a cellphone number where he could be reached and said he'd write when he had a more permanent address.

He hit the road going south and drove non-stop for the next few hours. When he grew tired, he stopped at a motel and went to sleep in minutes. The next morning, he was at it again.

It took him three days to reach her. He arrived in the late afternoon, squinting through the windshield at the house numbers. Ellen—now Maria—lived in a modest rented house in a working class neighborhood. She *had* been frugal, he mused, as he pulled into her driveway.

Nervously, he rang the bell. He heard footsteps and for a moment he had a sudden urge to flee. He didn't know what to expect. Would she be as distant as she had been during their last meeting? Would she be glad to see him? Would she throw herself into his arms?

The door opened. Maria stood there, smiling, wearing a light blue top and shorts. There was a glow about her, as if she had just come back from a jog. Jack tried not to stare. She had cut her hair, but otherwise looked very much as she had two years ago.

"Hello, Jack. I wondered if I would see you." She stepped back and allowed him to enter. She seemed tentative and Jack felt just as awkward. He followed her inside and they stood in the living room, more like strangers than old lovers.

Jack broke the ice first by being honest. "I'm glad you finally wrote to me. I'd just about given up hope. I figured you'd want to be left alone."

Ellen smiled and some of the warmth flowed back into the room. "I did, for many months. I tried to deny everything. Pretend it didn't happen. It helped to change my name, my hairstyle and my profession."

"You look great. I like your hair."

"Thanks." She seemed embarrassed at the compliment. "Can I get you a drink?"

He nodded and she went into the kitchen to fix them. He followed her and was pleased to see her making martinis—she had remembered his drink. She handed him one and he took a sip. The gin was cold and soothed his throat.

They moved back into the living room and sat on a couch, separated by a few awkward inches. He tried to make conversation. "What are you doing now? For work?"

"Oh, I'm a hairdresser." She laughed when she saw Jack's expression. "I know, I should be doing more. But I only work three days a week, four hours a shift and it's relaxing. Just cut hair and gossip with the ladies. I don't have to think much."

Jack wanted to hold her, kiss her, but he held off. She was so damn cute now, with her new haircut and bright attitude. She had come a long way since she had blindly obeyed him. And yet, there was something there. He could feel his cock stir in his pants.

"Can I take you out to dinner?" he asked suddenly.

She smiled. "Sure. I'd like that."

He waited while she showered and changed. She came back wearing a simple cotton print dress that zipped up the back and came down to her ankles. It gave no hint of the treasures within. Yet all Jack had to do was close his eyes and he could see her naked body again.

They went to a Mexican restaurant that Maria recommended. Jack had some trouble thinking of her as Maria. She seemed different, to be sure, but there was a lot of Ellen in her.

After the waiter had taken their orders, Jack boldly put his hand over hers. "I've been hoping you would contact me."

"I debated it. At first, it just seemed like a really bad idea, but as time went on, I felt we had some unfinished business between us."

"I've felt the same way, Ellen—I mean, Maria."

She smiled at the gaffe. "Yeah, but for the life of me, I can't think of what that should be."

Jack laughed. "Me, either. I just feel drawn to you."

"Oh, maybe you're just drawn to the so-called perfect woman I was to you—you know, all tits and cunt, no brain. Ready to spread my legs for you at any time."

Her harsh words shocked him, and excited him at the same time. "Yeah, right." He shook his head. "I guess it's true—all men are pigs."

"Yeah. But we women keep putting up with you guys." She spoke the truth, he knew, but there was a lilt to her voice.

"Maybe it's our rugged charm."

"Yeah. That must be it." She smiled again, lighting up the room.

The waiter came with the hot plates and for a few minutes, they ate, almost grateful for the silence. Jack worried he might say something stupid, something that would ruin everything. He tried to figure out what lay ahead and he couldn't. His id wanted El back, just like she once was. His ego knew better—she was different now, more self-assured. And yet he couldn't quite let go of the past. *God, listen to me*, he thought. *I'm a shallow, self-absorbed, sexist pig, just as she thinks I am. Just by thinking like this, I'm ruining everything.*

"What did you expect, from writing me?" He blurted and immediately wondered if he had been too bold.

She put down her fork and studied him, chewing nervously on her lower lip. Jack again resisted the urge to kiss it. "I don't have any expectations, if that's what you're worried about."

"I'm not worried." Suddenly, he grew tired of the banter. He decided to lay his cards on the table. "All right. Here it is: I think I want to be around you. At least for a while. Would that be all right with you?"

"You want to stay here? In town?"

"I want more than that. I want to stay with you. Or have you stay with me." He shook his head, knowing immediately it was the wrong thing to say.

"No, it's too early for that." She took another bite and swallowed carefully. "Let's take it slow, okay? I am flattered that you'd like to stick around. I thought maybe we'd just have a visit, then you'd be on your way."

"I'm at loose ends. I sold the business, you know."

"That went through? Moose said you'd been working on it. Is that what you really wanted?"

"Yes. It wasn't fun any more." He drank a sip of beer, thinking how it wasn't fun because she had no longer been there. "Besides, if I decide I want to be a big businessman again, I can always start another company."

She laughed and Jack remembered how he had liked that sound. "I'm sure this town could use an entrepreneur."

"Well, that's later. For now, I just plan to live the life of ease."

"Good for you. You deserve a break."

They finished their meal and Jack drove her back home. She opened the door and started to get out. He reached out and lightly clasped her forearm. "Is it too soon for me to come in?"

She hesitated. Then she said, "Just for a drink, okay?"

He nodded and got out. He cock was hard in his pants and he jerked at the belt to try to make it more comfortable.

He thought of all the times he could've made love to her and had not and wondered why he hadn't taken advantage of her more often. Was it because he didn't like the idea of sloppy seconds?

They went inside and Maria bustled about, turning on lights. She put on the radio, playing some soft jazz. "Martini?" He nodded. He wanted to grab her, crush her in his arms, kiss those pouty lips, and run his hands through her tousled hair. His erection became almost painful and he turned away, rather than see him.

But she did see him. She paused by the makeshift bar and carefully placed her glass on the counter. She came to him, her hand low. It touched his cock through his pants. He tried to turn away again, but she held him with her free hand on his upper arm. He allowed her to rub it, remembering all those times when she would touch him, suck him, and be naked for him.

He groaned softly, under his breath. Her hand went to the zipper and eased it down. His cock sprang out from his boxer shorts and into the soft palm of her hand. Her light, warm fingers enveloped the hardened shaft.

"It's just like I remembered it," she cooed.

"I thought you were just going to give me a drink and send me away."

"I meant to. I thought that's what I should do. But now, touching you, I'm thinking I was wrong." She caught his eye. "You feel it too."

"Yes." He wondered if she would ever be submissive again, or was that part of her past as well. He ached to relive those experiences, even as he felt shame to wish it so.

He leaned down and kissed her, sharing the spices from the meals they had eaten. She responded hungrily, her mouth open to his. Her hand never left his cock, moving up and down, tormenting him.

His hands went to the back of her dress and started to unzip it. He half expected her to say, No, Stop, but she didn't, so he eased her zipper down and allowed the dress to fall from her shoulders.

She wasn't wearing any underwear. Jack knew she had made a statement and he was glad, for he was on the same wavelength. Her breasts were just as he remembered them: proud and copper-colored. He glanced down and noticed the Sawyer logo was missing—she'd had it removed. He was glad—to still have it today would be obscene, not sexy.

He leaned down and hooked one arm behind her knees, then picked her up and carried her toward the bedroom. She giggled and hugged him. He put her carefully on the bed while he undressed.

Naked, he climbed over her. His hard cock danced over her thighs. "Wait," she said suddenly, putting a hand up against his chest.

He pulled back. "What? A condom?" he said, a little disappointed.

She smiled. "No, I just wanted to see if you'd wait."

He laughed and lay down on top of her. He kissed her and rubbed her nipples. He felt his cock touch between her legs and could feel the wetness there.

"What happened to your jewelry?"

"I didn't feel right, putting it on myself," she said simply.

He kissed her again and reached down between her legs to touch the core of her. Her slit was sopping wet and her clit a hard nubbin that strained toward his fingers. She groaned when he touched it.

"I think you've missed me," he said and pressed his cock into her about one inch. She shuddered and widened her legs for him. He teased her, moving his cock in and out in tiny thrusts until she cried out.

"Please!"

"Please, what?"

"Please ... sir," she said, teasingly and he rewarded her by plunging deep inside her. She gasped aloud and climaxed, holding his body tightly to hers. He gave her a few seconds to come down, then began to stroke. She came again ... and again—it was as if she had been saving up for months, years, even. His strokes increased and Maria climbed that mountain again, her mouth open, her eyes wide. "God," she whispered, "Oh, fuck me, fuck me."

He obliged and when he felt his seed ready to boil, he thrust hard into her and erupted, shooting his essence deep inside. They clung together like lost souls, loving this moment and each other.

Finally, Jack eased his softened cock out of her and lay beside her on the bed. "Wow," he said simply.

"Wow, indeed," she responded, resting her hand on his stomach.

"That was special. Very special."

"Yes, it was. Almost like old times."

He wondered about that "almost." Was something missing? He decided to change the subject. "I never did get my drink," he teased.

"You want it now?"

"Actually, yes, I do. But I'll get it," he said.

"What's this? The master to wait on the slave?"

"Yeah. Call it the new paradigm." He started to rise, but she grabbed his arm.

"No."

"What?"

"No. Please allow me."

Jack looked down at her, a wry smile on his lips. "It's just a drink. I'm not going to suddenly let you dom me."

"Good. Because you see…" She trailed off and Jack knew better than to break the moment. He waited. "I thought I was over it. You know, the submissiveness. I told you I had gotten it out of my system."

"I remember." He nodded, encouraging her to continue.

"But it's part of me. I know that now. The thing is, it's only part of me with you. Can you understand that?"

"Yes. That's why you haven't become someone else's girlfriend, right?"

"Right. I've dated. I've even had a few lovers in the last two years. But no doms. It didn't feel right."

"But it feels right with me?"

"Yes. So why is that, do you think?"

He shrugged and sat up. "Because we have some sort of connection, I guess. Something that each of us needed."

She nodded. "That's what I was thinking." She sat up and placed a hand on his cheek. "We should be angry at each other. We should want to be well rid of each other. Yet here we are, two years later, together again. I tried to go slow tonight, tell myself I didn't want to fuck you, but it was all I could think about."

"Me too. But I was afraid of rushing you, so I tried to be good."

"Oh, honey, you were good."

He laughed and pressed the hand against his cheek. "You weren't so bad yourself."

"So, bottom line—I want to go get you a drink. Don't feel weird about it, okay?"

"I won't. In fact, I think it's wonderful. I missed having you around and not just because you were good for business."

"But you didn't fuck me much, you know. You usually just handed me over to some other guys."

"I know. I was mixed up with anger and desire and the power of my domination over you, I suppose. I think I got as much enjoyment out of fucking you as knowing you had to fuck whomever I said to."

"Right. And you know what? I got just as much out of that as you did. Let's face it, I'm a slut at heart. I liked being at your mercy. Everything was out of my hands. And yet, that power in another man's hands could've been a disaster. In your hands, it just made me want to continue doing it forever."

"Yet you rebounded, after my arrest."

"Yes. There are two warring factions inside my head, the slut and the feminist. When I was with you, the slut loved it and the feminist was shocked by my behavior. Then afterwards, the feminist cheered and the slut slunk away, embarrassed. So I had to resolve it."

"And you have?"

Maria tipped her head. "As best I could, without having you around to talk to about it."

"So that's why you decided to write to me."

"Yes. I had to know. What I really wanted."

"I know it's too soon to tell, but—"

"No, it's not too soon. I knew it the moment you walked in. I just had to see if that's what you wanted."

"Yes, it's what I wanted too. Although I was sure you wouldn't. I mean, how could you, I thought. You were so thoroughly taken advantage of, I felt kind of like a real jerk, you know?"

She nodded. "I know. But from my point of view, I felt like a real low-class woman. A true slut. Among women, that's as low as you can go."

"But you're drawn to it."

"Just as you're drawn to having a slut around."

Jack scooted up so he could lean back against the headboard. "Slave, my darling, go fix me a drink," he voice was light, teasing. "And be quick about it or there will be punishment."

"Yes, master." She smiled and stood up, magnificent in her nudity. She started to turn.

"Wait." She paused, facing him, her breasts thrust out, her hips at a jaunty angle, the soft incurving line of her slit below. "I just want to look at you for a moment."

She stood there, smiling, as he admired her slim, copper body and how it curved so invitingly.

He sighed deeply. "Now, go make those drinks."

She winked at him and left. Jack put his hands behind his head and got the silliest grin on his face.

Epilogue

Jack looked out over the desert as he sipped his morning coffee. He loved the way the light played across the cliffs, changing from pale coral to ochre to flamingo to red. When he and El had gone on vacation in New Mexico three months ago, they had both fallen in love with the rugged beauty of the land. It had been a fluke that they had come across this house for sale. It was set well back in a canyon by itself, undisturbed by others and yet relatively close to Santa Fe, the capital. Jack ran a small machine shop there, although in truth, he spent most of his time at home, with his new wife. He allowed his foreman to run the business most of the time.

El—she had gone back to that name privately, at his request, although she remained Maria to everyone else—padded up the steps to the roof, naked, carrying a cup of coffee.

"It never stops being beautiful, does it?" she said.

Jack turned toward her, taking in her nut-brown body, once again adorned with the jewelry that he had purchased for her, long ago. He liked her naked most of the time and she was happy to oblige. No one else could see her and even if they could, so what? It was what he wanted. She loved to give him what he wanted for she got back so much more in return.

"No, it doesn't," he said, staring at her nakedness, his meaning clear.

She shook her head. "You are incorrigible."

He opened one arm and she stepped into his, pressing

her naked body up against his robe. With her free hand, she unfastened it and allowed her body to snuggle up against his bare skin. They sipped their coffee together, alternately looking at the desert view and each other.

"I'm glad you sabotaged your life," he said, rubbing a whiskered chin against her ear. She giggled and pulled away.

"If I had known that I would end up here, I would've done it long ago."

"Funny how things work out."

They separated and she glanced down to see his cock semi-hard. "Ohh, looks like junior is awake—again."

He chuckled. "He just can't get enough. After last night, I figured I'd be limp for a couple of days, at least."

She stroked him and his cock instantly came erect. "I think you're sadly mistaken." She put her cup down on the ledge and eased to her knees. Her hungry mouth opened to envelope him.

"Hey, did I say you could do that?"

"Thorry, maastr," she mouthed around his spear of flesh. "Wann me a thop?"

"No, don't you dare."

Their master-slave relationship had evolved in the six months since Jack had returned to El's life. He didn't bark out commands and she didn't mindlessly obey his every request. They had moved beyond all that. He was still the boss—her constant nudity was one reflection of that—but the relationship had deepened and mellowed. Simply put, they loved each other. She still had a need to be submissive and he played her like a fine piano, never hitting a sour note. But he never pounded on the keyboard. There were no outrageous demands, no sharing of her body with clients or strangers.

He did enjoy his little games. His current favorite was to make El wear a short skirt and a blouse with no underwear and take her out to dinner. The stares they got made him hard and often he would fuck her up in an alleyway on the way back to the car. He'd just press her up against a wall and enter her, hard and fast. She thrilled at the excitement without the danger. She would have gone a lot further, had he asked her to and she suspected he might, someday. *Whatever he wants, I'll do. Because I know he would protect me.*

"What shall we do today?" He asked, rhetorically, as she sucked on his hard cock.

"Mmmum, wat uh wanna uh?" Her mouth never left his cock.

"I don't know. Maybe we could go get some new clients..." It was a regular joke and she finally pulled away, leaving his cock glistening in the morning light.

"You want me to fuck them for you?" She knew her lines too.

"Maybe. I mean, you're a fine piece of ass and it's a shame not to use it."

"Aren't we using it?"

"Oh, yes, but I'm just being selfish, you know, to keep you to myself. Think of how big Sawyer Machining could be if we only applied ourselves!"

"Whatever you say, master." She returned to his cock.

Of course, that would never happen and they both knew it. Although they were fifteen hundred miles from his former business, they wouldn't risk another scandal. But talking about it was perfectly fine.

She began to deep-throat him and he soon felt on the edge of coming. He didn't want to waste his seed in her mouth. He wanted to plunge into that sweet pussy.

"Wait," he said, pulling back. "Get up on the picnic table."

She rose fluidly and lay back on it, lifting her legs to perch the heels on the edge. She looked so inviting. He allowed his robe to fall from his shoulders and posed there for a second, taking in the beautiful view. Then he eased into her and leaned down to kiss her coffee-flavored lips.

"You think this time will be the charm?"

"I hope so, although we can still practice, can't we?"

El had gone off the pill two months ago and they'd been trying to get pregnant ever since. He loved the idea of planting his seed deep into her womb, to grow a life there, to have children running around their large estate. He knew their lives would change drastically. No more casual nudity, no more fucking all over the house, no more open displays of domination/submission. Not that they considered human sexuality something that should be hidden away, but they knew that children might talk about it to their friends and that could bring about unwanted scrutiny.

El had been thrilled with the decision, although she would've gone on as they were just as easily. The last few months had been the happiest of her life.

Jack's cock filled her up and slipped in and out, eased by her copious wetness. She was always wet, it seems. Just being naked near Jack caused her to flow like a stream, waiting for his touch, his fingers, his cock. She moaned and opened her legs wider, wanting him to go deeper, if possible. She wanted to feel the head pierce her stomach.

El put her hands on his shoulders as they rose and fell. His cock seemed to grow bigger, if possible. She began to talk to him, telling him how good it felt, how hard he was, how everyone could see them up here on the roof if they happened to come down their road. Each remark drove him onward. She talked about how she had fucked other men for him, how their cocks had emptied themselves into her, how they compared to his—always unfavorably, of course.

"You have a big cock... it's filling me up... it's splitting me wide open. My god, honey! I can't take it anymore! I'm going to explode! Oh!"

With a roar, Jack came hard inside her, triggering her own climax. She could feel his sperm splash into her womb, taste it in the back of her throat. She let out a guttural cry and hugged him tightly. For several long minutes, they didn't move, his cock still buried deep inside her.

His cock softened and El could sense the fluids running down the crack of her ass and onto the picnic table. Her butt hurt a little and she wondered if she had splinters. It didn't matter a damn.

"If that doesn't make you pregnant, I don't know what will," Jack gasped.

"If it didn't, I'd be surprised."

He pulled out and a gush of fluids followed him. She reached down to cup it with her fingers and brought up some to taste. El started to get up, but Jack held her in place with a gentle hand.

"No, stay there. It will help the little sperm guys if you lie still."

She smiled and lay back. "But what about your cock? It so needs to be sucked clean."

He climbed up on the table next to her and pulled her head to his wet cock. She licked it, making loud slurping noises and causing Jack to giggle. He pulled back and admired his wife.

"Who would've thought we'd end up like this?"

El patted her stomach. "No one. I was nothing more than your sex object."

"And what a beautiful one you were, too."

"A slut, waiting for your orders."

"And you obeyed them to a tee."

"I had to; otherwise, I'd be beaten."

He laughed. "I didn't beat you enough, I can see that."

"That's true. I remember sometimes I'd do something bad, just to get a spanking."

"I know. You liked the spankings too much. That surprised me, I guess. If I had known, I would've made it a regular part of your work week. You know, have select people come in and give you a good thrashing on your bare bum."

"Ohhh, I would've hated that—and loved it."

"You are one sick chick, you know that?"

"Yeah." She rolled off and stood up. Jack's eyebrows came up.

"Hey! Are you sure you gave those little sperm guys enough of a chance?"

"No. I'm bad. I got up too soon. I'm defying you."

He tsked at her. "You little slut. Go get me my riding crop."

"Oh, no!" she said in mock horror. "Not that!"

"You heard me. Go get it."

She left, her bare feet padding downstairs. In seconds, she was back, the black riding crop in her hand. It was finely made, about twenty inches long, with a flat fold of leather at the tip. Jack swished it in the air for a few seconds, seeing El flinch, even as she licked her lips.

"Bend over the table," he ordered and she did so, gripping the edges with both hands. Her breasts flattened against the painted wood surface.

He eyed her perfect ass: heart-shaped and almond brown. He gave her a tentative slap and she flinched. "Oh, master, you're killing me," she said coyly.

He struck her again, harder and El groaned. He looked down and saw his cock was again becoming erect.

"God, what you do to me, woman," he said, hugging her tightly from behind.

"That's it? That's your idea of punishment?" She laughed, low in her throat.

"Hang on, I'm just taking a break." His cock pressed against slit and was immediately drenched in her fluids.

She sighed elaborately. "Very well, master. Have your way with me. I live to serve."

"The perfect woman," he said, slipping inside of her.

THE END